Stefan Radaković
Zašto? / Why?
22.09.2017

AF210543

Zašto?

Why?

Стефан Радаковић / Stefan Radaković

written
29.01.2017 - 29.08.2017
published
22.09.2017

inspired by the original that was previously written
as a private project
(25.02.2014 - 20.07.2014)

Bibliografische Information der Deutschen Nationalbibliothek: Die Deutsche Nationalbibliothek verzeichnet diese Publikation in der Deutschen Nationalbibliografie; detaillierte bibliografische Daten sind im Internet über dnb.dnb.de abrufbar.

Bibliographical information of the German National Library: The German National Library lists this publication in the German National Bibliography; detailed bibliographical data can be found online at dnb.dnb.de

Herstellung und Verlag   *Print and Publishing by*
BoD - Books on Demand, Norderstedt

ISBN: 978-3-8482-2422-7

Cover by Nick Ludwig
Model: Adam Radojević

Introduction

Welcome dear reader, the following 210 pages will lead you through the life of Branko, a gay Serbian teenager. This introduction shall serve as your crash course on everything you need to know about Serbia and will not spoil any contents of the plot. If you wish you can start reading, or stay here for some fun facts on the setting of this book!

The story is set in Belgrade, the capital of Serbia. Serbia is a country in southeastern Europe with about 7.5 million inhabitants, while its capital Belgrade houses about 2 million of them. Belgrade is a vibrant city full of cafés, bars and clubs. It is the biggest city in the former Yugoslavia and is home to the regions biggest LGBT community.

However, in terms of acceptance towards the LGBT community, Serbia is not such a fun place to be. According to the 2011 census of the Republic of Serbia, 84,5% of the population define themselves as Eastern Orthodox, making Serbia a deeply religious country. The Anti-Discrimination law of 2009 was barely passed in parliament with only 127 out of 250 votes (125 votes are required to pass a law) in favour of it. To date, Serbia has not recognised same-sex unions nor same-sex marriage and the abuse of homosexuals in society is high. Even though things have gotten better of the past few decades, the LGBT community in the country still struggles with a lot of issues on a daily basis that LGBT people don't have to face in Western Europe.

A little bit of recent history for you: In the 1990s the communist state of Yugoslavia fell apart in a violent civil war. The countries of Slovenia, Croatia, Bosnia and F.Y.R. Macedonia got their independence after years of bloodshed, while Serbia and Montenegro remained part of the newly founded Republic of Yugoslavia. Until today there are hostilities between Serbia and Croatia, even though the two countries share a common language and have shared a country for more than seven decades.

In 1999 after failing to give Kosovo, a southern region of the country which is populated by Albanians, NATO launched a three-month airstrike on Serbia and Montenegro and destroyed many parts of Belgrade.

In 2006 Montenegro declared its independence from Serbia via a referendum which Serbia recognised, however, when Kosovo declared its independence in 2008 Serbia didn't recognise Kosovo as a sovereign state and claims it as Serbian territory until today. Kosovo is still not a member of the United Nations despite being recognised by the majority of UN member states, it still lacks the approval of the UN a whole in order to join. Tensions between Serbia and Albania have been steadily hostile until today and the political turmoil between the countries rests until today.

When reading Zašto? you will encounter a lot of these issues and you will see how it influences the lives of the characters. Branko was born in 1997 so he and his peers were born after the civil war and were babies when the NATO bombardment occurred. However, the parents of the characters have all lived through that period which is reflected in their lives, views and actions. I really hope that you will enjoy this book and dive deeper into the themes and problems this book attempts to address. If you wish to know more about Serbia and the LGBT community in Serbia, I suggest using the internet for more detailed information, what you got here are just the basics. A great movie I can always recommend on the subject is "Parada". You can also find it in English.

Anyways, I really hope it will be a good a read for you!

С. Радаковић

Characters / significance

Branko Jovanović / serbian Teenager

Bojana Jovanović / his sister

Mr Dragan Jovanović / their father

Nenad / his brother

Diellza / his wife

Mrs Jadranka Jovanović / their mother

Milenko Jovanović / his brother

Marija / his girlfriend

Vesna / his girlfriend

Katarina / her best friend

Petar / his best friend

Ivan / his other best friend

Dejana / a friend

Sara / her friend

Jelena / her friend

Milica / a friend

Ms Prosetović / social studies teacher

Bojan / ministry worker

Luka / competitor from Croatia

Alex / competitor from Hungary

Daniel / competitor from Austria

Dušan / the one

Mr Radulović / psychiatrist

Act 1

Scene 1

The scene opens at the Kalemegdan fortress in Belgrade, Serbia. The date is February 14th, 2016. Branko, an 18-year-old, is sitting with his girlfriend Vesna at the edge of the wall, overlooking the district of New Belgrade, which is conveniently snowed in for Valentine's Day. Vesna is resting her head on Branko's right shoulder with his right arm around her. Branko stares into the distance. There's silence for a moment.

Branko: When you look around, what do you see?

Vesna: *(confused)* Uhm, well. I see the river, the city, the sky, the people, the fortress *(turns her face to him)* you. *(kisses him)*

Branko: And do you see any further meaning in the things you see?

Vesna: Well, not really. Some things are just the way they are. Why, what do you mean?

Branko: *(focuses his look into the distance)* You know, when I look around, I see a world which is constantly moving, everybody busy with themselves, and me as a tiny part of the entire picture. I wonder what is behind the scenes and what the meaning of what we see is. I wonder what I could find in the mind of others.

Vesna: *(pouts at him)* You still haven't figured which drawings you want to submit for the competition?

Branko: *(bursts out)* It's so annoying! There are so many good ones and I have to choose five, and I can't even decide on one and the submission is tomorrow! *(he puts his head down and smiles)* My sister wants me to take the one with her on it.

Vesna: You mean the on where she's sitting in Tito's garden? *(excited)* I love that one! Pick that one, it's so cute. Bojana will, like, literally die if you decide to go with that one, it's awesome, she'll love it.

Branko: And family does come first.

Vesna: You can also take the painting from Thessaloniki you did last summer! I am literally obsessed with that one.

Branko: *(stutters)* Uhm, well I haven't really thought about that one yet.

Vesna: *(pouts again)* Come on, do it for me, for Valentine's day.

Pleaaase

Branko: *(smiles)* Alright, alright. I'll take that one as well.

Vesna leans in to kiss him, but Branko is still staring into the distance so she opts for his cheek instead.

Vesna: You know, you could ask Ivan and Petar which one they like most. They're your best buddies after all and know you better than anyone else outside your family.

Branko: *(puts his hand on the back of his neck)* I guess I could call them over tonight since they only need to cross the street.

Vesna: *(smiles)* See, they do know you best. I still need some time to figure that thing you call your mind out.

Branko: We've only been together since the 8th of December, take your time, *(turns his head towards her)* and yes, I remembered the date. *(finally kisses her)*

Vesna: *(pulls a face at him)* Good for you. You'll have the 8th of March as one of our anniversaries. *(smirks)* I expect double the effort!

Branko: *(devoted)* I'll take care of everything you want!

Vesna: Well, my current need is to get out of the cold.

Branko: *(in a heroic voice)* Then we shall get you a cup of your favourite mocha.

Vesna: Ooooh! *(gets excited)* Somebody's taking his girl to Coffee Dream!

They stand up and leave the wall as they slowly start walking into downtown Belgrade.

Scene 2

The scene opens in the evening at the Jovanović's flat in central Zemun, a district of Belgrade. Branko is sitting with his parents and his little sister Bojana at the dinner table. His mother made sarma, a traditional Serbian dish, which is usually made on special occasions.

Branko: Uhm, mom, dad? Petar and Ivan wanted to stop by to help me with my selection for the competition.

Mr Jovanović: *(smiles)* Ah, sure, I haven't seen them in ages. *(looks* *over to his wife)* We saw Petar's parents today day in church. They invited us over for coffee tomorrow.

Mrs Jovanović: We were just talking about you guys and how much you've grown. It's still unbelievable that my second baby is graduating from school this year.

Branko: *(raises his eyebrows)* Yeah, because that's never been done before. It's not like-

Bojana: *(interrupts)* Speaking of the second baby. I texted with Milenko before his shift today. He said he's fine, and the weather in Malta is nice.

Mrs Jovanović: *(worried)* Oh dear, I really hope that he doesn't work too hard.

Mr Jovanović: Oh please, Jadranka, the boy is a man now. If he didn't have the brains to study he does have the brawn to work!

Mrs Jovanović: You know constructions sites aren't safe!

Bojana: *(in a soothing voice)* Mom. He'll be fine. He's just chasing his dream! Just as Branko is chasing his, and just as I'll be chasing mine. *(pauses for a second)* Given that I find one.

Mr Jovanović: I hope at least you plan on studying something proper.

Branko: *(upset)* Contemporary art is a proper field of study!

Mr Jovanović: *(in a sceptic voice)* To me it's just a bunch of colours, but you know what? If you manage to succeed at this competition and get to the finals in Budapest. Who knows? Maybe you are truly gifted. Maybe you'll be able to achieve something with your art after all.

Mrs Jovanović: *(enthusiastic)* Of course he's gifted. He might not get to the finals, but he will get a good score!

Branko: *(quieting down)* Thanks, mother.

Mr Jovanović: Boki, what are your plans for tomorrow?

Bojana: *(looks into her sarma)* I'm going out with the squad, there's this new café downtown and we wanted to check it out.

Mrs Jovanović: Oh, that's nice.

The doorbell rings.

Branko: *(runs to the door)* I'll get it!

Scene 3

The scene opens in Branko's relatively small room. His works are all over his huge desk and his bed. Ivan and Petar are observing the displayed stuff. They've been discussing it for a while.

Ivan: *(points around the room)* So, if we figured it out properly, we'll take Thessaloniki, the one with your sister, one from Višegrad, preferably one with the Drina bridge, the one from Amélie and one we haven't decided on yet.

Petar: I kinda like the one with the bombed buildings.

Ivan: Why on earth would you want to choose that one? It's just plain violence!

Petar: It represents our history. It shows what the world has done to us in 1999. It symbolises the strength of the people. I'm sure they'll want someone who cares about Serbian cultural heritage to represent us.

Branko: *(inspects the piece)* I don't know. They might take it the wrong way.

Ivan: Exactly! I'm against it.

Branko: I'm actually in favour of it.

Ivan: *(weirded out)* You what now?

Branko: Petar is right, we need something that represents the violent parts of our history. *(walks in circles)* Each piece gains its meaning in the selection. The bombed buildings represent our suffering. The Amélie one is for our social connectivity, our coffee culture. The Drina bridge our literature and cultural heritage, Andrićs mastermind. And the one with Bojana stands for the importance of family.

Ivan: You forgot Thessaloniki. The one that stands for love?

Branko: Huh *(is irritated)* Ah, yes and that one.

Ivan: Is something wrong?

Branko: *(slightly shakes head)* It's nothing

Petar: *(taps him on the shoulder)* Come on, don't fuck with us, somethings off.

Branko looks his friends into their eyes, takes a seat at his bed, while the two take chairs

Branko: *(shaky voice)* It's about Vesna. I... I don't think I can keep on doing this anymore. I'm simply not happy, and I know that she isn't either.

Ivan: Doubts this early into a relationship are never a good sign.

Petar: *(shakes head)* This is bad. Very very bad. Are you really going to let a girl like Vesna slip? Most of the guys would sell their left testicle for her!

Branko: She is a great girl. It's just that she's not the one for me.

Petar: *(interrupts)* Stop it! You two started off so well.

Ivan: Chill. She might not be the one for him.

Branko: I'm so confused. Nothing seems clear to me anymore.

Petar: Did you have sex?

Branko: Huh??

Petar: Did you fuck her?

Branko: *(in a disappointed voice)* No... We didn't! I never managed to get that far. Her parents were always at home, and the one time they weren't home, her dog was watching.

Ivan: Understandable, weird as fuck, but understandable.

Petar: *(confused, irritated, lost)* How can you not bang the hottest girl in class? What kind of fag are you?

Branko: *(annoyed)* Oh, come on.

Petar: I just want to help you.

Branko: And I think that it's not the help I need.

Ivan: *(looking out of the window)* Maybe you need to see a therapist?

Branko: *(raises an eyebrow at him)* The last time I checked, I was fine. I don't need a therapist, just because I didn't bang my girlfriend yet.

Petar: *(dements)* Ah, Branko's not nuts! He's just confused.

Ivan: Oh, trust me, I figured that out on my own.

Branko: Guys!

Ivan: *(turns his head towards him)* Just sleep on it.

Petar: Come on, don't be so sensitive. You know you can always call us if you need anything. You're like a brother us.

Branko: Thanks, guys.

Petar: *(punches him in the shoulder)* And we'll help you get some!

Ivan: *(starts laughing)* And here we go again.

They quickly switch the topic, talk for another 15 minutes, after which Petar and Ivan leave. Branko is left alone in his room.

Scene 4

Five minutes later, Bojana knocks at Branko's door and sticks her head through the door slip. She has a worried look on her face.

Bojana: Mind if I come in?
Branko: Uhm, sure.

Bojana enters the room as she closes the door behind her and takes a seat on the bed next to her brother.

Bojana: I… uhm, I…
Branko: Boki, what's wrong?
Bojana: I overheard you speaking. It didn't sound as if you were fine.
Branko: *(tries to avoid eye-contact)* What exactly did you hear?
Bojana: *(looks to the floor)* You said that you couldn't keep things up with Vesna as they were and that you weren't happy. *(looks him directly in the eye)* Is that true?

There's silence.

Branko: It's true, I'm not happy with my life as it is right now. And it's been like this for a while now.
Bojana: *(worried)* Why didn't you tell me anything sooner?
Branko: *(looks up to the ceiling)* I just didn't feel like addressing the issue was relevant. Sometimes it's the times I'm saddest where I behave as if everything was alright.
Bojana: *(frustrated)* That's not helping and it doesn't solve the problem.
Branko: *(rests his head against the wall)* Well what does solve the problem?
Bojana: Talking about it for instance!
Branko: This is Serbia. Men don't talk about their feelings.
Bojana: *(confused)* Not when it comes to family! You don't have to keep up with a bunch of social norms here. I'm your little sister and not one of your bros. There's a difference there.

Branko: Maybe it's just an instinct. I don't want to bother you with my problems.

Bojana: You obviously need help in finding a solution!

Branko: Well do you have one to offer?

Bojana: Break up with her.

Silence fills the room yet another time. This time Branko can't seem to break it, so the two simply stare at each other without any expression at all.

Bojana: You're not happy, so she can't be happy, so your relationship is unhappy, which turns into a toxic relationship and after a while you start asking yourself why you're torturing yourself, so why not just simply put a stop to this and end your suffering once and for all.

Again, silence fills the room. Branko's expression is still blanc.

Bojana: It's okay to be emotional, it's not okay to be a pussy.

Branko: *(raises voice)* Alright! Alright! *(lowers voice)* I guess there's no other way out.

Bojana: So how do you plan on doing it?

Branko: *(confused)* I can't decide that right now. I need to think about this for a moment.

Bojana: You seem tired. Get some sleep.

The two hug, Bojana stands up and heads for the door, as she reaches it, she turns around one more time.

Bojana: And remember. Family is always there for you!

Branko: *(smiles)* Thanks Boki, that really means a lot.

Bojana: *(smiles back at him)* Sleep well and dream in colours.

Scene 5

The next day, February 15th, Branko wakes up a little later than usual. It's about 12 am, as he strolls into the kitchen, to find leftover uštipci his mother put on the table. As he's eating his breakfast he listens to the television playing in the background.

Television: *(female news presenter voice)* The prime minister wished all Serbs a happy National Day of Serbia. In his holiday speech, he emphasised the importance of political stability in our country and commented on the issue of premature elections this morning as N1 is finding out. *(voice of the prime minister)* Today we are celebrating the existence of our nation. But we need to look into the future, to keep it prosperous and to keep moving forward. Even though this is the third time in four years that we have to hold a parliamentary election, I believe that it's in the interest of the people to go vote and to move forward. Let's leave our past behind! With the Serbian Progressive Party, we'll put in our best efforts to bring this country back into stability. We've done a lot, but we need to do more, and as your prime minister, I promise you, the people of Serbia, that we can make-

Branko switches the channel to a music programme which is far less politically demanding than watching N1.

Branko: *(to himself)* The people of Serbia. Progressive Party. *(he pauses)* Bullshit. They've done nothing but harm, they encourage the same right winged bullshit that fucked up Yugoslavia. They've done nothing to change the law or work on our rights. And how am I supposed to live in this country? How am I going to continue living, if everyone expects me to be something I'm not. **And why am I oddly fine with that?** In the west, it's supposedly different. There you don't need to hide from everyone. You're safe. You can accept it. Here, I can't even admit it to myself, let alone to others.

He looks around. No one is at home. So he stands up and walks to the bathroom and looks at himself in the mirror. He washes his face and looks again.

Branko: *(to himself)* It's time for you to say it. At least to yourself. No one else will know. It's just you. And you have to say it. *(keeps on staring at his reflection for a while)* My name is Branko Jovanović, I'm 18 years old, I was born in Belgrade. And. *(pauses)* I'm gay. My name is Branko Jovanović and I'm gay.

He lifts his back a little, looks at himself with astonishment. He has known for years, but this was the first time he said those words out loud. His heart fills with joy. He smiles at himself.

Branko: *(to himself, with joy in his voice)* My name is Branko Jovanović and I am gay.

Scene 6

The scene opens at the Serbian ministry of culture. Branko arrives in the main hall with his five paintings rolled up and with the application letter in his hand. He arrives into a room with tables which are all labelled with the categories. Branko looks for the table with the inscription САВРЕМЕНА УМЕНОСТ (contemporary art) which he finds right next to the table for САВРЕМЕНИ ПЛЕС (contemporary dance).

Branko: *(approaches the young woman at the table with a smile)* Hello, I'd like to sign up, please.
Woman: *(in a hectic tone)* Yes, sure. *(hands him a paper)* Could you please fill out this form? I have to take care of two tables at the same time. *(walks over to a girl at the neighbouring table)* So, is this the disc with the performance?
Girl: Yes. *(friendly, innocent tone)* My friends were here a little earlier, so I need to get my name on the collective application.
Woman: Alright. Fill out this form then. *(walks over to Branko)* Let me see your form. *(she takes the form out of Branko's hand and starts reading it)* Please present your five submissions and then sign this release. *(she hands him another form)* I'll need to get a confirmation from the office. I'll be back in a second. *(she walks into a hallway)*

Branko rolls out the five paintings to check if everything was in order.

Girl: *(glances over to Branko's paintings)* They're really beautiful.
Branko: Uhm, thanks.
Girl: *(points at one of the drawing)* Who's the girl in Tito's garden?
Branko: *(smiles)* That's my little sister. She's my everything.
Girl: *(puts a hand on her chest)* Aw, that is so sweet. I'm sure she must proud of you.

Branko: *(laughs)* I even got one of these red hearts from her. You know, the one that says "Najboljem bratu" (for the best brother).

Girl: *(grins)* What a cliché *(she continues to observe the painting)* You're really talented *(she looks at the bottom right on one of the paintings)* Б. Јовановић. That's a really cool signature. What's the Б for?

Branko: It's for Branko. *(stretches his hand)* Pleased to meet you.

Girl: *(stretches her hand)* Dejana, the pleasure is all mine.

Branko: *(looks over to her form)* Contemporary dance?

Dejana: Yeah. *(blushes)* Two friends of mine and I recorded ourselves dancing in my basement. We thought we could give it a chance.

Branko: Oh cool! What song did you choose?

Dejana: *(rolls her eyes)* Oh god, this is embarrassing. Well we did one to "Opasna Igra" by Nikolija, one to "Tri Čaše" by Milica Todorović and we topped it off with Sia's "Chandelier"

Branko: *(nods head)* That is some pretty good dance music.

Dejana: Isn't that like only what girls are into?

Branko: Uh, yes, but uhm, it has a clear danceable beat.

Dejana: True.

The woman returns with the leftover paperwork that Branko and Dejana fill in. As she releases both of them into freedom from bureaucracy, Dejana approaches Branko as he's on his way to the exit.

Dejana: Hey, where do you need to go now?

Branko: *(confused)* Home, why?

Dejana: *(grins)* I meant the direction.

Branko: Aaah. Zemun.

Dejana: So you need to take a bus from Zeleni Venac?

Branko: Yes.

Dejana: *(enthusiastic)* Great! I need to go to Novi Beograd, so we'll both need a bus from there. May I walk with you?

Branko: Yeah, sure.

Scene 7

In front of the ministry, Branko and Dejana are starting to walk towards Zeleni Venac as they cross Nikola Pašić square. The sun is shining.

Branko: The weather's nice today.

Dejana: *(suddenly a bit sad)* Yeah, I guess.

Branko: Is something wrong?

Dejana: I'm fine.

Branko: You don't seem fine. You seemed fine five minutes ago.

Dejana: *(takes a deep breath)* That's because, five minutes ago, I didn't have to walk towards my personal doom.

Branko: *(confused)* Novi Beograd is your personal doom? Wouldn't be the first time I heard someone say that. What's going on?

Dejana: It's just that. Urgh. *(pauses)* My boyfriend lives in Novi Beograd, I'm on my way to break up with that pig.

Branko: My God. What happened?

Dejana: *(tries to keep it together)* It's nothing.

Branko: It's something, but you don't want to talk about it.

Dejana: Exactly. *(sighs)* Although my friends haven't been really there for me either.

Branko: Mine are there for me, but can't ever seem to understand me, so trust me, I know how it feels to be alone in your mind.

Dejana: *(smiles)* At least someone who understands.

As there crossing Terazije square in front of the imperial hotel Moskva, Branko considers sharing some advice with Dejana, despite having just met her.

Branko: *(takes a deep breath and smiles)* It's funny how the world can be confusing when everything seems fine. I've been with my girlfriend for somewhat more than three months and I haven't been happy. Rather indifferent to be honest. *(keeps on smiling)* And I've decided this morning to break up with her because I don't want to be unhappy. You should rather be alone your entire life than spending a minute with a toxic person. *(throws Dejana a look)* It's something I read on the internet, but it is true.

Dejana: *(baffled)* How can you keep smiling while talking about this?

Branko: *(laughs)* Do you know this feeling where you're so fucked, that you can do is laugh?

Dejana: *(smiles back at him)* I believe I actually do.

As they approach the station, Dejana looks at the 67er bus which is standing in front of her. Branko pads her shoulder.

Branko: *(in a soothing voice)* It will be fine, trust me.
Dejana: Well, here goes nothing. *(She turns around)* Thank you, Branko, for being so nice to me.
Branko: *(shrugs his shoulders)* It's nothing.

She hugs him and enters her bus, as she watches him walk away towards his bus.

Scene 8

The scene opens in front of "Beograd" Department Store in central Zemun. Branko is walking home from the bus station as he sees Ivan who's just leaving the grocery store with three bags. Branko approaches him.

Branko: *(takes a bag out of Ivan's hand)* Mind if I help?
Ivan: My God, Branko, didn't see you there. Where are you coming from?
Branko: Uhm, the ministry.
Ivan: Ah, yes. Of course, how could I forget? How did it go?
Branko: It went well. I didn't do much. I Just signed up.
Ivan: Did someone suck the life out of you? You seem extremely expressionless.
Branko: I lost myself in my own thoughts on the bus.
Ivan: *(worried)* Oh, that bad?
Branko: I met a girl.
Ivan: *(totally confused)* A girl?
Branko: Yes, Ivan, a girl.
Ivan: But you have a girlfriend!
Branko: *(nervous)* Yes, dude, I know. I don't know why Dejana intrigued me so much. She was nice, kind, honest, direct. At least she seemed so. And I didn't see a threat in her. With Vesna, all I see is boredom, emptiness and a lack of a flame. *(calms down, saddens his voice)* I made a mistake and I need to change it.

Ivan: *(irritated)* Are you planning to do, what I'm thinking you're planning to do?

Branko: *(looks over to him)* I'm going to break up with Vesna.

Ivan: *(happy)* That's my man!

Branko: Ivan, what the fuck?

Ivan: You finally made a choice and it's your own one! I'm so proud of you!

Branko: *(still confused)* You want me to break up with Vesna?

Ivan: Yes! The only reason you're keeping this relationship at the moment are the expectations that are being put upon you. I know that, for example, Petar wants you two to stay together. He only wants that because that's what he thinks is best for you, and I'm just happy that you developed enough critical thinking to decide what works best for you! And I believe you'll be happier, bruh!

Branko: Woah, thanks dude. I guess you're right.

Ivan: *(takes the third bag from Branko)* All that's left is to execute it.

Branko: I'll try to get it done by the end of the week.

Ivan: I know it'll be tough, but trust me, it'll all be fine in the long run!

Branko: *(smiles)* I sure hope so.

Ivan: *(looks at the building behind him)* Well, this is my place. I'd love to hang, but I promised my parents I would join them for lunch.

Branko: Don't worry about it, bro. I'll chill on my own or with my sister.

Ivan: Dope. I'll see you in school.

Branko: *(starts crossing the street, waving)* See ya!

Scene 9

The scene opens in Branko's room. He's sitting at his desk making sketches of men. As he hears his door open, he quickly puts a blank sheet of paper over them and turns around to greet his sister.

Branko: Ey, you're back! How'd it go with the squad?

Bojana: *(walks over to the bed and lies down)* As always. We went to Ušće Mall, crowded as always, you could barely walk through to the shops. So we went to Moritz Eis and sat in the food court for like, hours.

Branko: Sounds cool.

Bojana: So, how'd your day go? All set for the competition?

Branko: Yup, all done. *(puts his elbows on his knees and his chin on his hands)* Now, we play the waiting game.

Bojana: Yeah, about that. *(pauses)* You're going to get the results by post, right?

Branko: Yes.

Bojana: *(softens her voice)* Would you mind not asking neither mom nor dad about the post?

Branko: *(confused)* Uhm, why?

Bojana: There will be a letter in there that they won't like.

Branko: Okay, now you're creeping me out.

Bojana: It's about Nenad.

Branko: *(slightly shook)* Our uncle? We haven't talked to him in years.

Bojana: Milenko did, ever since he moved to Malta. Turns out Nenad is quite successful nowadays. He runs a business in Tirana.

Branko: I thought he moved to Priština to be with his girlfriend?

Bojana: Yes, that was back in 2013, they've been in Tirana for a year now. He got the opportunity to start a business?

Branko: Our uncle is successful?

Bojana: Yes, and that's not everything. He is going to try to contact us!

Branko: And what does he have to do with my result letter from the competition?

Bojana: The thing is, you know father and him didn't talk to each other ever since our family denounced him.

Branko: I've been sad about it often enough. You know I loved uncle Nenad.

Bojana: Well he's pulling off what he's been denounced for. He proposed to his Albanian love and we're expecting our invitation to "beautiful" Tirana for the wedding.

Silence fills the room as Branko's eyes widen. He opens his mouth, closes it again. Then pauses for a few seconds.

Branko: *(in a low, worried voice)* Dad is going to freak out.

Bojana: I can imagine that they don't want to tell us about the wedding, so please don't ask about the post, they might know something's up. I'm sure the first thing mom will do when she sees your letter is call you. So can we keep quiet about this?

Branko: Of course we can. It's just a lot to take in right now.

Bojana: Trust me, I was shocked too when Milenko told me. *(pauses)* You know, he will be attending the wedding without telling our parents.

Branko: What? He said he can't afford to visit us, but he can afford flying to Tirana?

Bojana: *(calming him down)* Nenad is taking over the costs. In his letter, he'll offer us the same.

Branko: We might be going to Tirana?

Bojana: *(laughs)* As if our parents would allow us to do such a thing.

Branko: Only God knows.

Bojana: *(smiles)* The only thing I hope for is that our family will get less disturbing.

Branko: I'll light a candle for that next time we're in church.

Bojana smiles as tension is eased, they then start gossiping about the people from church, their neighbours and friends. Basically, everyone's a target.

Scene 10

Sunday, February 21st, 2016, 4:51 pm, Coffee & Factory in central Belgrade, in the basement floor, with no one but Branko and Vesna sitting at a table, and Vesna's blank expression.

Vesna: *(speechless)* You're not serious?

Branko: I believe I am. It's for the best.

Vesna puts her hand over her face.

Branko: *(reaches his hand out)* Please don't cry.

Vesna: I'm NOT going to cry! *(throws him a sharp look)* I'm just mourning at how pathetic this is!

Branko: *(confused)* Pathetic?

Vesna: Yes, pathetic! *(puts both her hands on the table)* Listen, I know that this relationship wasn't going to work out. I mean, our "date" on V-day. What the fuck was that? What kind of terrible telenovela is this? I knew we were going to break up, but I thought that at least we'd try to make this work. Otherwise, I would've given up a long time ago!

Branko: You would've?!

Vesna: Yes, of course! I was doing all the work at the end. Before you always wanted to hang out and planned the cutest dates. I fell for you Branko! And as that happened, everything stopped. Now I was the one who was pushing for us to hang out, to do stuff, I started cancelling plans because of you, I wanted us to work. How can you not see that? And then you come, and tell me that you want to break up, because you don't feel the spark anymore, well duh! That spark was long gone.

Branko: *(in a loss for words)* I… uh… I…

Vesna: Oh, so now your confidence is gone? *(pauses)* Tell, me, what's the real reason you're breaking up with me?

Branko: *(confused)* What do you mean by "real reason"? I told you that I simply don't have feelings for you anymore. The spark is gone and I can't see this working out. Trust me, it's not easy for me either.

Vesna: *(stands up)* Oh, this is really easy for you. *(throws 200 dinars (1,65€) on the table)* Pay once you leave. And I hope you'll get it up when you do it with her.

Branko: *(stands up as well)* I already told you that there's no one else and that I couldn't disrespect your parents like that.

Vesna: Bullshit, you were never that into me from the start. *(raises her arms)* I give up, this is so pathetic. Can I leave? I really need some time for myself.

Branko: *(takes the money on the table)* Sure, no worries. I'll get the bill. *(gives her her 200 dinars back)* Don't worry about it.

Vesna: *(rejects it)* Keep it. Get your next one a coffee. Whoever she may be.

Branko: I told you there's no one!

Vesna: *(starts walking away)* There might not be now, but there will be some day.

As she leaves the cafe, Branko puts the 200er bill into his pocket and takes a 500er bill from his wallet as he goes over to the waiter to pay and commence his walk of shame.

Scene 11

The scene opens at the Zemun Gymnasium the next morning at 9:35 am, as Branko exits his French class and is walking over to his classroom for social studies. He gets halted by Ivan and Petar.

Petar: *(grabs both his shoulders and shakes him)* What have you done? Are you nuts?

Branko: I have no idea what you're talking about.

Ivan: *(worried)* It's about Vesna. You should talk to her.

Branko: Did she tell you that we broke up?

Ivan: Uhm, no. She didn't say anything. I assumed it though, she was nervous as fuck.

Petar: Katarina told me that she told her yesterday but that she didn't want to make a big deal out of it in front of everyone.

Branko: What?

Ivan: She barely spoke to anyone, sat all by herself and just looked at funny Instagram clips. She's obviously distracting herself.

Petar: *(disappointed)* What the fuck did you do?

Branko: I… *(pauses)* I wasn't happy, she didn't seem happy either, so I sat her down yesterday and I broke up with her.

Petar: *(puts a hand on his forehead)* My God, you are stupid!

Ivan: I think he's right.

Petar: You what now?

Ivan: If he didn't feel anything for her, it was obvious that it would lead up to this!

Branko: Petar, please understand that I had no other choice.

Petar: You're a hopeless case, Branko.

Ivan: *(annoyed)* Will you stop? Can we just let this rest?

Ms Prosetović, their social studies teacher walks past them.

Ms Prosetović: You have three more minutes boys.

Ivan: *(smiles)* We'll be right in.

Ms Prosetović enters the classroom, Branko follows seeing Vesna on her phone by herself.

Branko: *(taking the seat next to her)* Are you fine?

Vesna: *(yawns)* Yeah, I'm just a bit tired. Didn't get enough sleep.

Branko: Listen, about yesterday-

Vesna: Hey! We're past that. It's fine. I'm fine. And I'll be fine.

The bell rings, as Vesna reassuringly smiles at Branko, calming him down.

Scene 12

Ms Prosetović starts the class off with putting on a comic of prime minister Aleksandar Vučić on a podium replying to the questions of a journalist.

Ms Prosetović: *(in a joyful, motivated voice)* In the spirit of the upcoming election, I wanted to start today's class with a somewhat controversial topic. So I'm giving you a comic we can work with. What can we see here? Yes, Katarina.

Katarina: *(descriptive, innocent voice)* We see our prime minister at a press conference. And in a speech bubble we can see a journalist asking him "Mr Vučić, what do you have to say about claims that you're gay?" and him replying "All I can say is that I have a beautiful wife and kids. So those claims are clearly false." At the same time, people in the background are shouting VUČIĆU PEDERU, implying that he, in fact, is a so called "faggot" or "pussy".

Ms Prosetović: *(smiles)* Very good. And what does this comic tell us about the social context of the situation? Branko.

Branko: It portraits the spread of information in society. So there's a common phrase being repeated all the time, that eventually people start believing it's true.

Ms Prosetović: Also. However, that's not where I wanted to go with this. *(sees Vesna's hand)* Yes?

Vesna: Maybe it's about wording. The misuse of a word, which is used to describe male members of the LGBT community in a derogatory way.

Ms Prosetović: *(surprised)* LGBT! Very good, Vesna. Today, we want to deal with social minorities, more specifically with the LGBT community. Is everyone aware what LGBT stands for? Katarina?

Katarina: Lesbian, Gay, Bi and Trans.

Ms Prosetović: Exactly.

Petar: *(interrupts)* Is this on the curriculum?

Ms Prosetović: Uhm. No, it isn't. I was thinking we could do something outside of the Serbian curriculum. We had colleagues from Norway here last week who showed us how they taught social studies, and they talked about talking about sexual orientation and social minorities in class. The other social studies teachers weren't too pleased with the idea. *(pauses)* But I thought I'd give it a try!

Petar: *(upset)* While would you want to talk about such an atrocity? Why should we even care about LGBTs? I don't give a fuck.

Ms Prosetović: Language!

Petar: *(rants)* Why do we have to give them so much attention? These people are not normal, they go against nature, they have a mental illness and treat it as if it was something to be proud of! They always want to parade around the city and cause nothing but trouble.

The class breaks into affirmative whispering on Petar's behalf. Branko sits there quietly.

Vesna: *(yells into class)* What's wrong with you people?! *(class is silenced)* Why do you care so much? Who cares if they parade in the city, isn't it just another great excuse to get drunk? It's also less violent than when you monkeys *(points at a few guys)* go to football games to beat the hell out of each other. At parades, it's radicals like you who beat up these poor people! Yes, they were born with a mental illness, but they can't do anything about it! Or do you blame your family members for having cancer because of the '99 bombing? *(utter silence)* Thought so.

Ms Prosetović: Okay, if this is such a sensitive topic, I guess that we can move on with the political system of Serbia.

Petar: *(interrupting)* Wait, teacher. Vesna has a point, but I would like to disagree. The cancer comparison makes no sense because mental illnesses are treatable.

Katarina: *(confused)* Isn't bipolar disorder a lifelong illness?

Ivan: *(checking Google)* There are multiple terminal mental illnesses. Homosexuality doesn't seem to be one of them. And according to our health ministry, it is no longer classified as an illness, yet psychiatric treatment is still available on a voluntary basis.

Petar: *(annoyed)* That's all because of the EU. If we don't adapt to their senseless laws they won't let us in.

Ivan: They're still not letting us in, even though we're adapting.

Vesna: *(triggered)* Are you for real now? The gays are not stopping us from entering the EU! How brainwashed are you on a scale from 1 to Progressive Party voter?

Petar: *(angry)* Ah, come on. What do you know about politics?

Vesna: *(frustrated)* Apparently nothing, because I'm a woman.

Ms Prosetović: *(interrupts her class)* Let's stop it here. How about we talk about what Petar just mentioned, the EU. How does EU society expect our society to adapt and vice versa?

As Ms Prosetović pushes the topic onto politics, she calms down her class and continues teaching.

Scene 13

After classes Branko sees Vesna walking home, he joins her to walk the usual chunk they used to walk together.

Branko: Hey, mind if I join you?

Vesna: No, I don't have much of a choice.

Branko: You have my utmost respect.

Vesna: What for?

Branko: For standing up for what you believe in.

Vesna: Aah, you mean the LGBT issue.

Branko: *(smiles)* Exactly.

Vesna: Do you remember my aunt Maja?

Branko: The one who lives in Stuttgart? She's was the young one, 24 or something?

Vesna: Exactly. *(pauses)* Well, I did it for her.

Branko: What do you mean by that?

Vesna: Well. Remember her friend from Germany? She came with her during her last visit.

Branko: Amina was it, right?

Vesna: *(pleasantly surprised)* Yes, my God, you were actually listening.

Branko: Of course I was!

Vesna: *(grins)* Anyways, Amina isn't her friend, she's her girlfriend.

For a second Branko's eyes open up wide.

Vesna: Do you see why I had my rant in class? When people say these hurtful things, I think about my aunt and what she had to go through to be herself.

Branko: *(shocked)* Wow. I did not see that coming. I should've though.

Vesna: *(smiles)* It's okay. In our family, LGBT has become the norm. It took my parents, my sister and me some time to get what was going on, but after actually reading about the topic, I realised that love is love.

Branko: *(confused)* You called it a mental illness in class and now you're promoting that love is love? I don't get it.

Vesna: Let's say I wanted to speak my mind without actually offending people. I don't think that being gay is a mental illness and the truth is that I do think that love is love. *(pauses)* That's why I want you to find love as well.

Branko: *(concerned)* What does that have to do with me finding love?

Vesna: Well, you know. I have a feeling that you might be. You know. It. That would explain your insecurities.

Branko: *(laughs uncomfortably)* Ahahahaha, you think that I'm gay?

Vesna: It was just an assumption.

Branko: Ah, Vesna, come on. You know me better than that.

Vesna: *(is uncomfortable)* Heh, I guess it was just wishful thinking.

Branko: Wishful thinking?

Vesna: *(nods)* Yeah, according to BuzzFeed's "Signs your boyfriend is

GAY" article, you're a total homo.

Branko: *(laughs confidently)* Is sexuality nowadays defined by what BuzzFeed tells you about it?

Vesna: Oh, I could take the sexuality test. Good idea!

Branko: *(grins)* Do that, and then let's go on a double date with your "girlfriend" and my "boyfriend".

Vesna: Deal! Well, this is my street. I'm off. Have a good one!

Branko: You too! *(walks away nervously)*

Scene 14

The scene opens at the Jovanović's. Branko's parents have guests over, so he quickly passes the living room, by greeting the guests and enters Bojana's room at the end of the hallway.

Bojana: *(interested)* Any news? How did your first day with Vesna as friends go?

Branko: Uhm, it was fine I guess. She seems really cool about it.

Bojana: *(excited)* Well that's great! No drama, no stress.

Branko: I guess you can phrase it that way.

Bojana: Well, in that case, I have news for you. *(pauses)* The wedding invitation was put into our mailbox today. I don't know if mom checked it yet, but, it's there.

Branko: *(confused)* How do you know that if you don't have the key?

Bojana: I passed the mailman this morning on my way to school. I saw him putting it in our mailbox.

Branko: Do you think mom saw them already?

Bojana: I told you, I don't know. I can't remember her acting a certain way that would give it away. I have no idea.

Branko: So we can't know for sure.

Bojana: Well done Watson!

Branko: Now we wait.

They sit and chat for a while. Branko then returns to his room as he reflects on Vesna's words.

Branko: *(to himself)* "Love is love". Vesna is completely right. What do we judge people for? Is love another behaviour that underlies societal norms? *(he takes a sheet of paper and tries to make a sketch of Maja and Amina)* If we love someone, why shouldn't we? Just because Nenad loves someone who belongs to a national group that we call our enemies. I mean okay, most Albanians are hostile towards Serbian and they do hate us, but they're not all that bad. I'm sure Diellza is a great girl, she must be, otherwise, Nenad wouldn't've given up everything for her. Now, that should be true love. And then there's the thing with gender. Yes I am definitely attracted to my own gender, but how the fuck am I supposed to live with that? Will I keep quiet my entire life? Currently, that sounds like a plausible plan. A wife and kids, a happy life, or at least for them and my family. I'll just draw the entire day and use viagra during the night. It's not a happy life, but living with a man isn't happy either. And no life isn't the answer. That would not be God's wish. God. God's wish. I mean, why would God create me this way if he didn't intend to. I haven't been to church in quite a while, it's about time to at least say a prayer. *(stands up and takes his prayer booklet)* Господе, …

Scene 15

Friday, February 26th, in the evening Bojana enters the kitchen to get a snack and sees her mother reading a letter with excitement.

Mrs Jovanović: *(enthusiastic)* Sweetie, where's your brother?
Bojana: *(looking for an eurokrem bar in the drawers)* In a pub with the guys, why do you ask?
Mrs Jovanović: His results are in! He made it to the finals. *(puts the letter on a pile of letters)*
Bojana: *(noticing the wedding invitations on the pile)* Oh wow, that's great! Should I text him?
Mrs Jovanović: Yes, please. Though, it would be better if someone told him in person.
Bojana: *(walks over to her room)* Then let me get a jacket.
Mrs Jovanović: Are you sure you want to go?

Bojana: *(walks back with a jacket on and her phone in her hand)* Sure, I'm always up for a beer.

She takes her phone to text Branko.

Where you at???

Uh, at a pub with the guys

I know that. 🙄 Which one?

Black Turtle, Svetogorska street

Can I join you? 😊

Let me ask the guys

She looks up from the phone to her mother.

Bojana: They're in the centre. He's asking the guys if I can come.

Mrs Jovanović: Oh, it would be great if you could join them! This is such a terrific moment! I'm going to text your father the news, he's still working.

Bojana: *(walks over to the letters)* I'll take the letter with me, so Branko can see it *(picks up the invitation)* Mother? What is this?

Mrs Jovanović: *(confused)* Isn't that the acceptance letter in your hand?

Bojana: No, it's from uncle Nenad and Diellza.

Mrs Jovanović: *(freaks out)* Hush! You are not supposed to see that! Please don't tell your father that you know.

Bojana: How long have you been hiding this from us?

Mrs Jovanović: A few days, your father and I have been discussing the issue.

Bojana: Discussing the issue? Are you really going to hold a grudge against uncle Nenad forever?

Mrs Jovanović: No, that's the thing. I want to convince your father to forgive his brother for betraying the family.

Bojana: He wanted to be with an Albanian woman. Love is love, mother. He didn't betray anyone.

Mrs Jovanović: He might not have, but your father feels betrayed nonetheless. So does his family and I am trying to fix that. He's invited us to his wedding in Tirana.

Bojana: And?

Mrs Jovanović: He said that he'll fly us all in, that we'll see your brother Milenko there. You know that he can't afford to visit us and since Nenad seems to be well off.

Bojana: *(disappointed)* So you're only considering forgiveness because he has money?

Mrs Jovanović: It is only natural for a mother to want to see her own son.

Bojana's phone rings, she opens Viber.

> The boys are fine with it, you can come

Great, I'll be there in 20! 😘

She looks up to her mother.

Bojana: *(taking the correct letter)* We'll talk about this later!

Mrs Jovanović: Before you go! Promise me you won't tell your brother.

Bojana: *(after pausing for a second)* I promise. I'll let him enjoy his day.

Mrs Jovanović: Honey, please don't be mad at me.

Bojana: *(disappointed)* I'm not mad at you, I'm mad at dad. He needs to start warming up to people. *(she leaves)*

Mrs Jovanović: *(yelling through the corridor)* Have a great night sweetie!

Scene 16

The scene opens at the Black Turtle pub. Ivan, Petar and Branko are finishing up their first round of beers.

Petar: *(looks to Branko)* I still can't believe what you've done man.

Branko: *(annoyed)* Can we let this rest?

Petar: Not wanting to be with Vesna is like not wanting to eat pizza in Italy.

Ivan: Petar, we get it. Branko's an idiot.

Branko: Hey! I'm not an idiot!

Ivan: Just let it rest already.

Branko takes a sip of his beer and looks at his phone.

Branko: *(talking while texting)* Bojana is asking if she can join us.
Ivan: Why would she want to do that?
Petar: Ah, Ivan, don't be like that. I haven't seen little Bojana in ages. Tell her she can come.
Branko: Will do. *(starts texting)*
Petar: *(staring at his glass)* I still can't quite grasp it. If I were you, I would've banged the shit out of her.
Ivan: We all would have, dude, we all would have. Branko's just a little different from the rest of us.

Branko stares nervously at both of them.

Ivan: *(standing up)* I'll go order us another round.

Two rounds later, Bojana shows up and joins the guys at their table.

Waiter: What can I get for you?
Bojana: *(smiles flirtatiously)* A blueberry beer, please.
Waiter: Coming right up *(leaves)*
Branko: *(surprised)* You drink? You're only 16.
Bojana: You started at 15, I know where you hid the bottles.
Branko: How did you...?
Bojana: Even mom found them, she probably just chose to ignore it.
Branko: That was supposed to be a secret spot!
Bojana: Yeah, "secret". I'm surprised I never found a porn stash. Guess that's all on the internet now.
Branko: *(embarrassed)* Boki!
Petar: *(laughs)* Hehe, I love your sister dude. She could hang with us more often.
Ivan: True, you never hang with us Bojana. Why today?
Bojana: Because *(reaches for her purse)* I need to give this to my brother *(hands Branko the letter)*
Branko: *(in disbelief)* Could this be what I think it is?
Bojana: Your results for the competition.
Ivan: *(amazed)* Whoah, dope.
Bojana: Go ahead, open it.
Branko: *(examining the envelope)* This was already opened.

Bojana: Yeah, mom couldn't really resist.

Branko: Well is it good?

Petar: Will you open the damn letter already?! Geez.

Branko: Alright, Alright!

He takes the letter out, reads over the words. As his eyes open up widely he stretches both arms into the air.

Branko: I made it to the finals! I'm going to Budapest!

Bojana: *(hugs him)* Congratulations!

Ivan: I knew you could do it.

Petar: I thought you were going to fail tremendously. *(laughs)* Just kidding.

Branko: This is so groundbreaking. It says the next briefing will be on March 4th, and the trip itself will last an entire week from April 10th until April 17th. I'll have an entire week of paid holiday!

Bojana: This is just what you needed! A week away from all the drama in your life.

Ivan: And who knows maybe you'll get to spend the week with that the girl you met at the signup *(as he continues to speak Bojana's and Petar's eyes widen)*, that is if she won. What was her name again? Dejana? Darija?

Branko: Ivan…

Ivan: I can't really remember. I remember you telling me about her though.

Petar: Were you unable to do it with Vesna because you had something with another girl?

Bojana: *(looks to Branko)* You were unable to screw your girlfriend?

Branko: That's none of your business, Boki, and I didn't know Dejana before the signup.

Ivan quiets himself down and observes the rest in their discussion

Petar: Did you break up with Vesna because of Dejana?

Branko: No!

Petar: Then how come there's this other girl?

Branko: I met her at the signup. We talked we clicked and she gave me a good piece of advice. There was nothing between us!

Petar: I see…

Bojana: Well, since Branko is probably not going to see her again. There's no reason to discuss it.

Branko: Well said sister *(stands up)* I'll get us another round to celebrate my success!

Bojana: Oooh! Free beer!

Scene 17

The scene opens on March 4th, 2016, Branko is on his way to the ministry as his phone vibrates. He opens Viber to see a message from Vesna.

Petar told me that you got into the finals

Congrats!

Thank you 😋

How are you doing?

Fine, I guess

I'm currently on my way to the ministry for a briefing

Oh cool.

What about you?

I've been alright

Listen, about us…

I wanted to tell you that I miss us

And that I miss the times we shared

So I was hoping we could meet sometime to talk about it

What do you think?

Uhm, sure

Are you sure you want to do that?

Yes, I want us to end on good terms

Do you have time tomorrow?

Hmm, I guess so

Let's go out for a walk on the quay

In Zemun?

Sure, why not, it's already almost 20°C

Sounds great. Meet you at around 2 pm after lunch?

Deal

Scene 18

The scene opens as Branko enters a briefing room in the ministry of culture only to find Dejana sitting on one of the chairs along with a few other people.

Branko *(in thoughts)*: This can't be true. The chances were close to zero.

Dejana looks up to him, smiles and waves him over. Branko takes the seat next to her.

Dejana: Hey, I was hoping to see you here.
Branko: *(irritated)* You were?
Dejana: Yes, I mean, your works were like, amazing.
Branko: I still didn't see what you've got.
Dejana: *(moves her shoulders trying make it look like she's dancing)* Well, you'll see in Budapest when our moves beat those other nations.
Branko: You're confident, I like that.
Dejana: I guess so.
Girl: *(walks in and over to Dejana)* There you are!
Dejana: I texted you that I would be inside.
Girl: And where's Jelena?
Dejana: I haven't seen her. *(looks through the room, turns to Branko)* By the way, this is Sara, she's one of my friends who's dancing with us.
Sara: *(waves over)* Hi, nice to meet you.
Branko: *(smiles)* Nice to meet you too. I'll assume Jelena is the third one.
Dejana: Yup. *(looks to the door)* Speaking of the devil.

Jelena walks into the room in her high heels, with a professional look and a bright red lipstick. She smiles to the girls. After her, a young man, in his mid-20s, enters the room.

Jelena: *(whispering)* Sorry I'm late. *(looks to Branko)* Hi.

Branko: Uh, hi.

Young man: Hello everyone and congratulations for making it to the finals. You are the nine chosen ones to represent Serbia at Europe's Competition of the Visual and Performing Arts for young talents. Or ECVPA in short. As you have received envelopes which include the necessary information you need for the trip. I'd just like to ask you to be at Belgrade's train station on time so we can meet before we enter the train. All candidates from Northern Serbia need to catch the train on their own from Novi Sad. About myself: My name is Bojan, I'm 26 and a graduate from Belgrade's FDU university with a degree in directing and management. I currently work with the ministry and am in charge of our ECVPA team, which this year comprises the nine of you. I will be your guide and your main source of information on the trip. Are there any questions? Yes?

Jelena: When will we receive exact information on our performances?

Bojan: The team in Budapest should upload the schedules in the coming days once all teams have been put together and briefed. Any other questions? No? Well, then I'd like to suggest a little introduction round if you don't mind? Who wants to start. You?

Girl: Uhm okay. My name is Milica, I'm 19 years old and I study sociology at the University of Novi Sad. My passion is photography and I will also represent us in that category.

The round continues as the others introduce themselves.

Sara: Hello, my name is Sara, I'm 18, this are Dejana and Jelena, also 18, and we are from the International School of Belgrade. We will represent us in contemporary dance.

Branko: Hi, I'm Branko, I'm also 18, somehow the only other guy here, and I will represent us in the category of contemporary art.

Bojan: *(smiles)* Thank you. Now, as you can see we weren't able to cover every category. Especially since our budget is fairly limited. I still hope that we'll have a great time nonetheless. That would be it for now, you're free to go. Have a great day!

The group stands up and everyone starts to mumble.

Dejana: Girls, do you have time for a coffee?

Sara: Sorry, Deki, I promised my brother I'd babysit my sister while she's out in the theatre with my dad.

Jelena: Yeah, I need to rush, I'm meeting Vuk in 10 minutes, so I'm alrealy totally late.

Dejana: Didn't you date someone else last week?

Jelena: That didn't work out, wish me luck girls. *(leaves)*

Dejana: Branko?

Branko: Me? Uhm, sure. I have time. I'd love to.

Milica: *(walks over to them)* Did I hear coffee? May I come with you, I don't want to take the next train back to Novi Sad.

Dejana: Sure! Why not? I know a great place in the Dorćol district, it's about a 15-minute walk from here.

Milica: Sounds great!

They leave the ministry and start walking towards the café.

Scene 19

At the Blaznavec café in Dorćol, Milica, Dejana, and Branko are discussing their expectations for the trip.

Dejana: So, guess we're going to Budapest in a month.

Milica: I know! It's going to be sooo awesome. I can't wait.

Branko: Yep.

Milica: So, do the two of you know each other?

Branko: We met at the signup.

Dejana: Seeing each other here was more of a spontaneous thing.

Milica: Oh, I see.

Dejana: You're from Novi Sad?

Milica: That's right. I study sociology there, photography is more of a hobby. *(points at Dejana)* You're at the ISB, I'm guessing you're graduating this year?

Dejana: *(smiles)* That is correct.

Milica: *(looks to Branko)* But you've been quite secretive, what do you study?

Branko: I'm also a high school senior. I'll graduate this year from the

Zemun gymnasium.

Dejana: The Zemun gymnasium? Not bad.

Branko: Oh, come on, you're at the ISB.

Dejana: The only thing that you prove by getting into the ISB is that your parents are either rich or diplomats.

Milica: Your case being?

Dejana: Diplomats. My mother was the ambassador of Serbia to Albania for 5 years, so I lived in Tirana and attended the international school there. We moved back in the summer of 2012 after the government changed.

Milica: That's so cool! Did your mother serve other places as well?

Dejana: She served a lot of countries and is currently serving in Angola, but she didn't want us to move with her and thought that my brother and I are better off staying with my father here. Before Albania, we used to live in Abu Dhabi with my mother, but I can't remember much of that, and before that, we were in Serbia.

Branko: That's highly impressive. I've never even been outside Europe or on a plane.

Milica: I flew once when my parents decided to go to Egypt a few years ago.

Dejana: *(a bit embarrassed)* I'm sorry, I shouldn't have said so much.

Branko: No, it's okay. You have nothing to be ashamed of.

Dejana: Trust me, I do. You know how it is here, everyone wants to be the richest, everyone wants to be the best. All the snaps, rich kids from private schools post claiming they're better than the ones from the state run ones. It makes me sick. And I don't want to be seen as one of them.

Milica: Oh, don't be a fool. It's fine. We're not responsible for the wealth of our parents. And maybe you lack something we have.

Dejana: *(after taking a short breath)* Well, I guess it would've been nice not to grow up with divorced parents.

Branko: Oh, I'm so sorry.

Dejana: It's okay. I'm used to it.

Milica: My mother remarried, I'm the child of the second marriage, but my older sister doesn't even know who her father is. It's said that he works on some construction site abroad.

Dejana: Every family has their struggles.

Branko: Tell me about it.

The group starts giggling as they switch the topic.

Scene 20

After a while, the group stands at Belgrade's main train station as Milica is about to get on the train to Novi Sad.

Milica: So I guess this is it for now.

Branko: Yeah, it was nice hanging out with you.

Dejana: *(hugs her)* Have a safe trip.

Milica: Thanks, guys, I'll see you when the competition starts! Bye.

She walks into the train as Branko and Dejana are left over at the platform.

Dejana: Do you happen to have any plans now?

Branko: Uhm, not really. Why?

Dejana: My parents aren't at home and I'm too lazy to cook, so I wanted to grab something to eat at Savanova. Wanna join?

Branko: Uh, yeah sure, I've never tried that place before.

Dejana: *(winks)* You'll love it, it's modern and very chic.

Branko: Well, I guess I gotta give it a try then.

They walk out of the train station over to the Sava river bank. At Savanova a few moments later, with food on the table and a table with river view, Dejana and Branko enjoy the sunset over Belgrade.

Dejana: *(takes a deep breath)* Uhm, remember that ex I was talking about last time?

Branko: The one you went to, to break up with?

Dejana: Yes. I don't see why men have the urge to be in charge.

Branko: Was he one of those who felt obligated to do everything a man is supposed to do? That's what killed me in my last relationship. I couldn't keep up.

Dejana: He was one of those people who, when I opened the door for him, took the door out of my hand and insisted on me passing through first, where I was like what the fuck can't you accept a simple gesture? *(face palm)*

Branko: *(raising an eyebrow)* But that wasn't the reason why you broke up with him?

Dejana: Not directly. It all just piled up.

Branko: You sounded very angry last time.

Dejana: Well…

Branko: What happened?

Dejana: Well. Sara, you met her, she found a picture of him on one of our classmate's phones.

Branko: Uhm okay. And?

Dejana: *(sarcastic tone)* Well, it would've been nice if he'd chosen to wear a little more clothing in the picture. Or any clothing at all to be fair.

Branko: Asshole.

Dejana: I feel much better now though.

Branko: Is the pain gone?

Dejana: Oh the pain was never really there. I suppose I was just looking for a reason to break up with him. I'm just amazed by how pathetic he is.

Branko: He is pathetic.

Dejana: Can I ask you something?

Branko: Um sure.

Dejana: How are you so non-typical compared to other guys here? Do you even date girls?

Branko: *(getting uncomfortable)* What do you mean?

Dejana: You're too soft for a straight guy.

Branko: *(deepens his voice)* But I am a straight guy.

Dejana: Really? Well, you know, in that case. *(nervous)* I know this seems kind of forced, but uhm, would you like to hang out more often?

Branko: Uhm, well. I just got out of a relationship myself, so I don't know if.

Dejana: Oh, yeah, that's totally fine. I'm sorry.

Branko: No, it's okay, don't worry about it. It's just, she wants to meet up tomorrow to clarify things, and I'm completely confused. *(pauses)* I literally have no clue what I'm supposed to do.

Dejana: It's fine, don't worry about it. I hope it goes well for you.

Branko: Thanks, I appreciate it.

They quickly change their subject as they break the awkward silence, despite a romantic sunset.

Scene 21

The next day Branko and Vesna meet up at the quay.

Branko: Hey.

Vesna: Hi.

Branko: You ok?

Vesna: I'm fine. I just wanted to talk.

Branko: *(worried)* Uhm, okay, what's up?

Vesna: Can you please be honest with me?

Branko: Of course, what's going on?

Vesna: What exactly lead you to break up with me?

Branko: *(stutters)* Oh, wow, this is, this is direct.

Vesna: I didn't want to beat around the bush. So what's the trigger?

Branko: *(pressured)* Jesus. Please give me a second.

Vesna: Uhm, okay, if you really need it.

Branko: *(after a pause)* I told you that I was not happy and that I felt like you were not happy either.

Vesna: You did.

Branko: And I guess that I realised things.

Vesna: What kind of things?

Branko: Well, what I may or may not want from life.

Vesna: And that is?

Branko: Well, I can't really say.

Vesna: Branko, are you a homosexual?

Branko: *(takes a step back dramatically)* VESNA!

Vesna: What?

Branko: *(angry)* Listen, just because I'm not that into you, doesn't make me a fag.

Vesna: The way we talked after the discussion in class. I… I kind of assumed it would be possible. You're a very sensitive guy and to some extent also quite feminine. I just thought it could be possible.

Branko: So you basically called me here to ask me if I'm gay?

Vesna: I thought you might need someone to talk to.

Branko: Jeez Vesna, I really can't figure out whether you're trying to be nice to me or nice to yourself.

Vesna: I don't know myself anymore. Our break up really hit my self-esteem, an explanation like that would've freed me from the guilt.

Branko: But there's nothing to feel guilty about. I'm the dick that dumped you. I don't want you to feel bad. *(hugs her)*

Vesna: Are you sure?

Branko: *(smiles)* Yeah, I am. Come on, let's take a walk, as friends.

As the situation calms down they start walking alongside the Danube.

Scene 22

With the walk with Vesna cleared, Branko finds himself home sooner than expected awaited by Bojana who's in the living room watching TV.

Bojana: You came back early, where were you?

Branko: I was out with Vesna. Where are mom and dad?

Bojana: I think they went one of our aunt's places, I don't remember which one, they won't be home by eight or nine. Why did you go out with Vesna, I thought you guys were a thing of the past?

Branko: We are, but we kind of aren't, it's confusing.

Bojana: Shouldn't you have figured out that by now? I thought you broke up with her?

Branko: I did but she wants us to still be friends and to stay on good terms with each other. That might be nice. But I can feel that there's this part of her that's still mad at me.

Bojana: *(confused)* Why is that so difficult for her? You are literally the one who broke up with her?

Branko: Yes, but my reason is that I just didn't feel the spark anymore.

Bojana: And that's not enough?

Branko: Apparently.

Bojana: Well, to be honest, you seem fine to me, so it doesn't seem like too big of a deal. Can I talk to you about the Nenad issue?

Branko: Uhm sure, any news on that?

Bojana: Yeah. I talked to mom on the day you got the results and a few days after that.

Branko: Why didn't you tell me anything?

Bojana: Because I promised mom to keep it a secret. *(she gets up to make get a bag of chips)*

Branko: Okay, but do you plan on telling me?

Bojana: Only if you promise to keep it to yourself.

Branko: I kept it to myself so far, don't worry about it.

Bojana: *(walks demonstratively around the kitchen)* So, she's thinking of convincing dad to forgive Nenad and to settle this once and for all. She wants us to go to the wedding.

Branko: To Tirana? Do you think dad would ever step foot on Albanian soil?

Bojana: He can't hold a grudge against his brother forever. It's a delicate subject and we all know that. But if we give him some time, he might come around. *(opens the bag of chips)*

Branko: That would be a good thing.

Bojana: I know. Mom plans to talk it through with him when you'll be in Budapest, as that would give her the sufficient alone time with him. I agreed to hang out with my friends a lot during that time.

Branko: And you're really convinced that this could work?

Bojana: Yes, this family has been making a fuss about this for way too long. It's just way too much drama.

Branko: Isn't going to Tirana going to create more drama?

Bojana: Yes.

Branko: And why is that okay?

Bojana: *(laughs)* Because it's all of our family at one place. How can you not have drama at such an event?

Branko: Good point.

Bojana: *(giving him the bag of chips)* Want some?

Scene 23

The scene opens on April 10th at Belgrade's main railway station at 7 am. Branko just got out of his bus and is meeting up with the group. Bojan is making a few announcements.

Bojan: *(points at a train)* So that one will leave at 7:36 and we'll be in Budapest at around 4 pm if everything goes according to plan. I'll see you on board.

The group separates as Branko, Dejana, Jelena and Sara walk towards the train.

Dejana: Let's go get a coupé!
Branko: A coupé?
Dejana: Yes, this train is divided into compartments for six people, we can take one for ourselves.
Branko: Awesome!

They enter the train and get settled.

Dejana: What's the time?
Sara: *(looks at her phone)* 7:25
Jelena: So this is it, we're going to Budapest.
Dejana: I really can't wait. It's been ages since I was there for the last time.
Branko: I've never been there before.
Jelena: Really, didn't you go there with your school?
Branko: No, last year we went to Bratislava, Vienna and Prague.
Dejana: Oh, trust me, you will love Budapest. I know that most Serbs don't really like Hungarian people, but Budapest is awesome. They have a really cool night life.
Sara: Don't we have pre-determined social events for the participants of our competition?
Dejana: *(is very excited)* Even better, a room full of young artists. What do you want more?

The train starts pulling out of the station

Jelena: Am I sensing hoeing opportunities?
Dejana: I'm a free woman. I can do what I want.

Sara: *(looks over to Branko)* I'm sensing that someone's uncomfortable.

Branko: I'm not! I just didn't think there'd be people hooking up at these things.

Jelena: Are you out of your fucking mind? You have young artists from all over Europe in one place under the influence of alcohol. What do you think is going to happen, haven't you ever been to a model UN?

Branko: A what?

Dejana: I think that's a thing only private schools do. That's not relevant. The point is: Yes, people do hook up there.

Branko: And why do you want to hook up there?

Dejana: Well, I guess I've been trapped in a relationship for so long that I want to enjoy my freedom for a while. You know? Let myself go. Sexual liberation is a thing, you know?

Branko: Trust me, I know what it feels like to be trapped, but is that the best way?

Jelena: Branko, trust me, hoe life is the best life. So you go, girl.

Dejana: Thanks, girl.

Branko quietly stops contributing to the conversation and rests his head on the window to get some sleep.

Scene 24

As the train arrives in Novi Sad, Milica joins the group in the coupé.

Milica: Sup bitches!

Branko: Someone washed their mouth today.

Milica: Only because I don't speak like a well "paid" politician?

Jelena: I like this girl.

Milica: So what's the T today?

Jelena: Well we started the journey talking about how hoe life is the best life, and are currently talking about the benefits of sleeping with officials.

Milica: Why that?

Dejana: I have a theory that no matter how high you set your standards, you would agree to sleep with someone to get out of something at some point in your life.

Milica: As in?

Dejana: You might not want to sleep with an ugly policeman to get out of a speeding ticket.

Milica: True, I wouldn't even want to sleep with a policeman.

Dejana: But what if you could sleep yourself out of a jail sentence?

Milica: Hmm. Good point. Would I do it? Depends on the benefit I guess.

Branko: Is this going to go on for much longer?

The discussion continued intensely up until the Hungarian border.

Jelena: But like, doesn't every university student have doubts whether their decision was utter bullshit or not?

Milica: Of course, I asked myself if I want to study sociology a thousand times, and I'm still not sure. I wanted to do an arts degree, but then I might as well directly apply for social welfare.

Sara: *(laughs)* Deki, maybe that's what you should apply for.

Dejana: Oh, screw you.

Branko: Did I miss something?

Dejana: Well, I thought of starting an arts degree in performing arts at the FDU.

Branko: Isn't it extremely difficult to get in there?

Dejana: Well they take around 20 out of 400 people who apply.

Jelena: But she has the talent to succeed at it. That's why we have been encouraging her. And this competition only proves it that you could one day be a valued actress.

Branko: You want to be an actress?

Dejana: Ever since I was little. I looked up to the likes of Seka Sablić and her extremely sarcastic and funny ways.

Branko: Since I come from a median income family, my mother always used to ask me: "What would you do if money was no object?" and I used to tell her that it was painting. And she encouraged me to do so, even though my father was against it. And now I'm here with you on this train, almost in Budapest.

Milica: Well said.

Branko: So, Deki, what would you do if money was no object?
Dejana: As if that were a question? I would just go for it.
Branko: Then that's exactly what you need to do.

Scene 25

The group arrives in Budapest at around 4 pm. Bojan assembles the group.

Bojan: So the Opening Ceremony is at 7 pm. We will go to the hotel now, check in to the rooms and then we will eat in the restaurant there. We will go to the opening ceremony later and after the official part is done, I will take the group that wants to leave immediately back home. You will each receive a public transit ticket for the length of your stay, so you will be fully mobile. You will also be given further details at the ceremony.

In the restaurant of the Leonardo Hotel, the group is eating as Branko shares a table with Milica.

Milica: I must admit that I've never stayed at a hotel this fancy.
Branko: Me neither to be honest.
Milica: *(looks over to the others)* They probably have.
Branko: Do I sense envy?
Milica: Not really. Growing up with money makes it easier to live and as long as you're not a spoiled brat you're good. Dejana is one of the nicest people I met in a long time.
Branko: I know, I hardly see people who are open hearted like that.
Milica: Those are the ones who typically get used.
Branko: And that's a shame for society.
Milica: Watch out for her. Please.
Branko: What do you mean?
Milica: She's in a vulnerable phase. She talked about the emotional damage she suffered on the train. That was after we crossed the border. You fell asleep.
Branko: Yeah, I didn't get any of that.
Milica: Anything? Wow, you sleep like a rock.

Branko: *(smiles)* And I'm cute when doing it.

Milica: There's also a non-serious version of you?

Branko: Sometimes.

Milica: Anyways, the girls and I want to make sure that she doesn't do anything stupid, feel free to join us.

Branko: I will. I wouldn't want her to get hurt.

They finish their meals and join the rest of the group to go to the Opening Ceremony.

Scene 26

At the opening ceremony, the organisers of the events are greeting, Branko is sitting next to Dejana on his left and the representation of Croatia on his right.

Dejana: *(extremely bored)* Oh God, how much longer is this going to take? I can't listen to this. I need a drink.

Branko: I think we'll all need a drink after this.

Guy: *(looks over to them, speaks in Croatian[1])* Will there be drinks after this?

Branko: *(in Serbian)* Yes, at least that's what the organisers told us.

Guy: Nice, looking forward to that.

Branko: Falling asleep as well?

Guy: Well I'm picturing my happy place right now.

Branko: I see.

Dejana: I think my happy place is somewhere in Slovenia. My grandma is from Lake Bled. I spent much of my childhood there.

Guy: Lake Bled is one of the nicest places in Europe. I personally find the Plitvice Lakes to be my happy place, but that's very patriotic of me.

Dejana: Did your supervisor even allow you to talk to Serbs?

Guy: Ha ha, very funny. We're not lunatics, you know.

Dejana: I'm teasing you.

Branko: She does that at times.

---

[1] Croatian and Serbian are almost identical and can be understood interchangeably without issues.

Guy: *(smiles)* Alright, that's a nice girlfriend you got yourself.

Branko: Oh, no, she's not.

Guy: Sure she isn't.

They keep on listening to the ceremony. After it ends Branko approaches Dejana. They start walking towards the drinks.

Branko: He thought we were a couple?

Dejana: Kind of, I mean we looked like one.

Branko: *(pours himself a glass of white wine)* Just because we're a guy and a girl sitting next to each other?

Dejana: *(pours herself a glass of red wine)* Most probably, people think like that. *(looks at the two glasses)* Also, we're totally not a match.

Guy: Don't opposites attract?

The Croatian guy appears with two other guys accompanying him.

Guy: I'm Luka, btw. *(points at the other two guys, continues in English)* These are Alex from Hungary, a gifted musician, and Daniel from Austria, a gifted painter.

They introduce each other.

Dejana: Oh cool, so you'll be competing directly against Branko in the painting competition.

Daniel: *(in an Austrian accent)* Seems like it.

Alex: And I'll be taking on Luka in the musical part.

Luka: My originals are no match to your covers.

Alex: We'll see about that on stage.

Luka: *(turns to Branko)* So what's the T on you two? How long have you been together?

Dejana: *(smiles)* Oh, we're not together. It's cute you'd think that.

Luka: So you're on the market?

Dejana: *(flirtatiously)* You can say so.

Luka: Sorry, I'm not really into that.

Dejana: What, me?

Luka: No, not just you, girls in general.

Dejana: Oh. Okay. *(looks over to Alex and Daniel)* And you guys?

Alex: Been dating long distance for almost two years by now.

Daniel: Ja.

Dejana: *(sips her wine)* I think I'm going to go find the girls. This is obviously a gay boys only round. *(walks away)*

Branko: I think I should go after her.

Alex: Why, don't you fit in this round?

Branko: Uhm, I don't know yet. *(awkward silence)* I'm going to go now.

Luka: I'll see you around?

Branko: *(walking away)* Yeah, sure.

Scene 27

At around 10 pm, with most of the crew tipsy, Branko stands with Milica and Dejana close to the doors as Jelena and Sara approach.

Jelena: Wanna go for a smoke outside?

Dejana: *(nods)* I could use a cigarette.

The girls start walking towards the door.

Milica: *(to Branko)* Aren't you coming with us?

Branko: I don't smoke, I'll stay here for a while and go to the hotel afterwards.

Milica: Suit yourself. *(walks away)*

Branko turns around and walks around the room as he is approached.

Luka: Well, well, look who we have here.

Branko: Woah, you really smell like wine.

Luka: Isn't free booze always an excuse to drink?

Branko: Yeah, you don't really turn it down.

Luka: You see my point. What are you up to?

Branko: I was about to get my coat and leave.

Luka: Whaaa? Why are you leaving man?

Branko: I guess I'm not really having the time of my life.

Luka: You need a drink.

Branko: No, I need to get home.

Luka: Oh come on.

Branko: What does it change for you? You can find other people to hang out with.

Luka: But the people from my team are so annoying. I don't want to be around them.

Branko: What about Alex and Daniel?

Luka: Yeah, I'm not going to be the third wheel on that one.

Branko: And what can I help you with then?

Luka: Hang out with me Branko.

Branko: I barely know you.

Luka: I want to get to know you.

Branko: Can't we do that another night?

Luka: We can.

Branko: Then let's do that.

Luka: *(stretches his hand out)* Promise?

Branko: I promise.

Luka: *(smiles)* I'll see you tomorrow then.

Branko: See ya.

Branko gets his coat and leaves the building.

Branko: *(to himself)* And another evening passes.

Luka: *(running after him)* Wait!

Branko: *(turns around, to himself)* Oh, God.

Luka: *(reaches him)* Let me come with you. Are you also at the Leonardo?

Branko: I am.

Luka: Then let's go together.

Branko: I thought you wanted to stay?

Luka: I changed my mind. The fun will start tomorrow anyways.

Branko: If you say so.

They both walk away from the hall.

Scene 28

The scene opens in a half-lit Soviet-era underground train blasting through the tunnels of central Budapest, with Branko and Luka sitting inside it, staring at the ceiling.

Announcement: A Ferenciek Tere következik.

Branko: So, where in Croatia are you exactly from?

Luka: I'm from Rijeka, but I study in Zagreb?

Branko: Something related to music?

Luka: Law. My parents wanted me to get a "proper" degree.

Branko: I can imagine how that must feel like.

Luka: Really? What do you study?

Branko: Nothing yet, I'm in my final year of high school. I want to go into the art department, but my father wants me to study something "proper". You know, law, economics, engineering.

Luka: Or Medicine.

Branko: Exactly. But I couldn't care less about any of those. Maybe politics, but even there I'd go crazy.

Luka: Trust me, I know how that feels. I feel like I'm going to drop out after my second or third year because I simply can't take it.

Announcement: Ferenciek Tere.

Branko: Ah, push through. What's 4 years of your life? It's better to waste a part of it than all of it.

Announcement: Kérem vigyázzanak, az ajtók záródnak!

Luka: *(annoyed)* This language is so weird. I hate it.

Branko: Why?

Announcement: A Kálvin Tér következik. Átszállhatnak az M4-es Metróra.

Luka: Do you really need an explanation?

Branko: I think I don't.

Luka: Hungarian is just so abstract. You have all of Europe with their language groups and then there's Hungary just going like: "Fuck you!" to the rest of Europe.

Branko: Don't forget Albanian.

Luka: *(laughing)* Am I sensing Serbian nationalism?

Branko: Totally. And now that I have lured you into my trap, I shall cut your throat.

Luka: Even with so many witnesses around us?

Branko: Why not? Besides, I always wanted to go to The Hague.

Luka: *(starts laughing)* Woah, that was dark.

Announcement: Kálvin Tér. Átszállhatnak az M4-es Metróra.

Branko: I can be funny if I want to.

Luka: Don't people think of you as funny?

Branko: No, they see me as shy and incapable. I'm more than that, *(stuttering)* I'm just. I'm just not that confident.

Luka: Shouldn't that change?

Announcement: Kérem vigyázzanak, az ajtók záródnak!

Branko: Yes.

Luka: So what's stopping you?

Branko: Do I look like I have a clue?

Announcement: A Corvin-Negyed következik.

Luka: I think you know what's stopping you from being you, but you're just too afraid to share.

Branko: I think you just can't see that I'm actually clueless.

Luka: *(stands up)* Fine. I'll buy it. *(pauses)* For now.

Announcement: Corvin-Negyed

Luka: Get up, we need to get off.

Scene 29

The next evening, Branko is sitting with the girls at Szimpla Kert (a large ruin pub consisting of multiple bars, fast food stands, dance-floors and rooms) which was reserved for the social event of day 1 of the exhibition.

Dejana: So, now I think that we might have a good chance in the next round, after seeing some of the competition.

Sara: Iceland is really up our ass, those girls are highly disciplined.

Milica: I believe that three of you can do it.

Dejana: How was your photography session?

Milica: They liked my works, I mostly had positive feedback. I'm supposed to exhibit my works at a school tomorrow and let Hungarian kids rate them.

Dejana: That sounds like a fun part of the competition. Is it just for the photographers?

Milica: It's also for the painters. I think, Branko, you're assigned the same school with me tomorrow?

Branko: Not sure. It's like at Köbanya something.

Milica: Yup, that one.

Dejana: Cool, so you guys will get to hang out a little. I always feel sorry when I see those lone competitors.

Branko: That's what these social evenings are here for. To meet the other teams!

Luka: *(appears)* I fully agree.

Branko: *(taken by surprise)* Jesus fuck. Can you not always appear out of nowhere?

Luka: I could try. I won't guarantee success though.

Branko: What's up?

Luka: You promised me I would get to know you.

Branko: I don't think I'm drunk enough for that.

Luka: Then let's go get a drink. It's on me.

Branko: Okay, I'd be down for a drink. *(stands up)* Girls, if you excuse me.

The two of them walk away.

Milica: Since when is Branko so confident? Do you think they're screwing?

Dejana: *(surprised)* What?

Jelena: Finally! Someone said it.

Dejana: Branko isn't gay.

Milica: Oh come, on it's so obvious.

Dejana: He's not. I asked me and he told me that he isn't.

Sara: You asked the dude if he's gay? Are you out of your mind?

Dejana: I was nervous.

Jelena: When?

Dejana: *(looks at Jelena)* Huh?

Jelena: When did you ask him that? I didn't see you spend a lot of alone time here.

Dejana: *(looks over to Milica)* On introduction day, after we brought you to the station, Branko and I went for dinner, and well, I. I kind of hit on him.

Jelena: *(shocked)* Oh my God, and you didn't think of telling us?

Dejana: He rejected me. I didn't want to talk to about it.

Milica: You like him?

Dejana: Yes, he's soft, he's sweet and he's caring. I feel like he would be the perfect boyfriend.

Milica: And that's why you asked him if he was gay?

Dejana: It was an embarrassing moment. I asked him, he denied it and then I told him that I liked him.

Jelena: *(hugging her)* Deki, what happened to you? That's not the confident Dejana I know.

Milica: Did you change?

Dejana: *(looks at Milica)* You don't know the abuse I've been through.

Milica: You said your ex cheated on you.

Dejana: Oh he did not only just cheat on me.

Milica: Oh, I'm so sorry.

Dejana: *(stands up)* I think I'm going to get myself a drink. I need one. Anyone want one too? *(the group stares at her)* Suit yourselves.

Scene 30

After getting them drinks, Luka leads Branko to a private section of the pub into a run down room with a run down couch, he sits on the couch while Branko opts for a simple chair.

Luka: *(sipping his cocktail)* What do you wanna know?

Branko: Huh?

Luka: Is there anything you want to know about me?

Branko: *(awkward giggle)* Are we having an interview over here? What an honour to be graced by a presence of the virtuoso of our times!

Luka: *(amused)* An honour it is! It's an offer you know you can't reject.

Branko: *(entertained)* True... a bold statement. How come you're so confident? Like, at all times?

Luka: I'm sorry, what?

Branko: How do you do it? Make yourself so likeable even when you're being arrogant. Were you the popular kid in school? How do you do it, Amadeus?

Luka: How I manage to seem confident?

Branko: Yeah.

Luka: That's quite simple. No matter how many self-doubts you have, you should always be yourself. Just by being you, you've already come far. Trust me, I'm not that confident, I beat myself up on a daily basis, but that doesn't have to see the light of day.

Branko: What's wrong?

Luka: Nothing is wrong. We all have our issues and dramas, there's nothing wrong about that.

Branko: I see.

Luka: And what's up with you. What's keeping you from being yourself?

Branko: What do you mean?

Luka: Come on, I've met you yesterday and I can already tell that you're always so tense, not able to let loose, serious as if you're an adult. It's as if you aren't in high school but are already retired.

Branko: My sister tells me that all the time.

Luka: If she's your sister, she must have a point.

Branko: Can you not question my life?

Luka: And where's the fun in not doing that?

Branko: Eh.

Luka: Oh come on. *(stands up to pull Branko over to the couch)* Come here. *(pushes Branko onto the couch)* Relax for a moment.

Branko: Are you going to force me to chill?

Luka: Yup.

Branko: *(lying there, looking up to the ceiling)* Okay, I'm calm.

Luka: Then, tell me, what's running through your mind?

Branko: A lot of things. I'm thinking about what you said.

Luka: *(turns towards him)* Uh huh.

Branko: I haven't been myself, and I haven't been doing what I wanted to do.

Luka: Why not?

Branko: I don't know. I just kind of… go with the flow. I do what's expected from me to do. Usually it doesn't really get to me, but sometimes I just wanna punch things. I'm aware I risk sounding like a fucking cry baby. Life has always been good to me. I just want more, I feel... trapped I guess.

Luka: Why are you not breaking free then?

Branko: What is hell am I supposed to do?

Luka: Maybe dare to take a risk every once in a while?

Branko: Like what?

Luka: I don't know, something like this maybe?

Luka kisses Branko.

Branko: Now we're talking.

Branko starts making out with Luka, as he hears a loud gasp.

Dejana: Branko?!

Branko: *(pushing Luka away)* Deki?

Dejana: *(stuttering)* I'm gonna... I'm gonna go. *(she runs off)*

Branko: Wait! *(turns to Luka)* Give us a moment. *(he follows her)*

Luka: *(to himself)* Now he broke free.

Act 2

Scene 31

After seing Branko and Luka kiss Dejana runs towards the rest of the group. Before she can make it to the group, Branko pulls her to the side.

Branko: *(frantic)* What do you think you're doing?

Dejana: What does it look like?

Branko: You're about to spill the T, I see it in your eyes!

Dejana: I'm confused. You said you weren't gay.

Branko: I lied.

Dejana: Why?

Branko: Isn't it obvious? Do you think I'd like to get beaten on the streets?

Dejana: Belgrade has changed.

Branko: Maybe to some extent, that doesn't mean that I'm not under threat.

Dejana: *(upset)*You could've told me.

Branko: But I didn't. As a matter of fact, I never told anyone.

Dejana: Am I the first?

Branko: Yes. *(annoyed)* And the only one for now.

Dejana: Why don't you want to tell the others?

Branko: I hardly even know them.

Dejana: But they will accept you. *(taps him on the shoulder)* You'll finally have people you can talk to.

Branko: I don't need people I can talk to, I have Twitter for that.

Dejana: *(taking out her phone)* You have Twitter? What's your username?

Branko: You're kidding me? As if I'd tell you.

Dejana: Oh come on, I put all of my rants on there as well.

Branko: No!

Dejana: Why? Do you share gay stuff on there and don't want me to see it?

Branko: I only share gay stuff on there, it's what Twitter is for! *(pauses)* My God, you're the first person I tell that I'm gay, and all you care about is my Twitter handle.

Dejana: I love it when someone spills T on Twitter.

Branko: Yeah, could you please not spill any in front of them?

Dejana: *(looks over to the group and back to Branko)* Are you sure?

Branko: Please, don't.

Dejana: *(calms down)* Okay. I promise I won't tell them.

Branko: Thank you.

Dejana: Are you okay?

Branko: *(quieter)* This feels weird.

Dejana: Awww, don't feel weird. Come here. *(she hugs him)* It's going to be alright. Come on, let's go have a drink together.

Branko: Uhm, I'd like to do something else.

Dejana: You want to go back to him, don't you?

Branko: *(smiles)* Yes, please.

Dejana: YAS qween! Go for it! *(gives him a high five)*

Branko walks back to Luka as Dejana joins the rest of the group.

Scene 32

The next day, Branko and Milica are at a school in the outskirts in Budapest, watching their works being presented to students.

Milica: So, about last night.

Branko: What about it?

Milica: You know, you and Luka. What did you talk about back there?

Branko: Oh, well, I asked him about his life in Zagreb.

Milica: What about it?

Branko: You know, his studies, his music. We talked a lot about his songs.

Milica: Oh, yeah, what kind of songs does he write?

Branko: *(hesitant)* Uhm...

Milica: You're lying.

Branko: I'm sorry, what?

Milica: Come on, don't lie to me.

Branko: Did Dejana tell you?

Milica: Tell me what?

Branko: Please don't bullshit me.

Milica: I'm not bullshitting you. She didn't tell me anything. It's just quite obvious that you're lying. You're hiding something.

Branko keeps quite as Milica stares at him. She then takes a deep breath.

Milica: *(tapping him on the shoulder)* I'm a lesbian Branko, you can tell me.

Branko: How did you…?

Milica: It was quite obvious. Don't take this the wrong way. I had a feeling you were, you know.

Branko: Yeah, I know. And now you know. *(sighs)* Are we done here?

Milica: Not quite.

Branko: What?

Milica: If you need someone to talk to, you know I'm here for you. I can speak from experience.

Branko: I know. But for now I don't really have anything to say.

Milica: Okay. *(turns her head)* I'll go check the rating.

She starts walking away.

Branko: Wait! I have a question.

Milica: *(turns around)* Yes?

Branko: *(frightened)* Do things really start getting better once you come out?

Milica: They might not at first, but after a while you'll start thanking yourself. Just keep your head up. *(smiles as she turns around)*

Scene 33

The next evening Branko, the girls from Serbia, Luka, Alex and Daniel are at a rooftop bar overlooking Budapest and the Danube river.

Alex: So, how does everyone like our city?

Dejana: It's beautiful. It has this European chic but it's not all too tacky.

Sara: Everything looks stunning from above. Especially at night.

Alex: Ah, it's these days that make me proud to be a Hungarian.

Daniel: It's also these days I am happy to be with a Hungarian!

Sara: You two are literally like, the cutest couple I've seen!

Jelena: Yeah, how long have the two been together?

Alex: Oh, that's a long story, you see…

Luka starts whispering to Branko.

Luka: What'd you say we ditch the others and go for a walk over the chain bridge.

Branko: Wouldn't that be kind of rude?

Luka: Oh come on they'll be fine with us. Plus, I really want to smoke one and don't want to go alone.

Branko: I'll keep you company then.

The two of them slowly make their way out of the bar away from the group and into the elevator.

Milica: *(whispering to Dejana)* Are you thinking what I'm thinking?

Dejana: *(smiles)* Someone is about to get laid tonight.

Meanwhile Branko and Luka are downstairs walking through the streets of Budapest towards the Chain Bridge.

Luka: *(smoking his cigarette)* So, tell me, how was your day? *(grins)* How does it feel to finally be a free man?

Branko: Huh?

Luka: Come on, tell me, how does it feel like to finally be out to people?

Branko: Oh that. *(laughs)* I don't know. I can't describe it.

Luka: Aw, you're sweet.

Branko: Oh, stop it.

Luka: *(smiles)* What? *(kisses him)*

Branko: Stop that, we're in public.

Luka: So? This is Budapest, you can be a free man here.

Branko: Yeah, just imagine that happening in Belgrade.

Luka: I wouldn't do this in some parts of Zagreb either. Although Zagreb has progressed enough there's still a 90% chance that at that exact moment I'm going to run into someone I know there.

Branko: So Zagreb is like the capital village of Croatia?

Luka: It's crazy, everyone knows everyone and you're just like kind of there going: Dafuq?

Branko: Do people there know you're gay?

Luka: Officially my friends know, unofficially all of Zagreb probably knows, gossip spreads fast.

Branko: Ouch, though crowd.

Luka: Yeah, as long as you're not ashamed of it, no bitch can hurt you.

Branko: Harsh words.

Luka: It's the truth, t b h.

Branko: Cruel world, huh?

Luka: Yeah, that depends. It's not always cruel. *(pulls him to the side, kisses him)* It's not cruel now. *(smiles)*

A few minutes later the two of them are standing on the Chain Bridge, overlooking the Danube river.

Luka: Now, if we got on a boat, would we get to Belgrade?

Branko: Yup, we would.

Luka: That would be nice.

Branko: Why so?

Luka: I've never been to Belgrade. My family is not really fond of Serbia and the Serbs, so I never got to go.

Branko: Belgrade is a chaos. It defies all logic and quite frankly is a terribly ugly city when you're looking for "European chic". It's the people that make the city what it is.

Luka: I should visit you once then.

Branko: I think Zagreb would be a nicer place to meet. That is, if we ever meet again.

Luka: I know our time here is limited. We will go back to living our boring lives once we're back home. I'm actually wondering what will happen to us.

Branko: What do you mean?

Luka: I like you, Branko, more than I'd maybe like to admit, but it is what it is. And I want to know how we can spend more time together.

Branko: I don't think I can give you a clear answer. I'll have to see once I'm back home if I'm even able to go anywhere in the near future.

Luka: I understand. *(takes his hands)* Promise me, you won't forget me and our time here.

Branko: *(kisses him)* I will never forget my true first kiss.
Luka: *(kisses him back)* Then let's make the most of the time we have left here.

Scene 34

The next morning Branko wakes up to the ring of a message on his phone. He opens Viber to find a message from Bojana.

Please tell me you're having the time of your life

> I am

> Don't worry 😊

Good 😌

I miss having you here

> I miss you too

Stay safe 💚

> I will 😘

Luka: Who even uses Viber nowadays?
Branko: *(shocked, puts phone away)* Would you mind?
Luka: *(smiles)* Good morning *(kisses him)*
Branko: Hi
Luka: You're cute when you're clueless.
Branko: You have no idea how often I've heard that.
Luka: Often?
Branko: Well, my ex used to say that from time to time. She found it cute, but irritable.
Luka: *(stutters)* W-Wait a second. She?
Branko: Yes?
Luka: I thought you were just gay, I didn't know you were bi.
Branko: I'm not bi.
Luka: So you have been lying to yourself?
Branko: *(hides under the blanket)* Yup, kind of.
Luka: *(pulls him closer, spoons him)* Oh God, Branko. How long do you

plan on keeping this up?

Branko: What? Lying to myself and others about who I am? *(pauses)* Not for very long, I see that there's much more to being gay openly.

Luka: Like living a normal life?

Branko: I wouldn't say normal. But at least it would be living, instead of hiding.

Luka: Agreed. *(pauses)* Hm, so if you're not bi, how did you sleep with your ex?

Branko: Simple solution: I didn't.

Luka: Then, there's one thing I don't understand.

Branko: What?

Luka: *(climbs onto him)* How are you so good in bed? *(kisses him)*

Branko: I watch an unhealthy amount of porn...

Luka starts laughing and lies on top of Branko.

Luka: I was always more of a learning by doing type. Or learning by re-doing. *(kisses him, pushes himself onto him)*

Scene 35

On their train back to Serbia, the group (Branko, Dejana, Sara, Jelena and Milica) are all sitting in a coupé together.

Branko: Guys, I think I have to tell you something.

Jelena: Yes?

Branko: Since you've all been so good to me, I feel like I should tell you, that I might like Luka more than anticipated.

Sara: So you're telling us that you're gay?

Branko: I thought you'd figured by now.

Dejana: *(displays her palms)* I didn't tell them anything.

Milica: Me neither.

Jelena: We thought so though.

Sara: It was kind of obvious.

Dejana: So what is it about Luka that you wanted to tell us?

Branko: *(insecure)* Well, you know. He's kind of the first guy I've been with, and I know it's just been a week, but I'm really starting to like this guy.

Dejana: We all have this connection to our first crush.

Branko: I had crushes before.

Dejana: But were they ever this serious?

Branko: I wasn't out, I couldn't act upon my feelings, and they were probably all straight.

Dejana: See, and that's why it's so different now. You're falling for someone who is probably falling for you.

Jelena: So what's the problem? Is it the distance?

Branko: Kind of, Zagreb is far away.

Sara: It's only like five hours by bus, totally manageable.

Branko: But it would be a financial burden. I'm middle class, nowhere near your standards.

Milica: I do get Branko. We don't always have 40 euros to spend on a ticket to Zagreb.

Branko: It's not the end of the world if we have to spend that once or twice, but it would add up quickly if it becomes regular.

Jelena: So what do you want to do? Do you want to forget him?

Branko: That's what I was thinking.

Sara: I think that's a good idea. That will come with time, once you're back home, it'll all settle.

Dejana: No, that's a shitty idea. I think Branko should keep Luka in his life.

Jelena: Why? It's only going to hurt him.

Dejana: Think of it this way: Branko, how many gay people do you know?

Branko: Personally?

Dejana: Only Luka, right?

Milica: And me!

Dejana: And her. Anyone else?

Branko: Not really. I have a few people on Twitter, but I never really met them.

Dejana: See, that's what he needs Luka for. Not to be there for him as a lover, but to have another gay man he text and talk about issues that no one of us understands.

Milica: She has a point.

Dejana: And if the distance bothers you, try using Twitter to meet someone.

Sara: Or get something like Grindr.

Branko: I haven't fallen that low yet, thank you.

Sara: Suit yourself.

The train pulls into Novi Sad's main railway station.

Milica: Well, this is my city. I need to get off now. Thank you for this amazing week, you're truly the coolest people I met in a long time. Please text me if you ever come to Novi Sad.

Dejana: *(stands up to hug her)* We will, please text us when you're in Belgrade.

Milica: I will. Bye, everyone!

She goes around hugging everyone and leaves the train.

Scene 36

In the evening Branko and Bojana are chilling in Branko's room. He tells her some of the stories from Budapest.

Bojana: *(impressed)* Wow, so you actually managed to win quite some prizes. Did they include cash?

Branko: I think I took home some 700 euros, but I want to save that for a special occasion.

Bojana: Anything in mind? The new iPhone?

Branko: No, I'd like to travel somewhere after graduation.

Bojana: Travel somewhere? Like to the seaside?

Branko: Yeah. I didn't swim in a long long time. I could consider it.

Bojana: Well you could go to Greece or Bulgaria, they have great offers there. Or you could go to Turkey by plane! You always wanted to fly some day.

Branko: Well, I was thinking Croatia.

Bojana: Croatia? Like Split, Zadar or Dubrovnik?

Branko: Actually, I wanted to look into Zagreb.

Bojana: *(surprised)* Zagreb? That's not even on the sea. Why on earth would you go there?

Branko: Well, I met this really cool guy from Zagreb and he invited me over, so I wanted to visit him.

Bojana: Can't he take you to some sea resort? It would be a shame to go to Croatia and miss what might be the most beautiful coast in Europe.

Branko: Is it?

Bojana: Of course it is. I'm not one of those nationalists who refuse to go to Croatia because they feel like they will get beaten because they're Serbs. The war is over.

Branko: True that.

Bojana: So tell your friend to go swimming with you.

Branko: Well he did say that he's from Rijeka.

Bojana: Then go to Rijeka. You deserve an amazing summer!

Branko: *(smiles)* I'll try my best. Thanks!

The conversation dozes off for a few moments until Branko takes on another subject.

Branko: Say, are there any news on uncle Nenad's wedding?

Bojana: Actually, yes, it seems like our father is warming up to the idea of actually going. Since it's in July, we still have a little time to spare.

Branko: Do you think he'll go for it?

Bojana: I don't know. I'd like to keep myself out of the issue. I talked to mom and she said that she'll take care of it. So she's on our side.

Branko: That's a good sign.

Bojana: *(in a calm voice)* Yup, now we wait.

Scene 37

Branko and his friends are sitting on a bench the day after his arrival enjoying the rising sunny temperature of up to 22°C

Petar: *(amazed)* 700 EUROS. Dude! That's two entire salaries. You're rich man. I always thought your hobby was a pointless waste of time, but shit man, I was wrong. You made it!

Branko: Oh please I had one somewhat important success, it could be the end of it as well.

Ivan: Or it could be the start of more than that. Try submitting your work to galleries, you might even get paintings sold.

Branko: I guess that would be something I could look into. *(pauses)* After graduation that is.

Ivan: Sounds plausible.

Petar: So tell us. What do you plan to do with the cash?

Branko: Well, I wanted to start going out more, you know, live a little. And I wanted to go on a holiday. Travel around a little bit.

Petar: Dude! Just combine both. You could totally go to Zakinthos, that's like the best party island in the world.

Ivan: What about Ibiza? You always wanted to fly.

Branko: That just sounded exactly like my sister. And, no I'm not really interested in Greece or Spain. I wanted to go to Croatia.

Petar: *(deepens his voice)* What the fuck do you want to do in Croatia?

Branko: Why does it seem like such a bad idea?

Petar: Don't they see us as the enemy?

Branko: Not really, I made friends with a guy from the Croatian delegation in Budapest.

Petar: Seriously? Peace with the Croats? That's gay.

Branko: Oh come on.

Ivan: *(in a calm manner)* Branko is right. We're no longer in the 90s, we weren't even born during the war. Why would we care so much about Croatia? We're still ethnically related to them.

Petar: Tell that to a Croat, he'll chop your head off.

Ivan: You're a moron sometimes. *(pauses)* Anyways, Branko, I feel like it's a good idea for you to go. I'm sure that Croatia is interesting. You might really like it.

Branko: I think so too.

Petar: I still think you're crazy. First, you break up with Vesna, then you win the double of a monthly salary in prize money and you want to go to Croatia with it? Hell, I wouldn't be surprised if you sucked a dick to get that money.

Branko: *(to himself)* I did do that though, I just didn't get paid.

Branko: I do still have dignity, you know.

Petar: I know, don't take me seriously, I just think what you plan on doing is a waste of money.

Branko: Then we'll have to agree to disagree.

Scene 38

April 22nd, 2016, the first Friday after Budapest, Dejana and Branko are sitting in a small café in Belgrade's downtown area of Dorćol.

Dejana: So how's your life been since you came back?

Branko: Well it's been alright. My ex ignores me in school most of the time. My friends are judging me for wanting to spend my prize money on Croatia and my sister is the only person I like talking to. Besides you, of course. *(smiles)* Otherwise I wouldn't be here.

Dejana: *(blushes)* Aw, thank you. So sweet of you. But, uhm, why do your friends judge you for wanting to go to Croaita?

Branko: My friends are not necessarily the most open minded people on the planet. They don't really get it and I can't really tell them that I want to visit Luka in Zagreb, because I'm not out to them yet.

Dejana: *(smiles)* So you do want to see Luka?

Branko: Yes. *(grins)* You were right. I do want to spend more time with him.

Dejana: Told you so.

Branko: We've been texting the past few days and it's been so nice.

Dejana: Aww, how sweet.

Branko: Anyways. If my friends are not quite keen on the idea of me going to Croatia, then how will they react to my coming out? If I choose to come out that is.

Dejana: You mean your two bros from school?

Branko: Yes, Petar and Ivan.

Dejana: I see. *(hesitant)* Do you think they'll accept it?

Branko: Accept me being gay? Hell no, they would probably beat me.

Dejana: Then why are you friends with them?

Branko: What do you mean, why am I friends with them? We've always been close.

Dejana: That doesn't make them good friends. When we're little we play with other kids because they are our age, but as we get older we have to surround ourselves with like-minded people in order not to end up in toxic friendships. Has it ever occurred to you that they might be the reason why you feel so scared of coming out? Don't let them run your life for you.

Branko: Oh come on, I would never fall under their pressure.

Dejana: During every walk we went for in Budapest you mentioned how you're beating yourself up because you gave into the pressure of being with Vesna and how happy you are now that you can finally let your true colours show. So why don't you do that now?

Branko: You got a point there.

Dejana: Listen, I can image coming out must be hard, but it's necessary to do it at some point in your life if you ever want to live a free life.

Branko: I know. And I don't think my friends will be a major problem. Since I won't have to see them after graduation. It will hurt distancing myself from them, but I feel like it's for the better.

Dejana: Then where's the problem?

Branko: My family, mostly my father.

Dejana: *(in a regretful tone)* Oh, I'm sorry. I should've thought of that.

Branko: My father doesn't even support my course of study.

Dejana: Well, in that case: If I were you, I would wait until I could support myself. Have you told your sister?

Branko: No, I'm scared of that too.

Dejana: Do you want my honest opinion?

Branko: Always.

Dejana: If I were you, I would tell her.

Branko: I want to tell her, but I feel like she's too young to understand.

Dejana: She's 16, I think she's old enough.

Branko: *(nods)* Yeah, you might be right.

Dejana: In Budapest, you described her as an angel and a blessing to your life. So why can't you tell your angel that you need her help to get back into heaven.

Branko: That's the one thing I never doubted.

Dejana: Getting into heaven?

Branko: Yes. *(pauses)* I am religious, I grew up realising that I'm gay through no fault of my own, and I do believe that God made me like this.

Dejana: *(starts singing)* I'm beautiful in my way, 'cause God makes no mistakes. I'm on the right track!

Branko: Exactly. So I still go to church and keep my spiritual side alive, it does help me quite a lot.

Dejana: *(annoyed)* Ugh, I didn't go to church for ages.

Branko: Then we should go together sometime. If you want to.

Dejana: I'd love that. You can text me when you usually go, I wouldn't want to disturb family time.

Branko: Yeah, my dad likes to go every week, but the rest of us doesn't really keep up with that. I usually go a few times every month. I'll text you.

Dejana: *(smiles)* Deal.

Scene 39

The same evening, Branko is hanging on his phone looking at funny memes on Instagram when he receives a text from Luka.

How was your day?

Are you getting used to WhatsApp by now?

It was good

Yes, it's a bit of a challenge,
but I like it more than Viber

I still don't get why you use that in Serbia?

It's kind of a thing, don't ask me why

Okay

What did you do today?

I was out with Dejana

We talked about quite a lot of stuff

I realised that I have a bunch of fake friends

Why would you say that?

> Because I feel like my two best friends from
> school would turn against me if I told them that
> I was gay

> And I don't want that to happen

Well, a coming out process does require us to
break out of our shell

And sadly we do have to leave some people behind

> Isn't that terrible though?

It is

But being gay in this region was never easy

And it won't be easy, especially not when you
still have to come out

> Then why should I even come out?

Because it's one of the most beautiful things you can do

You're finally free afterwards

Trust me

> Dejana said the same thing

Well, the girl has a point, listen to her!

> I know. I'm just scared that everything is
> going to change from now on

Everything will change from now on, trust me

But that's not a bad thing, it's a good thing,
because at the end of this long road is a
beautiful future waiting for you

> You're making it sound so easy...

Trust me, I know it's not

> So what do you suggest I do? Tell
> my friends and risk losing them?

I'm suggesting you don't do anything

Try to hang out less with them, get detached

It will hurt less when they find out and reject

I know it's a horrible thing to think about, but
you don't have any other options, and this one
doesn't hurt you as much

                    I think that I'll need some time to think about it

You do that

                                                        I will

One more thing though

                                                        Yes?

I wanted to talk about us

                                            What about us?

Listen, we had a great time in Budapest, and I
really enjoyed every minute we spent together

But

I hope you know that this can't go any further. If
you come to Croatia we'd have some fun and
it'd be great, but it wouldn't be anything more
than that

And I hope you know that

                                            Luka, I know

                            You're my first, so I do feel some
                            sort of connection towards you

                            Personally, I'm just happy to have
                            another gay guy to talk to

                    I haven't really met a lot of gay people in my life

Okay, good to know

Wait? So you've never been in a gay bar or club?

                                                        Nope

And you never met anyone off of Twitter?

                                                        Nope

Have you tried Grindr?

                    Nope, because the people on there are probably disgusting

Tru

So, you're like completely detached from the gay world?

                                                        I guess

What are you waiting for????

Get yourself out there!

Why should I?

Don't you want to meet people who understand?

People, who are not like your friends from school?

People, who actually get it?

I guess

My God, tell Dejana to take you to one of these places

So I should force my fag hag
to take her GBF to a gay bar?

Isn't that too much of a cliché?

It is a cliché, but everyone does it.

Just talk to her about it, okay?

I will

Okay, good

I have to go, talk to you soon, bye 😘

After the conversation with Luka, Branko takes his phone to Viber to text Dejana.

Deki, you said you wanted to join us for church?
Well if you want you can come tomorrow and join
us for lunch afterwards. How does that sound?

I'd love to! 😊

Scene 40

The next day after church, Dejana is sitting with the Jovanović's at the lunch table.

Mrs Jovanović: *(to Dejana)* Oh it's so nice to finally meet someone of Branko's new friends.

Dejana: Oh please, the pleasure is all mine. Thank you for having me.

Mrs Jovanović: Oh sweetie, you're welcome anytime.

Bojana: I like her.

Mr Jovanović: So you represented our country as well? Did you get any prize?

Dejana: We were 4th in contemporary dance, which is good, but unfortunately it wasn't enough to reach the top 3.

Mr Jovanović: Ah, that doesn't matter. It matters that you tried your best and did well!

Dejana: That's true. But it's still nice to win. Or come in second. *(throws Branko a smile)* You must be proud of your son.

Branko: *(blushes)* Deki, stop.

Mr Jovanović: To be honest, I am. I didn't think much of this entire art thing before, but he seems to have the talent for it. So yes, I am proud.

Branko: Oh. Really? *(smiles)* Thanks, dad!

Mr Jovanović: You're welcome son. If you continue to perform like this we can talk about getting you into art school.

Branko: Are you serious?

Mr Jovanović: Of course I am serious. When you, your sister and your mother went to light the candles at church, Dejana over here talked to me. She told me that the community in visual arts is very respectable and that if you're good enough you can make a living off of it. And you seem to be good enough to do that, and if you can be happy that way, nothing would make me happier.

Branko: Thanks, dad.

Mrs Jovanović: You know sweetie, the only reasons your dad and I wanted you to study something like economics, law or medicine is because we want you to have a good life and a job. Your dad is afraid that you're going to end up like Milenko.

Dejana: Who's Milenko?

Bojana: Our older brother.

Dejana: Oh, Branko never told me he had an older brother.

Bojana: Yeah, he's a deadbeat university dropout, who couldn't properly get an engineering degree, so he moved to Malta where he spent the past few months stuck on a construction site.

Silence.

Bojana: What? It's true.

Mrs Jovanović: So, Dejana what do your parents do?

Dejana: Oh, well my father is a graphic designer and my mother is a diplomat.

Mrs Jovanović: Oh, that's nice, did you move a lot?

Dejana: Yes, I did. I lived in Abu Dhabi and Tirana.

Mr Jovanović: You lived in Albania?

Dejana: Yes, that's correct.

Mr Jovanović: Did you encounter any problems? You know, because you are Serbian.

Dejana: Well, my personal experience is that the government dislikes Serbia because of the Kosovo conflict, but the people are perfectly fine. Sometimes you can get some rude comments, but most people you meet are quite alright. I think it is worse in the countryside or in Kosovo, but not in the big cities like Tirana.

Mr Jovanović: So you would say it's safe to go there?

Dejana: Oh definitely. If you know how to behave you'll be completely fine. Tirana might seem a little dangerous at first because it's a bit run down, but in general, you won't encounter any major problems.

Mr Jovanović: That is interesting. Especially since it's coming from someone who lived there.

Mrs Jovanović: Ah isn't that nice. *(smiles)* Dejana you are born to be a diplomat. Think of all the barriers you could beat down with your experience!

Dejana: Thank you Mrs Jovanović, I appreciate your words a lot.

Mrs Jovanović: *(taps her on the shoulder)* Please, call me Jadranka.

Mr Jovanović: You can also refer to me as Dragan.

Bojana throws Branko a hopeful look.

Scene 41

The scene opens after lunch, as Branko, Bojana and Dejana decided to go for a walk alongside the Danube.

Bojana: Dejana, you killed it over there at the lunch table!

Dejana: Oh please, I was just speaking my mind.

Branko: Bojana has a point though. You killed it.

Bojana: We're used to our dad being a bit more on the conservative side, so it was nice to see him warm up a little.

Dejana: Oh, really? Well, I didn't really get that impression of him. Sure, he seems a bit more traditional, but that doesn't make him conservative.

Branko: *(raises an eyebrow)* It doesn't?

Bojana: I think that's debatable.

Dejana: Well, I obviously don't know him as well as you two do. He just left a different impression.

Silence

Branko: *(nervous)* Boki, I need to tell you something.

Bojana: *(curious)* Now?

Branko: Yes, I wanted to do it with Dejana here, because...

Bojana: Because you don't have the balls to do it on your own?

Dejana: *(laughs)* Wow, she's good.

Branko: Yeah we get it, I'm a weakling, can we move on?

Bojana: Sure, what did you do? Did you kill someone? Did you steal something? What should I say to the police if they ask me?

Dejana: Oh wow, she's good.

Branko: *(confused)* No, it's none of that. Bojana, I'm...

Bojana: going to vote for Vučić?

Branko: *(shocked)* What? No! I'm gay.

Bojana: Phew! *(breathes out)* I already assumed the worst my bad.

Branko: *(perplexed)* So? Uhm...

Bojana: Listen, I don't care if you're gay, straight, bi or whatever, as long as you don't vote for the progressive party, I will love you no matter what!

Branko: *(touched)* Awww, that's the sweetest and most politically incorrect thing you could've said to me.

Bojana: *(opens arms)* Come here. *(hugs him)* I love you.

Dejana: Awwww, that's the sweetest and justifiably most political incorrect thing I've seen.

Bojana: *(smiles)* I want my brother to be happy, not stupid!

Scene 42

Branko and his family are standing at the polling station waiting for their turn to vote in the preliminary parliamentary election 2016. (April 24th)

Mr Jovanović: *(dressed up in a nice suit)* My second son is about to give his first vote, what a day to be a proud father.
Mrs Jovanović: We just need to stop Vučić from being in power.
Bojana: Milenko already texted me from Malta. He voted in the embassy this morning with a few of his colleagues.
Mr Jovanović: *(grumpy)* I hope he chose some appropriate party.
Bojana: He told me he supports DJB[2], the new party.
Branko: *(looks over to her)* I'm thinking of voting for them.
Mr Jovanović: They seem respectable. Though I'm probably going to stick with the Democratic party as always. Even though they're not what they used to be. What about you Jadranka?
Mrs Jovanović: Oh, well I was thinking either Democratic or Liberal.
Mr Jovanović: Liberal? *(pauses)* Interesting. I never thought highly of them, but I guess they would be good at EU negotiations.
Branko: Let's just hope for the best.

In the evening the family is sitting in front of the TV, watching the results.

Mr Jovanović: Motherfuckers
Branko: How did they get 48%?
Mr Jovanović: Because people in this country are radical and stupid. They probably stole votes. I bet you they either stole votes or bribed people into voting for them.
Bojana: *(reading the news)* 1000 dinars (ca. 8,30€) and a sandwich.
Mrs Jovanović: You know what I don't understand. Why do they have 131 out of 250 seats if they only got 48% of the vote?
Mr Jovanović: Because our political system doesn't give a voice to smaller parties. They have more than 50% of the votes for parties who acutally managed to get into parliament.
Bojana: *(looking up from her phone)* So what happens now?

---

[2] DJB: Dosta Je Bilo (literally: We have had enough)

Mr Jovanović: Nothing, Vučić secured his role as prime minister and we will be under his party's rule until 2020. Next year's the presidential election, let's see if we end up being an autocracy.

Branko: But will people vote for Nikolić again? He's been president for four years now and no one ever saw him do anything at all!

Mr Jovanović: Probably Vučić will put himself on the top. He'll have a problem with that election, but if he succeeds, we might as well end up being a dictatorship. We might as well be the next North Korea.

Mrs Jovanović: Oh, kids, your father is just exaggerating.

Bojana: I'm not going to cut my hair according to government standards anyways.

Branko: Do you have to do that in North Korea

Bojana: Google it.

Branko takes his phone out only to find conflicting articles on this rather sensitive and somewhat bizarre topic.

Scene 43

A few evenings later, Branko finds himself downloading the popular gay-dating app Grindr.

Branko: *(to himself)* Okay, since basically everyone told me to get out there, let's try this. Okay, so most of the guys here don't have a face pic, I'll cut out my head from my beach pic then. This was taken last summer in Greece, is it still accurate? Eh, I might have a few extra kilos now, but who cares. Okay, body type, height, weight, description, HIV status, check. Okay, so what's next? Oh a message.

First chat

Hey

                                                                        Hi

What are you looking for?

                                                                        Uhm
                                                            Nothing really

I just got started

Do you want me to get you started?

                                          Sure, why not

Second chat

(nude photo)

                                                    ???

First chat

Do you wanna come over then so we can get started

                                          What?! No

                    I didn't mean that by getting started

Then I'm not interested, sorry

Third chat

(face pic)

Hi

                                                    Hey

How are you?

                                    I'm good, and you?

Also good

Would you mind sending a face pic?

                    Not really, since you also sent me one

                                              (face pic)

You're cute 😊

                                              Thanks 😊

                                        You're cute too 😊

Aw, thanks

What are you up to?

                    Nothing really, just chillin' at home

Cool

Are you going to WB?

                                                    WB?

Yeah, the party

What party?

Don't tell me you're a gay guy in Belgrade and
don't know what WB is?

I really don't know

It's the biggest gay party in Belgrade, you have to check it out!

Look up WB Komjuniti on Facebook

You'll find the WB traffic light party on there

Trust me, it's awesome

Okay, okay, I'll check it out

After taking a precise look on the page. Branko takes out Viber to text Dejana.

Deki, what are you doing on May 14th?

Nothing, why do you ask?

I want to go clubbing with you

OMG, do I get to see a gay club?!

How did you know?

I was hoping you'd ask one day

OMG, this is going to be so lit
YAAAAS

Scene 44

May 1st, 2016 marks Easter in the Orthodox world. Branko and his family are at the lunch table as the fasting period is broken and their mother served a wonderful meal.

Mrs Jovanović: *(smiling)* Milenko called me this morning, he said that he's very sorry for not making it for Easter this year, but he's not spending it alone.

Branko: Is he out drinking with his work buddies?

Mrs Jovanović: Actually, that's what I thought as well in the beginning, but that's actually not the case. *(pauses)* He told me he has a girlfriend.

Bojana: What?! He hasn't said anything.

Mrs Jovanović: He wanted to tell us when it got serious.

Bojana: How long have they been together?

Mrs Jovanović: About four months.

Bojana: That bastard. And he didn't say anything?

Mrs Jovanović: No, as I said, he didn't want to tell people until it got serious.

Bojana: Does that loser really need four months for him to consider it serious? Damn. I mean I love him, but he can be such a dick at times.

Mrs Jovanović: *(deepening her voice)* Bojana, language!

Branko: *(distracted)* Dad, you're oddly quiet. What's wrong?

Mr Jovanović: Nothing is wrong. *(pauses)* But I do need to tell the family something.

Mrs Jovanović: What is it darling?

Mr Jovanović: *(puts his fork down)* You were right, Jadranka. We can't let the kids down and we need more dialogue in the family.

Mrs Jovanović: Are you saying that?

Mr Jovanović: Yes. Kids, you remember uncle Nenad and his girlfriend, Diellza?

Bojana: *(with a very bright smile*Yes, we do.

Mr Jovanović: Well, your uncle is getting married on the 14th of July and has invited us to his wedding in Tirana. I was reluctant to tell you at first but your mother insisted we go. Your brother is going to be there as well.

Branko: We're going to see uncle Nenad again.

Mr Jovanović: Yes, and we're going to Tirana. Your uncle will do our travel arrangements. *(smiles at Branko)* And guess what son? You'll be flying for the very first time!

Branko: *(in disbelief)* This can't be true.

Mrs Jovanović: *(happy)* Oh my God, darling, thank you for giving him a chance! It's so nice to see this family grow back together.

Mr Jovanović: Happy Easter to everybody!

Bojana: Happy Easter!

The family laughs together at the joy of success.

Mr Jovanović: *(to Branko)* Oh and one more thing.

Branko: Yes dad?

Mr Jovanović: Could you ask your friend a few things about Tirana? Like things to see, or any good cafés and restaurants your sister and you can go to while I help your uncle prepare his wedding.

Bojana: Jesus, dad, how long will be there?

Mr Jovanović: Ten days, we'll even to go the beach in Albania. I was with Nenad on the phone and Diellza suggested we could go swim a little in Durrës.

Bojana: *(amazed)* Awesome, this is even better than I expected!

Branko: *(takes out his phone)* I'll check with Dejana what kinds of tips she has.

Scene 45

After lunch, Branko and Bojana take a walk to enjoy the warm weather in Belgrade.

Bojana: *(streches her arms out)* I love it when Easter is in May.

Branko: Really?

Bojana: Yeah, it gets warm enough to go outside.

Branko: *(checks his phone)* Yeah, 26°C is pretty acceptable.

Bojana: *(giggles)* Barely!

Branko: *(looks to the ground)* I still can't believe our dad decided to go through with the wedding.

Bojana: I can't believe we're going to stay in Albania for ten days. Ten freaking days, we're basically going on holiday. In Albania! Do you know how special that makes us?

Branko: Pretty special, I guess.

Bojana: Out of all the countries in the world, we are going to see fucking Albania. Our sworn enemies. And we're going to own the streets of Tirana.

Branko: Yaas!

Bojana: Oh, wow. You really are a gay man. How did I not see that coming? *(gets excited)* OMG! You're going to be a gay man walking through the streets of Tirana, the most homophobic city in Europe!

Branko: Is it really?

Bojana: Well, when you came out to me, I googled being gay and videos on YouTube and I kind of watched them all. Now I know all about Grindr, heartbreaking coming out stories, your hooking up culture and being gay in Albania.

Branko: What the fuck is wrong with you and why do I love it?

Bojana: It was the first vice documentary that popped up, okay?! And they said Tirana was the most dangerous place for gay men in Europe.

Branko: *(concerned)* Are you trying to discourage me to go?

Bojana: What? No! I'm trying to encourage you to be brave! That's what Charles Gross told me.

Branko: Who's that?

Bojana: Look it up. He's like the gay YouTube God.

Branko: Isn't that Davey Wavey?

Bojana: Oh, right, yes. I learned a lot about anal sex and douching from him.

Branko: Okay, TMI. You don't need to know all of that stuff. That's something I should worry about, *(dramatic pause)* not you.

Bojana: But I want to be informed! Besides, I always google stuff when I'm bored. Speaking of which, there's this gay traffic light party on the 14th of...

Branko: WB?

Bojana: *(claps)* And you already know!

Branko: Oh a guy told me.

Bojana: A guy told you? Which guy? Luka? Luka lives in Zagreb though.

Branko: Uhm, no, not him.

Bojana: *(silly)* You little slut! Did you download Grindr?

Branko: I totally did.

Bojana: OMG, did you hook up yet?

Branko: No! I'm trying to find something meaningful.

Bojana bursts out in laughter.

Branko: What's so funny?

Bojana: *(keeps laughing)* You trying to find love on Grindr?! Ahahahah

Branko: Should I try Tinder?

Bojana: No you idiot. Just go that party and see if there's any good stuff there. You might get lucky, but don't expect too much!

Branko: Or I can carefully choose whom I want to talk to.

Bojana: That won't work. Branko, if there's one thing I know about you, it's that you have more luck than reason.

Branko: Hey! I'm not stupid.

Bojana: *(grins)* I love you no matter what!

Branko: *(confused)* I love you too…

Scene 46

On the evening of the 14th, Branko and Dejana are waiting in front of the Mikser House to get into the club, as they hear a loud voice yell at them.

Voice: Branko?! Dejana?!

Dejana: OMG, Milica?! What are you doing here?

Milica: *(approaching them)* It's the gayest event of the month, what wouldn't I be doing here?

Branko: She has a point.

Milica: What are you two doing here? *(to Dejana)* Are you fag hagging?

Dejana: *(laughs)* Kind of, yeah.

Branko: I didn't want to go alone.

Milica: It's a traffic light party, you have to go alone if you're single.

Branko: Yeah, that's the thing I didn't quite understand.

Dejana: Me neither, what's a traffic light party?

Milica: There's these neon bracelets that glow in the dark you get at the start. Green stands for "I'm single", yellow stands for "it's complicated" and red stands for "in a relationship".

Dejana: Aaah, I see the traffic light metaphor in that.

Milica: Exactly. There's also blue for "looking for a hookup" which combined with green means "one-night stand", and combined with red means "open relationship". And purple for "I'm married / pure".

Dejana: I think I'm going to go for yellow.

Milica: I'm going for green and blue.

Dejana: Ooooh, somebody wants to get some.

Milica: Well, I don't want to just party until the first train to Novi Sad. *(laughs)* I wouldn't mind snuggling up to someone in a warm bed if you know what I mean.

Dejana: *(demonstratively sassy)* Girl, I know what ya mean, and you need to go get some tonight!

Branko: I think I'm just going to stick to green.

Milica: Well you're a gay man, if you want sex you can just use Grindr.

Branko: You can say that out loud?

Milica: Oh please, don't be such a prude.

Branko: Hey! I'm not a prude!

Dejana: You kind of are.

Branko: Hey... *(quiets himself down)*

Scene 47

After getting the first two rounds of drinks the group is dancing on the floor.

Everyone: *(chanting)* TI MOJE ZLATO, TI MOJE ZLA-ATO, TI MOJE ZLATO, TI MOJE ZLA-A-ATO. *("rapping")* Ljubi, ljubi, ljubi, ljubi me ona

Dejana: *(yelling to Milica)* You see that girl over there?

Milica: Yeah.

Dejana: She's been looking at you this whole time.

Milica: What?!

Dejana: SHE HAS BEEN LOOKING AT YOU

Milica: REALLY?!

Dejana: YES, EVERY TIME AT THE REFRAIN

Milica looks back to her as the refrain chants.

Everyone: TI MOJE ZLATO

Milica: *(to Dejana)* OMG, she's totally eye fucking me!

Dejana: Go talk to her!

Milica: What?! No way?

Dejana: *(pushes her)* GO!

Milica approaches the girl, while Dejana looks to Branko.

Branko: Playing matchmaker?
Dejana: *(smiles)* You're next.
Branko: I think I'm good. *(looks to the DJ)* Oh, I love this song.
OTROVE TI MI DOĐEŠ KAO LEK!

Scene 48

A few iconic songs later, Branko and Dejana are standing next to the bar with two cocktails in their hands.

Branko: Say, why didn't you take red?
Dejana: *(blushes)* Uhm, because I'm not in a relationship.
Branko: So you went for "it's complicated". Who's going to hit on you anyways?
Dejana: Wow, rude. *(pauses)* Well, girls can hit on me here.
Branko: But you're straight?
Dejana: Most probably.
Branko: And what am I supposed to take from that?
Dejana: Let's say that I have considered the other side of the spectrum.
Branko: You're curious?
Dejana: Yes. And I know it sounds horrible because nowadays every straight girl wants to get with a woman just for fun but I was seriously considering if I could ever love a woman. And I'm not one of those straight girls who want to use a lesbian just for their own path.
Branko: Okay. Have you tried dating apps?
Dejana: I set my Tinder to guys and girls, but the girls on there never text me back! *(checks her phone)*
Branko: Try talking to someone here then?
Dejana: It's not that easy. I'm super anxious when it comes to that. *(sips her cocktail)*
Branko: Well, what do you want to then?
Dejana: I don't know. I'm drunk and confused.
Branko: You don't seem drunk, you might just be a little tipsy. *(taps him on the shoulder)*

Dejana: If I was just tipsy would I do this? *(kisses him)*

Branko: Dejana! *(pushes her back)* What the fuck?

Dejana: Oh come on, relax. Have some fun!

Branko: What's wrong with you?

Dejana: *(in a drunk voice)* What's wrong with you? You're acting like a dad, and you're not even a daddy.

Branko: I'm too young to be a daddy.

Dejana: *(snaps her fingers)* Then act your age bitch.

Branko: Okay, you're drunk.

Dejana: *(laughs)* There we go. *(calms down)* Stop being such a stuck up bitch. Jeez.

Branko: Oh God, you're a show.

Dejana: Why thank you.

Branko: Not sure if that was a compliment. *(looks to the bar)* Did you see Milica?

Dejana: Yeah, she was with that girl right at the bar.

Branko points to the bar.

Dejana: *(shocked)* Oh fuck, where'd she go?!

Branko: Do I look like I have a clue?

Dejana: Maybe she went home with that girl?

Branko: I think she would've texted us that.

Dejana: Are you sure?

Branko: Oh definitely. It would at least be on Snapchat.

Dejana: *(checks her phone)* But it's not on Snapchat!

Branko: Then we have to find her. And fast!

The two split up to see if they can find Milica.

Scene 49

After looking for Milica in the club, Dejana enters the bathroom to pee. She sits in a stall as she hears noises from the stall next door.

Girl: *(puking)* Arrrgh.

Guy: *(in a soothing voice)* Hey, it's alright. Just let it all out. We got you away from that mean girl now.

Girl: *(mumbling)* Uh-huh.

Dejana: *(knocking to the neighbouring stall)* Milica is that you?!

Girl: *(mumbling)* Heh.

Guy: I'm sorry, do you know her?

Dejana: I might.

She flushes the toilet and moves over to the stall only to find a vomiting Milica held back by a young man.

Dejana: Oh God, Milica what happened?

Guy: She won't answer you, she's about half asleep.

Dejana: This is terrible, what happened?

Guy: A dangerous girl was flirting with her. She's known in the scene for an overwhelming drug consumption.

Dejana: Oh poor thing. *(remembers)* Oh, shoot, I need to text a friend. *(takes out her phone)*

Guy: You have another friend here?

Dejana: Yes, he's looking for her as well. We lost her to that girl.

Guy: Okay, so you're her friends? I can trust you?

Dejana: Yes. *(pauses)* You can go back to the club, have fun. I'll take it from here. *(looks to him)* Why are you still here?

Guy: It's okay. I wasn't having any fun either, and I want to make sure she gets home safely.

Dejana: You're sweet.

Guy: Plus, when your friend gets here, he can help me with carrying her outside.

Dejana: Sounds like a plan.

A few minutes later Branko rushes into the stall.

Branko: *(breathless)* Oh good, you're here. I was already reluctant about going into the girl's bathroom.

Guy: This is an LGBT event, the bathrooms are gender-neutral.

Branko: Are they?

Guy: Yes, they are.

Branko: Oh okay. *(pauses)* Wait a second, who are you?

Dejana: This guy was nice enough to help Milica when she almost collapsed. *(whispers)* So be nice.

Branko: Ok, ok, I'm sorry.

Guy: It's okay. Could you help me carry her out of the club?

Branko: Yes, of course.

Branko and the guy take over carrying Milica out of the club, while Dejana makes sure to clear the path through the crowd.

Scene 50

Outside of the club the four walk under Brankov Most (bridge) and assemble.

Guy: Okay, so it's about 2:15 right now, the last wave of night buses is in 15 minutes. Is there one we can take to get her home?

Branko: She lives in Novi Sad.

Dejana: She can sleep at my place.

Guy: Which district do you live in?

Dejana: Dedinje.

Guy: Well fuck, nothing runs there at this time.

Branko: I live in Zemun. She can stay at my place.

Guy: Is that the 15N?

Branko: Yes. That should do it.

Milica starts crying. She get's hectic.

Dejana: If we go to my place, I can call a cab. She can't go take a bus like this.

Guy: Then you'd have to go alone, I don't have the money for a cab back home.

Dejana: You can stay at my place.

Guy: Won't that get crammed?

Dejana: I live in Dedinje[3]. It'll be fine. I'll call a cab. *(takes out her phone)*

Branko: *(laughs)* I'm guessing you're in for a sleepover then.

----

[3] Dedinje is the richest area in Belgrade, is mostly consists of large houses and Villas. Dejana is implying that her place is big, simply by saying that she lives in Dedinje.

Guy: *(smiles)* Guess that's not too bad of an option. Spending time with random people, isn't that what clubbing is all about?

Branko: Kind of. *(pauses)* I'm Branko, by the way. And my friend calling the cab is Dejana, and the girl we're holding is-

Guy: Milica. I know. Your friend yelled her name when she found her.

Branko: Heh, yeah.

Guy: I'm Dušan. Pleased to meet you.

Act 3

Scene 51

The scene opens on the night of May 14th, 2016 to the 15th. Dejana, Branko and Dušan leave the cab with drunk Milica and enter Dejana's house.

Dejana: Okay, we should get her to my room, she can sleep with me.
Dušan: *(holding Milica)* I feel like that's a good idea. Which way is your room?
Dejana: Upstairs.

As they walk in they are greeted in a luxurious house on a hill overviewing Belgrade at night.

Branko: I've never been to your place before.
Dejana: It's a bit far out of the city.
Branko: *(amazed)* But this is amazing!
Dejana: Nah, I don't like to brag too much about it.
Dušan: If I were you, I would show off.
Dejana: Yeah, well, *(smiles)* I have my humble ways.

They reach Dejana's room and leave Milica to rest, as they walk downstairs to talk.

Dejana: So my dad and my brother are away for the weekend. They're doing a father-son bonding thing in the mountains. Zlatibor or somewhere down there. So technically you two could each have your own room, but I'd rather have the two of you stay in the guest room because I don't want to let anyone stay in their rooms.
Dušan: Your mother doesn't live with you?
Dejana: Oh she's in Angola.
Dušan: Oh. *(impressed)* Well. To each their own.
Dejana: She works there. Anyways, would you mind?
Branko: *(looks to Dušan)* I don't have a problem with it.
Dušan: Me neither, as long as the bed is big enough for two people.
Dejana: *(gestures)* Oh trust me, it is.

She walks over to the guest room, only to unveil a bright room with a king size bed and a stunning view.

Dušan: *(amazed)* Yeah, this is fine. This is totally fine.
Dejana: It's a little run down, but it does the trick.
Branko: Oh shut up. *(throws himself on the bed)* This is amazing. *(pauses)* I'm tired.
Dejana: I'll leave you two to it then.
Dušan: Oh, one more question, where's the bathroom.
Dejana: *(points to another door)* Right over there. Your own small bathroom with a toilet and shower. There should be towel there too.
Dušan: *(mesmerised)* Damn, how rich are you?
Dejana: My father is a graphic designer and my mother is a diplomat. Plus both of them inherited a lot. Why does that even matter though?
Dušan: Most people I've met from richer families are usually spoiled bitches.
Dejana: Well you haven't met me then.
Dušan: I most certainly haven't. I guess I'll get a chance to in the morning?
Dejana: I guess you will. *(turns to the door)* I'm off, I need to get some sleep.

Dejana leaves.

Scene 52

Left alone in the room, Branko and Dušan get ready to go to sleep.

Dušan: *(a bit nervous)* Say, do you mind if I just sleep in my underwear?
Branko: No, go ahead. I'm going to sleep without my pants anyways.
Dušan: *(taking his pants off)* Don't you find this a tad bit weird?
Branko: *(taking his pants off)* Do you want to make it more awkward?
Dušan: *(laughs)* Can it get more awkward?
Branko: Yes, of course, it can. *(smiles)* I could ask you why you chose to wear the yellow band?
Dušan: Oh that's a bit complicated.

Branko: That's what it stands for.

Dušan: Yeah.

Branko: What happened?

Dušan: Well, I was with this guy who was a total loser and the relationship kept suffocating me up until it ended. I was tired of putting up with his lame bullshit, so I chose to become a hoe and fuck my way through life.

Branko: Why didn't you take a blue band then?

Dušan: I did…

Branko: But you took it off.

Dušan: It dropped when we left the club.

Branko: I see, an accident so to speak.

Dušan: Yeah, it hasn't been a really successful night. *(takes shirt off)* At least I helped someone and that does feel good. *(pauses)* Branko?

Branko keeps staring at Dušan's chest.

Dušan: *(approaching him)* Or will it be a successful night.

Branko: *(moving away)* I don't think so.

Dušan: Are you sure? We have this room to ourselves and I kinda caught you checking me out.

Branko: I'm pretty sure. I'm not into screwing a guy and never seeing him again.

Dušan: Are you sure you're even gay?

Branko: Yup, pretty sure.

Dušan: Then why don't you want to sleep with me?

Branko: Why is it that we sleep with each other first before we get to know each other? I mean sure, you're hot, probably the best shot I have at sleeping with someone like you, but what's the benefit if I have no clue who you are?

Dušan: Isn't that how it works? I don't like it either, but whenever I like a guy, I feel like I have to fuck him before I get to know him.

Branko: Oh bitch please, who said that you'd be the top.

Dušan: Well, I kind of assumed, that. Uhm. You know. You're a bit shy and passive in your acting. So.

Branko: So you assumed I'm a bottom?

Dušan: Kind of.

Branko: Oh God. You're really what's wrong with the gay community. *(lays down and turns his back on him)*

Dušan: *(lying on his back)* And you're different.

Branko: Am I?

Dušan: Yes, you have something other guys don't really have.

Branko: Oh yeah. *(turns to him)* And what is that?

Dušan: I don't know, but I do want to find out.

Branko: So what do you suggest we do?

Dušan: How about I take you out on a date? A real date.

Branko: Oh wow. Are you really serious?

Dušan: Yes, I am. I want to be proven wrong. Show me that you can date a guy without sleeping with him first.

Branko: Fine, I will. *(grabs his phone from the nightstand and hands it to Dušan)* Here. Add yourself on Facebook or give me your number.

Dušan: *(smiles)* And can I be sure you'll text me?

Branko: I promise.

Dušan: *(hands the phone back)* Here you go. It's a date then.

Branko: It's a date. *(pauses)* Well, good night then.

The two lay down to sleep.

Dušan: *(quietly)* Can I at least spoon you.

Branko: *(tired)* Go ahead, I don't care.

Dušan hugs Branko as they both fall asleep.

Scene 53

The morning after Branko wakes up in Dušan's arms.

Branko: *(slowly waking up)* Hi

Dušan: *(smiling)* Good morning.

Branko: *(smiles)* Morning.

Dušan: Do you want to see if the others are awake?

Branko: Yeah. Let's check the kitchen.

The two walk out only to see Dejana in the kitchen and Milica drinking coffee.

Dejana: Good morning guys. I'm making omelettes, do you want some?

Dušan: Oh, I'd love some! Thank you.

Branko: Sure, thanks. *(looks over to Milica)* There's our drugged lesbian! Are you alright?

Milica: *(tired)* Yeah. I still don't know what happened. I drank too much and then she gave me a pill. She told me that I'd feel better.

Dušan: Look. I know you don't know me, but-

Milica: Dejana told me what you did for me. *(smiles)* Thank you, I don't think I'll ever be able to repay you.

Dušan: Oh please, let that go. I just wanted to tell you that I heard about that girl you were with. She's known for drug abuse, and for dealing. My ex was an addict and I think she was his dealer.

Milica: *(surprised)* Oh?

Dušan: I dumped him when I found out.

Dejana: Wasn't that a bit too harsh from your side?

Dušan: It would've been fine if it was just weed, but it wasn't. And just look at your friend. You see what these things do to people.

Branko: He has point.

Dejana: *(to Milica)* I still can't believe you got drugged. That's like a girl's worst nightmare. Dušan, I don't think you know how much we owe you for this.

Dušan: Oh please, it was the least I could do.

Dejana: *(angry)* If I ever see that bitch again, I'm totally going to cut her throat.

Milica: Don't kill her though. I want to have the last cut.

Branko: Oh God. *(to Dušan)* Don't worry, my friends aren't always psychopaths.

Dušan: Oh please, it's fine. I think I'm at about their level of crazy.

Milica: *(chants)* Yaaaas!

Dejana: *(moves away from the pan)* So the omelettes are done, guys. Let's eat!

Milica: Oh thank God, I'm starving.

Dušan: *(to Branko)* I think I like your friends.

Branko: Yeah, they're that perfect mixture of adorable and creepy.

Scene 54

Later that day, Branko returns home, he walks into the living room to find his family watching TV.

Bojana: *(excited)* There he is! We were wondering where you were.

Mr Jovanović: We didn't receive any texts so we thought that you were partying until the morning. *(laughs)* Your mother already thought you got kidnapped.

Mrs Jovanović: *(shy)* I was a bit worried, but you seem to be well.

Branko: *(smiles)* I am. Milica came to visit from Novi Sad so she was in the club with us. We all had a sleepover at Dejana's afterwards.

Mrs Jovanović: Oh, that's really nice. You and Dejana seem to be really good friends.

Mr Jovanović: Is there anything going on between the two of you?

Branko: What do you mean?

Mr Jovanović: Well do you like her?

Branko: Oh, I see what you mean. I like her, I really do, but for now somehow just as a friend.

Mr Jovanović: Too bad. Dejana is a good girl. She's very intelligent and polite. She would be good for you. Vesna was nice too, but she was more of a status symbol.

Branko: I know, it was best for the two of us to split.

Mrs Jovanović: Oh, sweetie, don't feel pressured by your father. Just stay friends with her, if that's what feels right to you.

Branko: It does.

Mrs Jovanović: And that's great! Anyways, your father and I have been invited for dinner tonight, we need to leave in about 15 minutes, I left some moussaka for you two to heat up in the oven. Will that be enough? *(she walks over to the kitchen)*

Bojana: *(happy)* Awesome. Definitely.

Mrs Jovanović: I'll go get ready then. *(nagging)* Dragan, don't just sit there, get changed!

Mr Jovanović: Ah, women. What else would I do if I didn't have your mother? I'd be lost, that's what I'd be.

Branko: *(to himself)* You're lost already.

Scene 55

After their parents left, Branko was telling Bojana everything about the evening, while she was heating the moussaka. She placed it on the table as he finished.

Bojana: *(shocked)* So you're telling me Milica almost had an overdose?

Branko: I don't think it was that bad. But it wasn't very fun either.

Bojana: Wow, she dodged a bullet right there. She's lucky that guy came along.

Branko: Yeah, I think Dušan saved all of our asses that night.

Bojana: Yeah. So how was sleeping with him?

Branko: Oh my God, Bojana, I didn't sleep with him!

Bojana: But you said you shared a bed.

Branko: If that's what you meant by sleeping with him, then yes.

Bojana: That was not what I meant. I was actually hoping that you did actually have sex with him.

Branko: No, I didn't have sex with him. But if you must know, he invited me on a date.

Bojana: *(excited)* OMG! Now we're talking. When?!

Branko: We haven't yet set a date, but probably Friday.

Bojana: This is so exciting. You might actually have your first ever gay date!

Branko: Hey! I had a date in Budapest!

Bojana: Yeah, but Luka lives in Zagreb, it was obvious that wouldn't go any further than a few nights of sex and endless texting.

Branko: *(slightly salty)* With the texting already being over.

Bojana: You stopped texting with Luka?

Branko: We just kind of lost touch.

Bojana: Well that's all the more reason to date Dušan! You need to have another gay man in your life. It doesn't matter if you're together or not, you need someone you can talk to you about your gay stuff.

Branko: Can't I do that with you or Dejana?

Bojana: You can. And you know I'll always be there for you, but know that only a real gay man can understand how a gay man feels. Imagine Dejana and I were talking to you about your periods. You can feel sorry for our pain, but you don't know how it actually feels like.

Branko: That was a gross but accurate comparison.

Bojana: Oh come on, just because you're gay doesn't mean that you can be grossed out by the female body. *(takes her phone)*

Branko: You know that I never managed to sleep with Vesna because of that?

Bojana: Oh wow. *(looks up from her phone)* So that's the reason why the relationship went downhill.

Branko: Wasn't that kind of obvious?

Bojana: Yeah, I didn't spend that much time thinking about it.

Branko: You don't have to. I'm glad it's over.

Bojana: Yeah. Anyways, back to Dušan. So what are you going to wear for the date?

Branko: Uhm, my dark blue shirt.

Bojana: Oooooh, you're falling for him!

Branko: Am not!

Bojana: You plan on wearing your dark blue shirt. You only wear that on special occasions.

Branko: Okay, so I might have a little crush.

Bojana: That's so fucking cute. Does he have Instagram?

Branko: Yes.

Bojana: Give me his name. I wanna stalk him.

Branko: Dušan Kovačević

Bojana: *(typing it in)* So let me see. *(looks at profile)* What?! *(turns the phone to Branko)* Is that him?

Branko: Yes, that's him.

Bojana: And this guy asked you on a date?

Branko: Yes.

Bojana: *(stares at phone)* He's hot as hell. *(looks up)* You really have more luck than reason.

Scene 56

Wednesday, May 18th, 2016, Ivan went to a café with Branko to talk after school.

Ivan: Petar and I didn't see you around this weekend.

Branko: Yeah, I was kind of busy. Dejana, Milica and I went to a club.

Ivan: *(worried)* And we didn't see you around last weekend as well.

Branko: I spent that weekend with my sister.

Ivan: Branko, what I wanted to say is that we barely see you.

Branko: Oh. *(looks into the distance)* Well, I guess I've been hanging around a lot with Dejana lately.

Ivan: And that's not a bad thing. It's just that we think you might be angry with us.

Branko: *(looks to the ground)* Oh, I see what this is about.

Ivan: Ever since Petar and Vesna started dating you stopped hanging out with us.

Branko: That has nothing to do with that. They got together when I was in Budapest. The same time I started hanging out with Dejana. It's a pure coincidence.

Ivan: So you're not mad at Petar for stealing your girl?

Branko: *(slightly enraged)* Why the fuck would she be my girl? Girls are not property to be taken by us me.

Ivan: I know that girls are not property, but it was a dick move to take your girlfriend from you.

Branko: I broke up with her, he had the right to do so.

Ivan: And you're not mad at him?

Branko: I'm not.

Ivan: *(confused)* Then why are you avoiding us?

Branko: I'm not avoiding you!

Ivan: You're constantly with Dejana and you always act like you have something better to do.

Branko: I like hanging out with Dejana. Is that such a crime?

Ivan: You said you weren't dating her.

Branko: I'm not.

Ivan: Then why are you spending so much time with her?

Branko: Because she understands me better than anyone else.

Ivan: Oh, here we go again. Branko, we've known each other since kindergarten, Petar and I know you better than anyone else. We're guys though, we don't talk about this emotional stuff.

Branko: And maybe that's just what I missed.

Ivan: You really are a fag sometimes.

Branko: And you can be a dick at times.

Ivan: Oh come on, don't be such a pussy.

Branko: I might be a pussy, but at least I have my pride.

Ivan: What's that supposed to mean.

Branko: Well I'm tired of being Petar's little bitch. Why live my life for him?

Ivan: *(confused)* What the fuck are you even talking about?

Branko: You might not understand it now. But you'll get it one day. *(signs the waiter that he wants the check)*

Ivan: So you don't want to hang out anymore?

Branko: Why would I do something I'm not comfortable with?

Ivan puts both of his hands on his face and doesn't answer.

Scene 57

The scene opens at Belgrade's Republic Square on Friday, May 20th at around 6 pm, with Branko waiting for Dušan, texting Dejana frantically.

I'm so nervous…

Why? It's just a date

Relax 😏

You're going to have dinner and a drink afterwards

What could go wrong?

I really want to make a good impression

Okay

And I hope that he'll like me

So be yourself

And what if he doesn't like me?

Don't be a teenage brat

If he doesn't like you for you, he's not the one

It's literally that simple

I know that, but we all adjust to some extent

Then adjust to be sweet

Make him feel like his presence is important to you

All while being yourself and by that, being the caring one

Me? The caring one?

I think I'm the one that needs to be taken care of

And that's what makes you a good caretaker

You know what to do

So you'll figure it out

Eh, I really hope so

OH GOD

HE'S APPROACHING ME 😨

YAS!

YOU GO QWEEN

Oh God 🤢

Just suck it up and go for it!

Love you 🦇

lyt 🖤

Dušan approaches Branko as he gives him a wave.

Dušan: *(going in for a hug)* Hi
Branko: *(hugs him)* Hey

Scene 58

The scene opens in Smokvica restaurant. A beautiful 100% organic food ambience in the centre of Belgrade in a living room like atmosphere with Branko and Dušan sitting at their own table by a window with a candle.

Dušan: So, what are you currently doing education-wise?
Branko: I'm currently a high school senior. You?
Dušan: Same.
Branko: Cool. So what do you want to do after graduation?
Dušan: I want to study economics.

Branko: Really? You really want to?

Dušan: Well, not quite. I wanted to study politics because that's what I could see myself doing, but I don't feel like getting assassinated. So I wanted to go for sociology, but for my parents, that is not an option. So I guess I'll go through four years of economics and hope for the best. What about you?

Branko: Well, I am hoping to get a degree in arts, but if that fails I'll probably do something useful. The usual, law, engineering, heck I might see you in economics then.

Dušan: But you will try to get into arts?

Branko: Definitely. I wouldn't miss that opportunity for the world.

Dušan: I do admire your passion.

Branko: Why don't you try to do what you love?

Dušan: I don't know. I just don't think it's enough.

Branko: If you really want to do it, do it.

Dušan: *(contemplating)* Maybe I want to do economics so I have chances of finding a job.

Branko: And what would you do if money was no object?

Dušan: I would go into politics.

Branko: Then do just that!

Dušan: But what if that's a bad idea?

Branko: It's not a bad idea if you're doing what you love.

Dušan: Are you sure?

Branko: Yes. *(pauses)* I myself was thinking of studying German or French so I can pursue my passion over there. You know find some steady job in Munich or Stuttgart and work my way up from there. All with the goal of doing what I love one day. Because if I don't chase my goal, is my life worth living?

Dušan quiets down staring into his glass of homemade lemonade as Branko leans back.

Dušan: There are many things in life that can make you happy. Some are easy to obtain, others aren't. I live for other things. For the hope of living in a country where I can lead a normal life, get married and have a family. But I know that I may never achieve any of that and for that, I'm just looking for survival. It might not sound as brave as what you're doing but I'm trying to think of it as the realistic option.

Branko: You are right in terms of that, but what good does it do to be stuck in a classroom learning about things you absolutely have no passion for?

Dušan: Serbia's economy is shit, Branko, we all know it. There are people who finish university and still end up being ice cream vendors. I don't want to be one of those people.

Branko: In that case you need to stick out of the crowd. You need to be passionate about it.

Dušan: Be passionate about economics?

Branko: Yes.

Dušan: *(laughs)* And how do you think I should do that?

Branko: Have you tried organising your financial life? Make savings plans and strategies of how to get the most of your money. Look at ways to improve your spending plans and the market you have around you? Start with the little things.

Dušan: I could open a bank account.

Branko: See! Dive into the world of economics and find something you love.

Dušan: Hmmm, you're right. I will. Thanks, Branko! *(flirtatiously)* I guess I can learn a thing or two from you.

Branko: Oh trust me, I feel like I learned a lot from you.

Scene 59

The scene opens in the house as Branko comes back from his date.

Bojana: *(merrily skipping up to him)* So, tell me all about it, how was your date.

Branko: Hush, I don't want mom and dad to know.

Bojana: Mom and dad are out with friends. So how did it go?

Branko: It went very well. I realised that I could also study French instead of arts. Dad would be happy.

Bojana: Why on earth would you study French after dad gave you the permission to study arts?

Branko: *(convinced)* Because the economy is crippling.

Bojana: What the fuck is wrong with you?

Branko: Why? Don't you think that there's something wrong with our economy?

Bojana: No, it's not that you idiot. What does the economy have to do with you studying French?

Branko: *(dramatic hand gesture)* Everything! *(laughs)* Just kidding. No, uhm, when I talked to Dušan he was talking about his fear of finding a job etc. and I realised that if I study arts in Serbia, I'm basically bound towards unemployment.

Bojana: Oh good, so you realised why dad din't want you to study arts in the first place. So why French?

Branko: Because I'd like to study arts there.

Bojana: *(laughs)* You are out of your mind.

Branko: Look at it this way, if I can't study arts there, I'll still have a degree in French so I could work in France, and if that fails I can become a French teacher here. It might not be a high salary, but it's a secure job and there's a shortage of French teachers. So it's a win-win situation for my future.

Bojana: It does make sense. *(pauses)* And I guess dad would be happy to hear that.

Branko: See! I'll think about it when I start applying for universities. I mean, why not? I was also considering German as an alternative because I already have that in school, but my grades aren't too shiny.

Bojana: And you think you'll do better in French?

Branko: I always wanted to learn French.

Bojana: Uh huh. Whatever. So how was the date? Did you fuck on the first date?

Branko: Oh my God, no. We went for a walk through Dorćol after dinner and maybe kissed twice or so when nobody was looking.

Bojana: So why didn't you start with that instead of complaining about the goddamn economy?

Branko: I don't know it's not of relevance yet. I'm not really falling for him yet.

Bojana: But you like him?

Branko: I'm intrigued. I wonder where this is going.

Bojana: So you have a second date fixed?

Branko: Yeah.

Bojana: And, when is it?

Branko: We're going on a walk tomorrow.

Bojana: *(starts jumping)* OMG, yaaas qween slay.

Bojana hugs her brother with excitement.

Scene 60

The following day Branko and Dušan are walking alongside the new river quay of Belgrade Waterfront, a multi-million revitalisation project for the city.

Dušan: So then my other friend was like: "I'm not a wine expert, I just drink it" and my gay friend immediately tweeted it and it got like 10 likes within two minutes or so.

Branko: That's quite a lot.

Dušan: Yeah. By the way, I went through your Twitter the other day. It's quite cool. Not many followers, personal stuff, a few good songs.

Branko: The other day? Before our first date?

Dušan: Yeah. I was a bit nervous. So I wanted to make sure we don't run out of things to talk.

Branko: Aw, that's sweet though. What did you think of my Twitter?

Dušan: I liked it. You have some funny stuff. A lot of it is #relatable. And you try to be deep but fail to express yourself in 140 characters. It's quite cute.

Branko: Oh please, what's cute about that?

Dušan: I could see that you're a painter. You need visuals to express your emotions because words aren't enough for you.

Branko: Well, I'm not known for being good with words.

Dušan: What are the worst phrasings you used?

Branko: I can't think of anything specific. But I usually just passively sit around in group conversation because I lack words.

Dušan: Interesting. I didn't get that impression with you.

Branko: Dejana doesn't have it either. I always talk when I'm around her. Maybe it's because I'm really comfortable around her.

Dušan: Does that make you comfortable around me?

Branko: *(smiles)* It does.

Dušan: I'm really glad to hear that. *(pauses)* So. What kinds of groups make you quiet down then?

Branko: I'm usually the quiet one when I'm with my school friends.

Dušan: And only because you can't find the words to say?

Branko: By now I think that it's because I don't have anything to say.

Dušan: How come?

Branko: I don't know. I feel detached. I didn't tell them that I'm gay because I know that they won't accept it, but I don't want to give up those friendships either.

Dušan: I know what you mean.

Branko: You do?

Dušan: Yeah, I lost a lot of my friends that way, every gay guy does. I told people at my school, then they started telling around, one told my parents, and by now I don't have any of my old friends left. I found new ones because I figured that they weren't really my friends.

Branko: I fear that that will happen to me.

Dušan: As I said, it happens to everyone here.

Branko: What about your parents?

Dušan: I was very lucky with them. My mother works in an international company and is much more open-minded than other women her age, and my dad took some time, but by now they both came to terms with it and love me nonetheless.

Branko: Wow, that's great.

Dušan: I know, I got really lucky with them, and I know that other gays have a much more difficult time.

Branko: Ugh, don't make me think about it.

Dušan: You're not out to your parents yet?

Branko: Nope. Only to my sister and my new friends. I'm scared of telling my parents and I don't want to tell my old friends.

Dušan: Then don't. You don't have to tell anyone unless you want to. Keep it simple. Tell those who matter and those who will accept.

Branko: I prefer not to think about it.

Dušan: You know what might make you feel better?

Branko: What?

Dušan: Ice cream. Let me take you to Moritz Eis, undoubtedly the best ice cream in town.

Branko: Hmm, I guess that will make me feel better.

Dušan: (*singing*) So when I scream, you scream, and when you scream, ICE CREAM!

Scene 61

Sunday, the day after the second date, Branko and Dejana are sitting in a boutique café in central Belgrade.

Dejana: So he literally bought you ice cream to make you feel better? (*pauses*) He's a keeper!

Branko: Yes, that was so sweet of him. And it was undoubtedly the best ice cream in town.

Dejana: Moritz Eis is genius, I can't believe you never heard of them.

Branko: Well, I grew up with Frikom.

Dejana: Yeah. I'm going to take you Ice Box after this, you need to try the best frozen yoghurt in town.

Branko: I never even had frozen yoghurt.

Dejana: Exactly. (*pauses*) Anyways. He is so sweet. I should become a gay man. You're way more romantic than straight men.

Branko: Are we?

Dejana: I can't remember my exes ever doing something for me that was out of their way. Except for some flowers and paid dinners. But that's something I can get myself.

Branko: A different type of girl, are we?

Dejana: Well, not really. I just feel like a guy should do those little things that make a girl happy. Like, do you know a song that Dušan really likes?

Branko: Let me think. I'm not quite sure but he told me about some special dance move he always does in the club when Uno Momento comes on.

Dejana: Oooh, Severina, he's the classy type of dude.

Branko: I like Severina.

Dejana: Well, perfect. So here's what you can do to be more romantic. Make a playlist with various types of songs and put Uno Momento in there. He'll be happy to hear it, and he can show you his dance move.

Branko: Can't I just play all of Severina's albums?

Dejana: That takes the effect of surprise out. Make a playlist with English songs and then insert Severina into it.

Branko: Hmmm, that does sound really nice.

Dejana: Trust me.

Branko: Wait a second!

Dejana: What?

Branko: I know what I can play.

Dejana: What?

Branko: When he suggested ice cream yesterday, he sang something. I want to find that song.

Dejana: How does it go?

Branko: *(speaking, mumbling)* So when I scream, you scream, and when you scream, ICE CREAM!

Dejana: No clue. *(takes phone)* But Google should have an answer for me. *(typing)* It's "What's Cooking" by Las Balkanieras.

Branko: Can you send it to me?

Dejana: Sure thing. *(typing)* Done.

Branko: Thanks! I guess I'll take Dušan out on a picnic or something.

Dejana: Just buy two Sommersby and take him to Kalemegdan. That's low commitment yet cute and won't be too obvious in public.

Branko: True, I can't be exposed.

Dejana: Unfortunately.

Scene 62

That evening Branko is at the phone looking at his apps, noticing that he hasn't used WhatsApp in a while. He opens it to see Luka online. He texts him.

> Hey
>
> I haven't heard from you in a long time

How's it going?

Heyyy

I know. I've been super busy

I'm so sorry

How have you been?

I've been good

I met a guy recently

And I thought about what you said
about my friends from school

Ooooooh, that's great 😍

What's his name? What does he look like?

Did you decide to ditch the ignorance
for your own wellbeing?

Yes

YAS QWEEN 💕 😍

Be you. Be fab 💁

You can do so much better than them

I'm proud of you

So tell me more about your guy 😊

What's his name?

His name is Dušan

I was out at a gay party with Dejana and
Milica and met him there

(Dušan's profile picture)

This is him

Wow. He's even hotter than me

Damn

You must be the luckiest man in Belgrade

Don't overdo it

We just started dating

Okay, okay I won't

But you're good? You're happy like that?

I am, I really am

It's just nice to have someone to
talk to and to have someone here

I see

I know, that's the one thing I couldn't give you

And it's better this way

We'll stay friends

One day I might stop by Zagreb

Come with Dušan, I wanna see the dude myself

Make sure he's real and stuff

God, you're terrible

I'll see what I can do

We're going to Albania this summer

Your family is going to Albania?

What the fuck?

My uncle is getting married to an Albanian woman

So we're going to Tirana for the wedding

A Serbo-Albanian marriage??

That's crazy, that's like out of this world 😱

I know

My family is not really that normal as it seems

I know, they have you after all 😜

Oh come on!

What?! 😂

Scene 63

*The following week on Friday evening Branko and Dušan are sitting on
top of the Kalemegdan fortress wall with four bottles of Sommersby and a
pink loudspeaker playing Branko's playlist*

Dušan: *(looking at the speaker)* Can I ask you something?

Branko: Sure, go ahead.

Dušan: Why is your loudspeaker pink and glittery?

Branko: Oh, it's my sister's. I don't own one so I borrowed it from her.

Dušan: So you could play me your playlist?

Branko: I feel like you get to know a person through the media they consume. The magazines they read, the music they listen to, the art they value. It all gives you an impression of my personality.

Dušan: I see. So if I were to bring my playlist next time you would know more about me?

Branko: *(throws him "that look")* Most definitely.

Dušan: Hmm, then I'll guess we have something planned for our next date now.

Branko: *(smiles)* Gladly.

Dušan grabs Branko's shoulder when he pulls his face towards his and stops.

Dušan: *(hesitant)* I shouldn't.

Branko: Why you kissed me before?

Dušan: *(pulls back)* There are too many people that could see us here.

Branko: Oh come on, what's the worst that could happen?

Voice: *(joyfully from the background)* BRANKO?!

Branko: *(eyes wide open in disbelief)* Vesna? Petar?

Vesna: *(smiles)* Hello. Hello. What a surprise.

Branko: *(petrified)* What are you doing here?

Vesna: We're on a date here.

Petar: I remember you taking her here very often. I figured she likes it here.

Branko: I see. And you didn't figure out that I could be here?

Vesna: You always took me to the Novi Beograd panorama, so we figured you didn't like being by the wall.

Dušan: He suggested the Novi Beograd panorama, it was my idea to come here.

Vesna: Ah, I see. And you are?

Dušan: Dušan, Branko's friend. And who are you two?

Petar: (*full of himself*) I'm Branko's best bro. We've known each other since kindergarten.

Vesna: And I'm his ex. I can't believe that Branko didn't tell you anything about me.

Dušan: Oh he did mention it. We didn't talk about it a lot.

Petar: So where do you know each other from. Did you also go to Budapest with Branko?

Dušan throws Branko a nervous look.

Branko: We met through Dejana. I was out clubbing with her and another friend, and she got drunk so Dušan here helped Dejana and me get our friend back home.

Dušan: Yeah. And we started hanging out after that.

Petar: Interesting. Branko has been distancing himself lately from his pals back at school.

Branko: Oh, I was simply distracted the past few weeks.

Petar: I see.

Branko: Well, don't let us bother your date.

Vesna: Oh no, don't worry about it. May we join you?

Dušan: Oh sure, it's no problem feel free.

Branko throws Dušan an angry look.

Scene 64

The group sits together on the fortress, drinking.

Dušan: (*confused*) So let me get this straight. You two were together, then you broke up with her and she's now with your best friend?

Branko: Yup.

Petar: And apparently he's not mad at me.

Branko: Well it was a dick move. But I'm not mad at you.

Petar: I know it was a dick move, and I'm sorry.

Branko: It's okay. You two seem to be doing fine, and I'm happy with my life as well. So don't worry all too much about it.

Petar: I won't. Thanks, bro.

Vesna: (*to Dušan*) Are Branko and Dejana a thing?

Dušan: I'm sorry?

Vesna: Branko is spending so much time with her and it seems like they really like like each other.

Dušan: Well, Vesna, you're not the only one with that theory. *(looks to Branko)* I thought the same. But I can assure you that Branko is a happy single guy. *(winks)*

Vesna: *(to Branko)* Be honest. Did you see anyone after we split up?

Branko: I was seeing someone in Budapest.

Vesna: *(surprised)* You were?

Dušan: *(really surprised)* You were?

Branko: Yeah. She was representing Croatia. We had a short fling.

Petar: So that's why you wanted to go to Croatia! It wasn't about your friend, you wanted to get some of that puss.

Branko: So to say.

Vesna: What's her name.

Branko: *(hesitant)* Lana.

Vesna: *(smiles)* Tell her that she's a lucky girl.

Branko: But I'm not seeing her anymore.

Vesna: And that's why she's a lucky girl.

Petar: Ooooh! Burn!

Dušan: *(laughing)* I love this girl.

Vesna: *(giggles)* Thanks, everyone does.

Scene 65

The day after the awkward double date, Branko is in the living room with Bojana as the door rings. Bojana gets the door and Ivan enters.

Bojana: Ivan? What a surprise. What are you doing here?

Ivan: I came to talk to Branko.

Branko: What's wrong?

Ivan: Are your parents home? You might want to hear this in private.

Bojana: They went out for a walk.

Ivan: Wow, are they ever at home?

Bojana: Not really, *(laughs)* it's quite nice.

Ivan: Cool. Anyways, would you mind leaving us alone?

Bojana: Sure, no problem. I'll be in my room.

Branko: No, please feel free to stay. *(to Ivan)* I don't keep secrets from her. You can talk to both of us.

Bojana: Aw, you're too sweet.

Ivan: Ah, whatever. Do you still have Vesna on Snapchat?

Branko: You know that I don't like Snapchat.

Ivan: *(sits down on the sofa)* Well then you might want to stay seated.

Bojana: What's wrong?

Ivan: You might want to sit down too.

Branko: Okay, you're starting to freak me out.

Bojana: Spill the tea, Ivan.

Ivan: Vesna quasi-outed you on Snapchat.

Silence fills the room.

Branko: I'm not gay, Ivan.

Ivan: Will you stop lying to me and everyone around you?

Branko: *(angry)* What do you want from me?

Ivan: The truth. There is a snap of you sitting on the Kalemegdan wall with another guy and a follow-up snap of the four of you sitting there and drinking.

Branko: So it's four friends hanging out. What's the big deal?

Ivan: The big deal is the snap before that.

Branko: But you can't see it's me.

Ivan: But the snap after that proves that it's you.

Bojana: *(worried)* Ivan is right. This is problematic.

Branko: So, let people think what they want to think.

Ivan: I don't think it's that easy. People will poke fun at you. But we need to make them believe that it just looked like you were gay and that the snap was taken at an unfortunate moment.

Branko: I didn't even see her.

Ivan: I know. And I will stand by you if you're 100% honest with me.

Branko: Okay.

Ivan: So, please, be 100% honest with me. Are you gay?

The room is silent for a while until Branko pulls himself together.

Branko: Yes, I am.

Scene 66

After Ivan has left Bojana and Branko continue the discussion.

Bojana: *(furious)* Are you out of your fucking mind?

Branko: He's my friend. I wanted to tell him!

Bojana: You know that this mistake could ruin you?

Branko: I don't think that Ivan is capable of doing that.

Bojana: He just looked at you when you told him, apologised, said that he needed a while to process this, and left.

Branko: Which doesn't have to be a bad thing.

Bojana: *(yells)* How on earth is that not a bad thing?

Branko: He might just need some time to process this. I don't think that he would intentionally harm me.

Bojana: Then you need to sort it out with him! Soon!

Branko: I will. Don't worry, Ivan has always been a rational guy.

Bojana: I'm afraid he could turn into an instant asshole.

Branko: He won't, trust me. I mean, he came here to warn me about the possible shitstorm I'm going to get at school on Monday.

Bojana: You have to talk to him before Monday.

Branko: I could ask him if he has time tomorrow?

Bojana: That would be your best bet.

Branko: *(takes out phone)* Let me text him.

Bojana: You need to talk to Luka, Milica or Dušan first.

Branko: Why?

Bojana: Because you're at an important crossroad in your life. You need to talk to another LGBT person. I'm afraid I won't be able to help you as much.

Branko: Oh, please, Bojana, don't say that. You are the most supportive sister a brother could ask for. What you're doing is amazing and I will be for ever grateful for that. *(emotional)* Thank you.

As he hugs his sister, his phone vibrates.

Bojana: Is it Ivan?

Branko: *(looking at his phone)* Yes. He says he's going out with Petar and Vesna tomorrow, and that I could join. I should probably stay out of that.

Bojana: No! You should go!

Branko: What?

Bojana: Go and see what the situation is like. Act normal, as if everything stayed the same. It will lower their suspicion.

Branko: And what if I open my big mouth again?

Bojana: You won't, because you won't want to hurt Vesna's feelings, and because you don't know how your support will be in that situation. I think you can manage that and that you will get a better overview.

Branko: Well, then there's only one thing left to do.

Bojana: Yes?

Branko: Tell them that I'll be there. *(sends text on his phone)*

Scene 67

The next day, Branko, Petar, Vesna and Ivan are walking alongside the Danube quay.

Ivan: You know, Vesna, it's interesting to finally see you as part of the group.

Vesna: Thanks. I like hanging out with you guys. It refreshing not to always bitch about the world with the girls.

Petar: Oh I can believe that.

Vesna: *(handing her phone to Branko)* Hey, would you mind taking a photo of Petar and me for Snapchat?

Branko: Sure. *(takes picture)* Pose!

Vesna: *(taking her phone)* Thanks!

Petar: *(to Branko)* You've been awfully quiet.

Branko: Huh? Yeah. I don't know.

Vesna: *(worried)* What's wrong?

Branko: I don't know how to feel about your Snapchat, Vesna.

Vesna: What I just posted a snap of you and your friend, nothing spectacular.

Branko: You purposely made it look like I was gay on that snap.

Vesna: *(smiles)* Well that was the entire joke.

Petar: Oh come on, suck it up. It's just a joke.

Branko: Bitch please, you would be the first one to whine about it, if someone accused you of being gay.

Petar: I wouldn't mind.

Ivan: You're lying. Not only to us, but also to yourself.

Vesna: The only reason I did this to Branko is because he's the only guy who can take such a joke. He might seem weak, but his masculinity is not as fragile as those of you dumbos.

Petar: My masculinity is not fragile.

Vesna: Bitch what? You took your shampoo with you when you stayed at my place because you didn't want to smell like peach dreams.

Ivan: *(laughs)* Okay, that is idiotic.

Petar: Could you not expose my weaknesses to my friends?

Vesna: See, that's exactly what I like about Branko. He constantly shows his weaknesses. You use that to pick on him so you can feel a little better about yourself, but all men have this weakness. And it takes a lot to be a real man and show it.

Branko: *(mesmerised)* Oh wow. Thank you.

Vesna: You're welcome.

Branko: I guess one of the reasons I don't like that about myself is because I don't want others to think I'm gay.

Ivan: True. Most people at our school follow your "iconic" snap stories, and I can see that impacting Branko's reputation.

Petar: School will be over in a few months anyway.

Ivan: It isn't over yet though.

Vesna: Okay, I see how the story offended you. I'm sorry.

Branko: It's okay.

Petar: *(still in a crisis)* So you think my masculinity is fragile?

Vesna: I think we should talk about that once we're alone.

Scene 68

After parting from the group Branko texts Luka.

My life is so fucked up right now

What's wrong???

Are you okay?

I'm fine

It's just

Urgh, I'm walking 😣

Give me a second

Okay

(3:04, voice message)

So that's my situation

Hmm, well fuck

Are you sure that your friend will keep quiet?

It's the best bet I have

Hmmm

Well, personally I'd talk to him on my own

My sister suggested that as well

But we ended up being a group

Well, in that case, why don't you approach him after school or something?

You don't need a lot of time to tell him to keep quiet

Just talk to him and be like

(0:17, voice message)
Hey, so like because what you know now, I just wanted to tell you to keep quiet and let this stay between us, is that okay with you gurl?

I don't think I can use this amount of sass

That was a joke, you dummy

Oh God, you're up for a ride

Does your lover boy know about this?

I haven't talked to him about that yet

Why didn't you?

He could be a great support system for you!

We only had a few dates. I don't want approach him with a marriage like commitment all of a sudden

I don't think it would be fair towards him

Branko, trust me, he will want to help you

If you're really not fine and in a crisis

He will be there for you

That is if he really likes you

I think he does

Then what's stopping you from reaching out to him?

It's your best move

And talking to Dejana about it, all hail that qween

Trust me

I will, I think you're right

I'm always right

Sure you are

Alright, thank you very much and we'll text soon enough

Keep me posted

Bye

Scene 69

The next Friday, Branko and Dušan are lying in bed at Dušan's place.

Dušan: *(after hearing Branko's story)* So our thing here is famous on social media now? Cool, it's like being published on lovesexla's couple shoutout.

Branko: Could you take this a little more seriously?

Dušan: I am. The thing is, it's in the hands of Ivan. When are you two meeting to talk?

Branko: Tomorrow.

Dušan: So as long as you can make sure that he will keep the information to himself, you're fine.

Branko: Not really, there are rumours that I might be gay at school.

Dušan: So what? As long as no one confirms them they are just rumours. Also, school is almost over, and you won't have to worry about that.

Branko: And what if it leaks out to my parents?

Dušan: Then I will protect you, along with your sister, Dejana, and all of your other supporters. You'd be surprised how many people will be on your side. Don't worry about all the things that could happen. The fat lady hasn't sung yet.

Branko: *(cuddling up to him)* You're alright. I just feel so alone in this situation.

Dušan: You're not alone. You have so many people. You have me.

Branko: I know. Thank you for that.

Dušan: Oh please. I'm always going to be there for you.

Branko: Always?

Dušan: Listen, there's something I've been meaning to ask you.

Branko: What is it?

Dušan: Well, I remember saying that you're not like the others and that I wanted to get to know you the traditional way.

Branko: Yes?

Dušan: And now, now that I know you, I see this beautiful person in front of me. And I think to myself: "My God, I want to be with that person"

Branko: Do you want to take this to the next level?

Dušan: *(nervously)* I want you to be my boyfriend.

Branko: *(smiles)* Even though I'm a wreck, huh?

Dušan: You're a beautiful one, and also my wreck. *(kisses him)*

Branko: Well then. Yes, of course, I will be your boyfriend. *(kisses him)*

Dušan: I think you can't imagine how happy that makes me.

Branko: Oh trust me, I can imagine.

Dušan: *(climbs on top of him)* Wanna celebrate that?

Branko: Are we alone?

Dušan: My parents said you could stay the night, remember?

Branko: Yeah. *(kisses him)*

Dušan: Well they're out for the evening, so is my brother.

Branko: That changes the game.

Dušan: Let's do this then. *(starts making out with him)*

Conveniently the number of this scene explains what happens next.

Scene 70

The next day Branko arrives home.

Mrs Jovanović: Branko, there you are! How was clubbing?

Branko: It was great.

Mrs Jovanović: *(checks her phone)* You slept on your friends couch?

Branko: Yeah, he offered me to stay so that I don't have to wait for the bus or take a taxi.

Mr Jovanović: That's good. It saves you time and money.

Branko: Exactly. *(pauses)* I have to get changed and take a shower.

Mrs Jovanović: Where are you going now?

Branko: Ivan and I planned to hang out today.

Mrs Jovanović: Oh, that's nice. Say hi to Ivan and tell him to thank his mother for the pie recipe she gave me.

Branko: I will! *(runs off)*

After his shower, Branko is getting dressed in his room, Bojana enters.

Bojana: So what's the deal now?

Branko: *(covers himself with a towel)* Would you mind knocking? Jeez.

Bojana: Don't be such a wuss. So?

Branko: *(looking for a pair of jeans)* I'm going to meet up with Ivan, so I can try to make sure that he will keep my secret.

Bojana: Do you think that you can trust him?

Branko: I hope so, we will have to see.

Bojana: Please take care.

Branko: Don't worry, I will!

Bojana: Any other news?

Branko: *(smiles)* Uhm, well.

Bojana: Your smile is too bright. It's creeping me out.

Branko: *(whispers)* Dušan is now officially my boyfriend.

Bojana: I would scream so hard right now, but I don't want mom and dad to hear us. Why didn't you tell me before?

Branko: It happened last night.

Bojana: You could've texted me!

Branko: I wanted us to spend the moment together. You're the first one I'm telling.

Bojana: What? Oh God. *(takes out her phone)* I'm going to text Dejana.

Branko: You have her number?

Bojana: I added her on Facebook.

Branko: Okay, tell the her the news I guess, I'm in a bit of a rush right now. *(heads for the door)*

Bojana: Have fun! Love you!

Branko: Love you too!

Branko walks past the living room greeting his parents and walks out.

Scene 71

After that Branko meets up with Ivan at a Coffee Dream in New Belgrade.

Branko: So, I guess we have something to solve.

Ivan: Listen, Branko. I knew you were gay before you told me. I figured it could be an option when Petar started all of this Vesna drama with you, forcing to be with her.

Branko: Trust me, I knew that way before that. Petar just helped me cover it up.

Ivan: Okay, what now? *(worried)* Are you going to seek any help?

Branko: Uhm, excuse me?

Ivan: You're not?

Branko: Why would I seek any help?

Ivan: Maybe because you need it?

Branko: Ivan, there's nothing wrong with me being gay.

Ivan pauses for a second then turns to the side and points in the direction of a church.

Ivan: You're religious, aren't you?

Branko: That has nothing to do with me being gay.

Ivan: Oh that has everything to do with you being gay.

Branko: Okay, instead of just vaguely telling me why being gay is wrong, why don't you give me some proper arguments?

Ivan: Uhm. What do you mean?

Branko: Why do I need to get help. What's wrong with me?

Ivan: I don't know man. You're sick, you need some help.

Branko: But I don't want help.

Ivan: You need it! *(faithfully)* Branko, you can change.

Branko: I can't change, Ivan! Don't you get that? I tried to change, I wanted to change. While I knew that being with Vesna is a huge mistake there was this one part of me. This one part of me that hoped that I could change. But you know what? I never did. I never changed. Even though I myself sometimes want to. Do you think that I like being gay? Having to hide? Being discriminated against? I fucking hate it, but there's nothing I can change about it. And I still need to accept that, and I hope you can too.

Silence fills the conversation. Then Branko continues.

Branko: All I wanted to ask of you is to be a good friend.

Ivan: I'm not going to support your sickness unless you get help.

Branko: *(in a cold tone)* I don't expect that from you. I just want you to stay quiet about it. I told you because I trust you, and I need to be sure that I can trust you.

Ivan: Don't worry. I won't tell anyone. I want you to get better and I don't want to make it worse for you. You're still like a brother to me.

Branko: Thank you. I hope I can count on that.

Ivan: In some way, you will always be able to count on that.

Scene 72

After the meeting with Ivan, Branko is on the phone with Dušan.

Dušan: I can't believe you still want to be friends with that guy.

Branko: I just don't want to distance myself from him too much. Now I'm walking on thin ice.

Dušan: You're putting too much pressure on yourself.

Branko: Do I have a choice?

Dušan: You could just calm down and accept that he won't be there for you.

Branko: *(nervous)* I'm trying to grasp my head around that.

Dušan: Look, you should focus on other things in life.

Branko: Like our relationship?

Dušan: Sure, why not, give your boyfriend some attention. *(laughs)* No, seriously focus on your family, you're going to Tirana soon. Prom lies ahead.

Branko: *(frustrated)* Ah, f*ck, prom.

Dušan: What about it?

Branko: That will be an evening full of drama.

Dušan: I wish I could be there to see it.

Branko: Aw, I wish I could take you.

Dušan: *(dramatically)* Don't even think about that, we'd cause a scene.

Branko: Is it too much to ask to take your boyfriend to prom?

Dušan: We are not in the West, this is Serbia.

Branko: I know. And it makes me sad.

Dušan: So what is your plan for prom then?

Branko: Go there with my family and getting drunk with my sister.

Dušan: Isn't she like 16?

Branko: As if you didn't drink two years ago.

Dušan: Point taken. Anyways, I promised my mother I'd go grocery shopping with my brother, so I'll have to hang up.

Branko: Okay. Say hello to your mother, send my kindest regards.

Dušan: I will. She told me that she likes you.

Branko: Aw, that's nice.

Dušan: Yeah. *(pauses)* Uhm, Branko.

Branko: Yeah?

Dušan: Before I hang up.

Branko: Yes?

Dušan: You mean a lot to me.

There is silence on the line.

Branko: You make me happy.

Dušan: You too. I'll talk to you soon. Bye.

Dušan hangs up.

Branko: *(to himself, smiles)* Fuck, I am so lucky.

Scene 73

A few days later Dejana and Branko are sitting in café with Dejana having a huge smile on her face.

Dejana: Yes! *(claps)* Yes, of course, I'll come to your prom.
Branko: Really? Oh my God, thank you, I'd love to have you there.
Dejana: No worries, I'll be your cover up.
Branko: *(surprised)* That's not why I invited you.
Dejana: Admit it, you've considered the benefits of it all at least once.
Branko: Ehm...
Dejana: I'm not mad. I'd be happy to meet your friends.
Branko: Yeah, my "friends".
Dejana: Even though Ivan and you are having some drama right now, I bet it'll be a fun night.
Branko: *(insecure)* I wouldn't be too sure about that.
Dejana: It's prom. It's that one night where everyone forgets all their problems and enjoys the fact that those twelve years of school are finally over! *(pauses)* My God, I can't wait for it to be finally over.
Branko: Same, it's about time.
Dejana: So, why are you not looking forward to it?
Branko: I don't know.
Dejana: You're dreading that you're not spending the evening with him?
Branko: Yeah, I guess it's a little bit of that.
Dejana: Unfortunately, not everyone will get their fairytale moment. He won't be at your prom and you won't be at his, and it's not because you don't care about each other, it's because of the problem you'd encounter with others.
Branko: That's accurate.
Dejana: Look, I completely understand that you want to share that special moment with your boyfriend, but now that's not possible. And the good news is that there will be so many special little moments in your relationship. You'll be happy.
Branko: I really hope so.
Dejana: Aren't you happy in your relationship?

Branko: Oh, I am happy, it's not that. It's just. I am happy in the relationship, but I am not happy with my life. The relationship is not a "solve it all" solution for all of your problems, and I'm terrified of being outed and living with the consequences.

Dejana: I see. Well, have you thought about coming out to your parents?

Branko: *(dramatic)* Of course I have, and of course I won't do it.

Dejana: Well look at it this way: In your current situation you run the risk of being outed and facing the consequences, but if you come out to your parents separately, it might result in a milder outcome.

Branko: *(calms down)* I haven't thought about that yet.

Dejana: You should! It could be a lifesaver if you tell your parents yourself instead of someone else doing it.

Branko: That's very true. *(pauses)* Fuck.

Dejana: What's wrong?

Branko: Dejana, I feel like I have to tell my parents that I'm gay.

Scene 74

After the meeting with Dejana, Branko returns home

Mrs Jovanović: There's our little star! *(walks over to hug him)*

Mr Jovanović: *(in a proud voice)* There you are son!

Branko: What's going on?

Mrs Jovanović: *(walks over to the counter and grabs a letter)* This came for you in the mail.

Branko: What is this?

Mrs Jovanović: It's a letter from the Serbian ministry of culture, they're thinking of giving you an EU scholarship.

Branko: A what?

Mrs Jovanović: It says it in the letter, they want to place you at a university in the EU for a year as part of an EU development programme for young artists.

Branko: What would that mean?

Mr Jovanović: You could be going abroad, my son!

Branko: *(overwhelmed)* Oh my God, this is awesome!

Mrs Jovanović: They want to see you in the ministry, to talk about possible options on how you could obtain the scholarship.

Branko: Oh my God, this is great. Did they mention anything specific?

Mrs Jovanović: No, you're supposed to call them, they left a number.

Branko: Oh wow, I need to call them right now.

Mrs Jovanović: Wait until next week. At least on the letter, it says to wait until next week.

Branko: Oh God, I can't wait.

Mr Jovanović: Be patient, all the things we want will eventually come to us.

Branko: You're right. Thanks, dad. *(pauses)* Actually, there's one thing I wanted to tell you.

Mr Jovanović: What is it? Is it important?

Branko: I invited Dejana to my prom, so she'll be going with us.

Mr Jovanović: Oh, yeah. Sure, no problem.

Mrs Jovanović: Oh, that's nice. I really like Dejana, it would be nice if she comes to prom with you.

Branko: I thought so too, *(smiles)* she's a good friend.

Mr Jovanović: Well, I'm glad you're meeting the right people on your art excursions.

Branko: *(laughs)* I am too, dad, I am too.

Scene 75

The evening before Branko's prom, Branko and Dušan are hanging out at the Sava quay at a quiet end with hardly any people.

Dušan: *(interrupting silence)* You've been awfully quiet today.

Branko: I've been obsessing about my prom tomorrow.

Dušan: *(relaxed)* Ah, it's just prom, it's nothing special.

Branko: Really? How did yours go last week?

Dušan: It was okay, there was just one key thing missing?

Branko: What?

Dušan: My boyfriend.

Branko: Aw, you're too sweet. *(kisses him)*

Dušan: It's true. It wasn't even half as cool without having you there.

Branko: You're just saying that to make me feel better.

Dušan: Not really. I mean it, and you will feel the same tomorrow.

Branko: What do you mean?

Dušan: Well, you're there, surrounded by all of your friends, most of them have dates, all of them dance with their girlfriends, except for you. And it's not because you're single, but because you can't take your boyfriend to prom without risking being the trash talk of the night, or worse, physical escalation.

Branko: Was there physical escalation at your prom?

Dušan: Not really. Well, two of the guys from my class got wasted and threw a few punches. But nothing out of the ordinary.

Branko: Oh.

Dušan: So, I guess my advice for tomorrow would be: Just push through and try to be with your friends as much as you can.

Branko: You know it's been awkward with my friends recently.

Dušan: I know, but you have Dejana there, and your sister. You'll be fine. I'm sure of that.

Dušan hugs him and holds him.

Branko: I wish you were there. So we can at least have one dance together.

Dušan: I wish for the same thing. But we will have to accept the fact that that will never happen.

Branko: I know, I know. God, I wish I could live in some place like Sweden.

Dušan: Yeah?

Branko: Yeah, imagine it, a place where we could be free. Where it wouldn't matter if we're gay, straight, bi, trans, pan, poly or whatever. We could be free.

Dušan: The scholarship has been bugging you a lot?

Branko: I just want to get a chance to escape this place and live somewhere where I could be free.

Dušan: Try not to think too much about it. Think about it without any expectations and see where it will take you. You never know what you could get. Don't forget that Bulgaria is in the EU as well.

Branko: I guess you're right. Damn it! Don't ruin my day.

Dušan: Okay, okay. I won't. Here. *(takes earphones out of his pocket)* How about I make it better?

Branko: What do you want to do?

Dušan: *(gives him one earphone)* Stand up!

Branko: *(stands up)* What is this supposed to be?

Dušan: *(grabs his waist and arm)* Our very personal prom dance.

Branko: Oh, shut up.

Dušan: *(smiles as the music to Dernière Danse ques in)* May I have this last dance?

Branko: You may. *(kisses him)*

The two start slow dancing as the sun sets over Belgrade.

Scene 76

June 18th, 2016. In preparation for prom, Branko, Bojana and Dejana are in Bojana's room, with the girls getting their makeup done and Branko trying to get the suit to fit.

Branko: *(heavy breathing)* Milenko was so much smaller at my age.

Dejana: *(doing her eyelids)* Or maybe you're just fat.

Branko: Hey! I'm slimmer than most of my class.

Bojana: We know. You're going to look hot.

Dejana: *(to Bojana)* Will this do the trick?

Bojana: I think you're good to go.

Branko: *(confused)* Uhm?

Bojana: You should do drag once, then you'll understand our struggle with being beautiful.

Branko: Uhm, no thanks.

Dejana: Ey, there's no shame in that. Have you ever seen RuPaul's Drag Race? Those acts are amazing! I would give anything to be as witty as Katya.

Branko: The wannabe Russian?

Bojana: Watch your mouth! She's not a wannabe Russian. *(in a Russian accent)* She is the true representation of the emancipated yet traditional eastern European woman!

Branko: That doesn't make any sense.

Dejana: *(ratchet)* Oh that made perfect sense, sweetie.

Branko: Is it just me or do you girls get wittier when doing your make up?

Dejana: Oh this is our natural element of femininity.

Bojana: It's what get's us the rich men.

Branko: *(shocked)* Oh wow.

Dejana: *(in a Russian accent)* Behind every real lady, there is a rich man. Now, I know feminists might not be happy to hear this, but then again, they are never happy.

Dejana and Bojana laugh.

Branko: Where did you get that from?

Dejana: A Lithuanian YouTube video.

Bojana: Eastern European Lady School.

Branko: Never heard of it.

Dejana: You should really watch more YouTube, it'll ease your mind.

Bojana: Take it easy and start with like Tyler Oakley or Connor Franta. *(smiles)* You know someone who can show you the gay version of the American Dream.

Branko: Yeah. Okay. Whatever.

Scene 77

After making an entrance at prom, Branko and Dejana walk over to Petar and Vesna who are accompanied by Ivan and Katarina.

Vesna: *(hugs Branko)* Hey! There you are.

Branko: Hi.

Vesna: And who's this young lady?

Branko: This is my date, Dejana.

Dejana: Hey, everyone, nice to meet you.

Vesna: Oh, so you're the Dejana everyone has been talking about, I'm Vesna, this is my friend Katarina…

Petar: *(whispering to Ivan)* A part of me thought she didn't exist.

Vesna: … and this is my boyfriend Petar.

Petar: Oh, yeah. Hi, pleased to meet you. *(shakes Dejana's hand)*
Vesna: So, do you guys want to dance?
Dejana: *(smiles)* Sure, why not.
Petar: *(whispering to Ivan)* She's even hotter than Vesna.
Ivan: *(whispering to Petar)* Well if I were Branko I would've replaced that with that as well.
Petar: *(whispering to Ivan)* Oh shut your mouth.
Vesna: Sweetie! Are you coming?
Petar: *(distracted)* Huh! Yes! Coming, my love.

The crowd hits the dance floor as Severina songs are being played at maximum volume. After a while a slow dance part is introduced, Branko takes Dejana to dance.

Dejana: Your friends seemed very awkward around me. Petar was whispering the entire time.
Branko: I think they're just intimidated.
Dejana: *(laughs)* That would be the first time that men are intimidated by me.
Branko: Oh please. *(spins her)*
Dejana: It's true. Let's not deny that here. Anyways, what's the deal with them?
Branko: It's been very awkward with them ever since I distanced myself from them and it kind of peaked when they caught me with Dušan.
Dejana: Well, they know nothing for sure, except for Ivan.
Branko: Exactly.
Dejana: Have you thought about covering it up forever?
Branko: Yeah. I mean it's prom. After tonight I won't have to see anyone here anymore and I can spend my time with the people who matter. *(spins her)* We can hang out more.
Dejana: Aw, you're too sweet. Dušan really is a lucky man.
Branko: *(smiles)* I'm the lucky one, he found me after all.
Dejana: It's just cute seeing the two of you together.
Branko: Well, unfortunately, this is not the scenario where that could happen.

Dejana: Oh stop thinking about that. You're here with me, and from what I can tell, all your friends are jealous as fuck right now. So that counts for something, right?

Branko: I guess it does, my stunning bride. *(spins her again)* You're turning this night into a fairytale.

Scene 78

Later that evening Vesna, Katarina, Dejana and Branko are sitting at a table.

Katarina: So you just rocked the streets of Budapest together? That's awesome.

Dejana: Yeah, it was quite the trip. I found it very cool. And it was great to hang out with Branko.

Branko: It's awesome to meet so many new people at once.

Vesna: Yeah, Dejana, we really heard a lot about you. Every single time Branko had to take a rain check to be exact.

Dejana: Oh, so I'm his excuse for when doesn't have time?

Vesna: Well you two seem to be spending a lot of time together lately.

Dejana: That's true. It's just cool to hang out together.

Vesna: So what's the status on the two of you now?

Branko: I told you a million times, there's no status between us.

Vesna: *(to Dejana)* Listen, sweetie, I know I'm his ex and that it might be difficult for you to admit to me that you're dating him now. But trust me, I'm totally chill.

Dejana: Oh, I believe you, but there's no status between us.

Katarina: But you are his prom date?

Dejana: Yeah, and he's mine. No one likes to go to prom alone.

Branko: I thought this would be a nice way for all of us to spend some time together.

Dejana: Isn't it tiring for you to constantly dig around?

Vesna: I don't know. Maybe because it seems so obvious.

Dejana: Well, you might never know.

Scene 79

A few drinks later Ivan and Petar are chilling outside of prom smoking a joint.

Petar: I just don't get it.

Ivan: Don't get what?

Petar: How does he always get so lucky?

Ivan: Who?

Petar: Branko you dipshit. *(pauses)* I just don't get it.

Ivan: Well, I don't envy him.

Petar: Have you seen Dejana? That girl basically just slays everyone.

Ivan: You mean her tits?

Petar: Her tits are pure perfection. Branko must feel like a king having those in bed.

Ivan: I don't think they're sleeping together.

Petar: I feel like you know more than I do.

Ivan: I might. I don't know.

Petar: So tell me, what's the secret?

Ivan: Branko is not necessarily the guy you think he is.

Petar: What?

Ivan: Listen, I'm worried about him. I need to help him, but I can't do it on my own. You need to forget your jealousy to see that.

Petar: What? Branko needs our help?

Ivan: Yes. He doesn't know it, but we need to help him. He's our bro, and we won't let him down.

Petar: Okay, okay. What is it?

Ivan: Branko is gay.

Petar: *(silent)* He's what?

Ivan: You heard me. Dejana supports him so she's acts like a cover-up.

Petar: *(angry)* That bitch.

Ivan: Listen, we need to help him. We need to get him to therapy before more people find out or else he will be ruined.

Petar: Ivan! Don't you see what that will do to us though?

Ivan: What do you mean?

Petar: Uhm, we are friends with a fag, if they going to drag him into the mud, we're going down with him. They won't just talk behind his back, but behind ours too. We're so fucked.

Ivan: And that's why it's important that no one else finds out. But this should be about him, not about us.

Petar: And how are we going to get him to go to therapy?

Ivan: We need to show him the right way.

Petar: Hmm. *(pauses)* I think I know what I have to do. *(walks away)*

Ivan: Petar, wait! *(runs after him)* Don't do anything stupid! *(sees him walk away)* Oh God, why are all my friends self-centred bastards?

Scene 80

The morning after Branko walks onto the dining table with his family sitting there already having breakfast.

Mrs Jovanović: *(in a moderate tone)* You seem to be a bit dizzy.

Branko: *(sitting down at the table)* Urgh, I'm fine.

Mr Jovanović: Bojana told us you went a little crazy at the afterparty.

Branko: *(cutting bread while looking at his sister)* A little crazy?

Bojana: Well, except for drinking more than I thought was humanly possible, you didn't do anything stupid.

Mrs Jovanović: But then again, all of your friends were drunk.

Mr Jovanović: Exactly. *(looks over to his daughter)* Boki, would you like to go to your room?

Bojana: Uhm, why would I want to do that?

Mr Jovanović: Your mother and I wanted to talk to your brother first before we talk to you about it?

Bojana: Can't you do that now? I mean if you're going to tell me anyways.

Mr Jovanović: I feel like it would be best if we do it separately.

Mrs Jovanović: Dragan, let her stay. We need to talk about this as a family.

Branko: And what does that have to do with me?

Mr Jovanović: *(in a strict tone)* You'll stay quiet for the next 15 minutes.

Bojana: Dad, what's going on?

Mr Jovanović: You mother and I received a very troubling call yesterday.

Bojana: Okay, what's going on?

Branko: Who called you?

Mr Jovanović: Stay silent! You don't get to know who called. All I need you to do is to answer a single question.

Mrs Jovanović: They told us something deeply disturbing and we just wanted to check if it's just a stupid rumour.

Bojana: Can you get to the point for Christ's sake?

Mr Jovanović: They told us that Branko has been talking stupid things about himself. They told us that you, my son, started telling everyone in school that you're gay.

Silence fills the room

Mr Jovanović: So, are you? Are you really gay? Answer me.

Branko: *(takes a deep breath)* I am. And what are you going to do about it?

Act 4

Scene 81

After a while into the conversation on Branko's coming out to his parents he sits at the table in full shock.

Branko: A PSYCHIATRIST? Are you out of your mind?

Mr Jovanović: We need to know if what's going on with you is normal.

Mrs Jovanović: Your father feels like this would be the best way for you to get over this phase you're having.

Bojana: Are you out of your mind? It's not just a phase and he doesn't need a psychiatrist to get back to normal!

Mr Jovanović: You'll be seeing a therapist as well.

Bojana: *(angry)* Me? What?

Mr Jovanović: Look at you! Your mind is twisted as well. You can't support that kind of sodomy.

Bojana: It's not sodomy to love people of your own gender.

Mr Jovanović: It's a sin for Christ's sake! Why are the two of you so brainwashed that you can't see that? There are some unfortunate homosexuals who suffered a genetic defect, but Branko just got under the wrong influence!

Bojana: There is no wrong influence.

Mr Jovanović: Oh yeah, what about his "boyfriend"? That isn't influence, or what?

Branko: How do you know about that?

Mr Jovanović: I know it from the call.

Bojana: Will you finally tell us everything they said to you? And maybe who of Branko's friends betrayed him like that?

Mr Jovanović: That was a call made by a true friend. Only a true friend would want to help Branko when he needs help the most. The fact that even you supported him disappoints me in your judgement, Bojana. Go to your room. Jadranka, go with her, I need a moment with my son.

Mrs Jovanović: Come on, Bojana we should leave. *(stands up)*

Bojana: *(standing up)* You disgust me!

The two leave Branko with his father behind.

Branko: Dad, it's not what it seems like.

Mr Jovanović: Who is he and why is he manipulating you? That guy of yours.

Branko: I'm not going to talk about him.

Mr Jovanović: You'll talk about him with your psychiatrist then. For now, you will only be allowed to leave the house when you go to school, therapy, the ministry and Dejana's prom. And you will stop plotting your sister against me. Did I make myself clear?

Branko: You can't be serious?

Mr Jovanović: Oh I am serious.

Branko: So you're going to lock me in here?

Mr Jovanović: It's just a temporary measure until we know what's going on with you.

Branko: Nothing is going on with me.

Mr Jovanović: Stop denying your illness and face your problem!

Branko: Okay, fine, I will. But if I already must go to a psychiatrist I'll choose to talk to him about it.

Mr Jovanović: Fair enough. Go to your room, and leave me alone for a while. You will find the right way, my son. I do believe that you can do it.

Branko: I'm not going to comment on that.

Branko stands up and walks over to his room.

Scene 82

The following day Branko is texting Dušan everything that happened.

What the fuck? This is really the worst case scenario

The worst case scenario would be if they threw me out
Don't summon the devil honey. Please.

Okay, okay

I just don't know what to do anymore

Comply with them

See that therapist

And then see how you can escape

I guess that's my only option

Hang in there, it's not the end of the world

I'm sure they'll come to terms with it

And what if that doesn't happen?

Then you'll a new lifestyle you need to deal with

It does get better in the end

That's what they all say

I really hope so

When will I get to see you again?

I feel like that will be a problem from now on

They allowed me to go to the ministry tomorrow after school

My appointment is at 2 pm

So we could meet in the city at around 3 pm and I can tell them it took longer?

I'll pick you up from the ministry

Aw, thanks sweetie

You're the best!

Stay strong!

Meanwhile in the chat with Dejana

Do your parents live in the fucking stone age?????

Oh God

This is unacceptable

We'll fight this, don't worry

I'll pretend to be your girlfriend for now

I think we can convince them

No!

I'm done hiding

I want to live this lifestyle now

Full blown gay

Yas qween! 🎉 🎉 🎉 🎉

But, you know
Be careful
It might not work out for you

I feel like I should be all in

I'll support you all the way

I'm here for you 🖤

And I can't wait to see you at my prom
Since they won't let you out

I can't wait either
Yeah, I'll talk to them once we're back from Albania

You better get this sorted
Or else I'll come to have a word with your parents

You're on fire

Why wouldn't I be? My best friend is under attack!

This is unacceptable

Hang in there, I'll come and get you 🖤

Thanks!

Scene 83

On Monday Branko is sitting across from Bojan in his office.

Bojan: Hello Branko.
Branko: Hey.
Bojan: So you got the letter and know what I'm going to talk about that.
Branko: You wanted to see if you could get me into this EU programme?
Bojan: Yes. So, what the scholarship includes is us paying for you to study at a university in the EU for a year, while creating various

paintings and works for exhibitions around Serbia. That would be the deal. You can study anything you like, depending on the capacity of the university. You'll be financed by us and paid for your work.

Branko: Wow, that seems like a lot of money. Why does Serbia even fund that?

Bojan: The EU funds the majority, we fund another part of it so we can get your work for our exhibitions. After a year you will come back to Serbia to continue and finish your studies here. If you choose to stay in Serbia you'd still get the offer to exhibit for us. You can also stay in your designated country, but we won't finance that.

Branko: Okay, that sounds nice.

Bojan: So as I found out from the University of Arts in Belgrade is that you applied to study there. Is that correct?

Branko: Yeah. What about that?

Bojan: Well, the University of Arts would like to take you. So in order for us to do this, you'd have to cancel your studies there, at least for the first year.

Branko: Oh, well…

Bojan: You will have some time to think about it.

Branko: What would be my other options?

Bojan: Well, our funds are not very high, Branko. We could offer you Zagreb or Ljubljana if you want to study at a University where you can speak Serbian, though for Ljubljana you'd need to learn at least some Slovenian. Or you can study in English in Sofia. Do any of these sound good to you?

Branko: I'm not quite sure. You must know, it was my dream to study at the University of Arts in Belgrade, and if I could get a job working part-time for your exhibitions, that sounds like a great deal.

Bojan: You don't seem very tempted?

Branko: I am, because it could open new possibilities, but is the university in let's say Sofia, really that much better than in Belgrade?

Bojan: I would say that they're at about at the same level.

Branko: Exactly. That's why I'm a little reluctant. I'm sorry.

Bojan: Don't worry about it. Take some time to think about it and get back to me by the 15th of July.

Branko: By the 15th July? That's almost an entire month.

Bojan: Yeah, take your time, it's really not a hassle.

Branko: Wow. Thank you! Thank you for this opportunity. I know how rare it is to get this, and I promise you to make the best of it.

Bojan: I believe in you Branko, that's why I chose you.

Branko: Thank you, sir.

Bojan: You're very welcome. *(smiles)* Now go, enjoy the rest of the day and take your time.

Branko: Thanks, I will.

Branko stands up and leaves Bojan's office.

Scene 84

As Branko exits the ministry he's greeting by his worrying boyfriend in front of the main entrance.

Dušan: *(giving him a tight hug)* Oh God, I'm so happy you're well.

Branko: I'm okay.

Dušan: *(starts walking towards the park in front of the parliament building)* How have they been treating you?

Branko: To be completely honest, I don't think that they treated me any different than usual. They were a bit quieter, but otherwise, everything was oddly normal.

Dušan: I find that a bit suspicious.

Branko: I don't.

Dušan: How come?

Branko: I think they're just unsure. I can feel that they love me like they did before, but they feel like they did something wrong and that that's why I'm gay. And they believe that I can still change. So they're not treating me like the enemy, rather like a sick child that they need to take care of.

Dušan: *(points at a bench)* Wanna sit down there?

Branko: Sure. Anyways, where was I. Ah, yes, I feel like they're treating me with pity.

Dušan: *(sitting down on the bench)* Do you think they'll loosen their measures on you going out?

Branko: *(sitting down)* I think they will. I'll talk to them once we're in Albania. I think there will be so much family drama, that my issue will become irrelevant.

Dušan: And that will make them loosen the measures?

Branko: I sure hope so.

Dušan: All I can do is pray for you.

Branko: Oh please, stop it with the praying.

Dušan: Huh? I thought you're a believer?

Branko: I am. It's just. I have been listening to so much bullshit about how I need to find the way of God and my way out of my sin and being "that".

Dušan: Being "that"?

Branko: My dad avoids saying that I'm gay, so instead, I'm "that".

Dušan: Oh, what a lovely way to describe your son.

Branko: Indeed. Anyways, where was I? Ah yes. Finding the way of God. Well, after so much religious indoctrination, I feel like I need a break from the church.

Dušan: Don't you think that you can find peace in prayer?

Branko: I think I can find peace in prayer. It's just.

Dušan: Listen, God created all of us. I think it's safe to say that he thought through how your life is going to pan out. And you're blessed! I mean they offered you a scholarship.

Branko: Yeah. Zagreb, Ljubljana or Sofia for a year and then I'll go back to Belgrade.

Dušan: Hey! That's not all too far from here. I won't have to suffer as much.

Branko: Who said that I'm going to take it?

Dušan: What? You should take it!

Branko: I'm not sure. The University of Belgrade took me as well.

Dušan: Wait, you have a safe place at the University of Belgrade?

Branko: Yes.

Dušan: Urgh, that is a tough choice.

Branko: I know.

Dušan: Do you want my advice?

Branko: Yes?

Dušan: You should go.

Branko: *(surprised)* What?

Dušan: I know this university has been your dream, but imagine that you could move to another country. Away from your current problems! You could be free. Trust me, I out of everyone here, well maybe except for your sister, want you to stay here the most. But in such troubling times, your interests should come first.

Branko: I will really need to think about it.

Dušan: It's only a year, and afterwards you can come back to Belgrade and see how it unfolds. Maybe you'll manage to stay there as well if you can finance it. Did they say anything about an extension?

Branko: Yes, I'd have to fund it myself.

Dušan: And when do you need to confirm the first year?

Branko: I have until the 15th of July.

Dušan: So 5 days after you come back from Albania.

Branko: Exactly.

Dušan: Think about it once you're back. I'm pretty sure that Albania will change the game.

Branko: I think that has been obvious since the 1990s.

Dušan: Heh. Touché.

Branko: So your vote goes towards leave?

Dušan: Yes, I'm brexiting the shit out of you!

Branko: Maybe I'm just a gay Theresa May. I know I have to leave, but secretly I want to stay.

Dušan: If it helps, I know our relationship isn't even a month old, but I think with patience it could survive that one year. Besides, you'll visit often, and I'll give my best to see you.

Branko: Thanks, that means a lot to me.

Dušan: I won't leave you for such a thing! I promise.

The two kiss as no one is looking, crying in their final embrace for now.

Scene 85

At the dinner table, Branko and his family are discussing the events of the ministry.

Mr Jovanović: Personally, I think the ministry is giving us a great deal, but I would still like to see how your therapy will go, before deciding anything.

Mrs Jovanović: I think that a year abroad will do good. I mean, he could meet so many new people and get a new perspective, maybe that's just what he needs.

Mr Jovanović: You're right Jadranka, but letting him go could let things get out of hand.

Mrs Jovanović: I feel you locking him in is things getting out of hand. We can't forbid him to live his life. He needs to see on his own that what he's doing is wrong.

Mr Jovanović: Are you against me as well? Is this entire family against me?

Bojana: No one is against you. We just love Branko as much as we love you and think that he deserves a chance to do his thing on his own.

Mr Jovanović: Well that's easy for you to say if you wholeheartedly support his sin! It's a shame that you're letting your brother cloud your judgement.

Mrs Jovanović: Dragan, cut the crap and let's eat like a normal family for once.

Mr Jovanović: Okay.

The family eats.

Mr Jovanović: One more thing.

Mrs Jovanović: Oh for Christ's sake.

Mr Jovanović: It's about our trip. I checked the luggage allowance on Air Serbia and I felt like our bags were a little too bulky for flying. I wanted to ask the family if you wanted to go suitcase hunting on Sunday? Everyone will get a new suitcase. Nenad helped us financially.

Bojana: Jeez, how much money does he have?

Mrs Jovanović: Oh he made a fortune doing God knows what.

Bojana: So we have a rich guy in our family, we were just too stupid to realise it.

Mrs Jovanović: Oh, please, don't talk like that. We didn't talk to him for various reasons over the years.

Bojana: With various reasons you mean dad's nationalist attitudes?

Mrs Jovanović: You know that our history is complicated and that the war tore us apart. Our thinking went with it.

Mr Jovanović: I was a bit stupid. Mad. And for some reason I still am. But I'm giving it a chance.

Bojana: And if you gave one to your brother, you should give one to your son.

Mr Jovanović: Oh I am giving Branko a chance.

Branko: You are?

Mr Jovanović: Yes, my son. And that's exactly why you're going to see a psychiatrist.

Branko, shattered in his hopes just continues eating. There's silence at the table.

Mr Jovanović: Your mother and I are invited for coffee tonight. Don't leave the house and don't let anyone in. You're still under protection.

Bojana takes her phone and types. Branko looks at his phone, only to see a message from Bojana:

The only person we need protection from is him…

Scene 86

After their parents left, Branko is left with this immense feeling of panic.

Branko: I don't know if I'm going to keep this up.

Bojana: Calm down. I know, dad is upset with you and he probably won't really come to terms with it, but I don't think that it will be a permanent state.

Branko: So you think that this will be over soon?

Bojana: I wouldn't say "soon", but if you choose to go abroad you might get a chance at winging this.

Branko: But I don't really want to go.

Bojana: What? Why?

Branko: If I stay, I can go to the university I always wanted to go!

Bojana: But you can do that afterwards as well. The scholarship is only for a year!

Branko: Yeah, but why would I bother. Besides, maybe if I go, I'll extend it and I'll never come back.

Bojana: But that's also not a big deal!

Branko: It is to me.

Bojana: *(after a short pause)* Is it because of Dušan?

Branko: Maybe. Boki, I finally found myself. I finally managed to come out, have a boyfriend and have friends who support me.

Bojana: But that's not going to work with our parents' mindsets being like that.

Branko: Don't you think they can change?

Bojana: I do, but frankly, I don't think it's going to happen anytime soon.

Branko: So you think that I should just leave?

Bojana: *(gesturing with her hands in panic)* It's like God's giving you a sign to go, and you're not getting it!

Branko: I'm thinking about taking it, but I don't want to leave everything behind! It's a painful thought.

Bojana: Okay, look. You still have some time until the deadline, so wait to see how the situation develops, if you can see a light at the end of this dark tunnel, then sure, stay here, but if it all fades to black, then you need to get the fuck out of here as fast as it's possible.

Branko: Damn it. You're right.

Bojana: Is it worth a thought?

Branko: *(feeling defeated)* It's worth a thought.

Bojana: Good.

Scene 87

At his first therapy session, Branko meets his psychiatrist Mr Radulović for the first time. As a retired doctor, the sessions take place at Mr Radulović's apartment in a private therapy room in the Crveni Krst area of Belgrade.

Mr Radulović: *(after finishing his introduction)* So that would be everything regarding my career. Do you have any further questions for me or about the work I do?

Branko: Yeah, I'd have one question.

Mr Radulović: Please, feel free.

Branko: Do you know why you have been chosen to be my therapist?

Mr Radulović: My daughter is married to one of your father's school mates, so that's why I decided to take you. I'm a year or so into my pension, so I only work with previous clients or with special requests. I decided to keep my job and do the work voluntarily, which is why I want to help you.

Branko: *(smiles)* I'm thankful to have this opportunity because I might need some guidance.

Mr Radulović: I know, but all of what you're thinking is cureable.

Branko: Curable?

Mr Radulović: Your father explained the situation to me when I met him to review taking you in as a patient. And from what I've heard your homosexuality seems to be a temporary state?

Branko: A temporary state?

Mr Radulović: You see, there are two types of homosexuality. One is a genetic defect, a mistake of nature so to speak. In such cases you can only learn how to live with it. The other is a social construct. And as your father told me, you seem to be the second type. Your surroundings influenced you and your thinking.

Branko: You're making me feel like I'm not normal.

Mr Radulović: Oh please, don't get me wrong. What you're feeling is completely normal, and it happens to many people. But you don't have to feel this way, and you could change if you wanted to.

Branko: *(hesitant)* Well…

Mr Radulović: Okay, let's look at it from this way. Are you happy this way? Are you happy with your gay identity?

Branko: Well. I am really happy with it because I made myself feel comfortable enough in my skin. I learned how to embrace it and I think that I'm learning how to love a guy, and now that I'm in this progress I just feel like my father wants to cut it off and that's what makes me unhappy.

Mr Radulović: Do you think that he's right in what he's doing?

Branko: No, I don't. I know that he thinks that he's doing the right thing, but that just keeps hurting me. I really don't know how to deal with this situation, and I don't think that changing is the right thing for me to do.

Mr Radulović: Well, the only way you can change your sexuality is if you yourself choose to do it. Many studies, even in the Western World and at the Swedish university I worked at, found that sexuality is a fluid component of our identity. That means that if sexuality is fluid you can change it. However, it won't work if you just do it to please your father. That's not going to change anything. So let me ask you, do you want to change.

Branko: *(determined)* No.

Mr Radulović: Well then. I would like for us to talk about your childhood and to find the root of your homosexuality. What you do with that information is up to you, it's only my job to help you understand yourself. Maybe your thinking will change once you know where your sexuality comes from.

Branko: Uhm, okay, let's give it a try. I'm obligated to be here anyways.

Mr Radulović: Well, then, tell me about the first thing you can remember…

Branko goes on, talking about his childhood and his upbringing.

Scene 88

After the therapy session Branko texts Dušan.

> I swear to God I'm going to go insane if
> I have to keep this up much longer 😫

What did he say were the
causes of your "gayness"?

> Apparently the close relationship I
> have with my sister and my mother

"you needed a male figure in your
life, but you only got a female one"

Maybe I looked up to my mother because she's the
only person in our family to have attended university

What the fuck? My dad is a fat and lazy
conservative fuck literally 90% of the
time, why should I want to be like him?

Listen, I know you're frustrated, I would be too

But...

Try to keep it up

I talked to my mother about your situation and she
told me, that if you could get the therapist to declare
you as unchangeable, your parents would be forced
to accept their decision

And how do you suggest I do that?

Just keep up the act, give it your all

What act?

That it's a genetic defect. Act like you're
devastated about being gay and that you don't
want to be gay, but don't change at the same time
so that the therapist deems you clinically gay

How the fuck do you know about that differentiation?

My dad also contacted therapists when he found
out, so I know a thing or two about it

Never had to go through that though

Lucky you

Well, I could try, but I feel like if I tell
him that I want to change he'll use
some sort of weird method against me

You need to learn to be resistant

But it's a constant force applied to you

Those sessions are intense

Then you need to learn to beat it!

I believe in you 💕

I'll do my best

Thanks

It means a lot to me

You mean a lot to me

And you mean a lot to me 🖤

Scene 89

June 25th, 2016, At Dejana's prom, Branko arrives only to find Dejana in a gorgeous blue dress talking to her friends (Jelena and Sara)

Dejana: *(looks to Branko)* You made it!
Branko: *(hugs her)* I wouldn't miss this for the world.
Dejana: Thank you, that means a lot to me.
Jelena: *(smiles)* Nice to see you again. It's been a while.
Sara: How have you been?
Branko: Oh I've been great. And yes, it's been a while.
Dejana: Guys, would you mind letting Branko and me speak?
Jelena: No problem, talk to you later then.

The two leave.

Dejana: *(in a worried tone)* Now, seriously, are you alright?
Branko: I've been better but I'm hanging in there.
Dejana: I'm so proud of you for staying this strong. How was your first therapy session?
Branko: Can we talk about that some other time? I don't want to ruin your prom.
Dejana: Don't worry about it. Tell me. I'm worried.
Branko: Okay, okay. Don't worry about me. The therapy sessions are bearable, and my dad is busy because of the trip to Albania anyways.
Dejana: You're leaving in 5 days, right?
Branko: Yup.
Dejana: And until that you're still pretty much grounded?
Branko: For the most part, yes.
Dejana: Okay, I guess it's going to be calling each other from now on.
Branko: My mother recently got mad at my dad, so I can imagine him changing his mind in the near future.
Dejana: Let's hope that happens in the near future. What are you

going about Dušan? *(waves to people in the crowd)*
Branko: I don't know. I have to stick to messaging for now.
Dušan: *(approaching)* Or at least after tonight.
Branko: *(turns around)* Dušan? *(starts shaking)* What are you doing here?
Dejana: I'm going to leave you two alone for now. *(leaves)*
Dušan: Dejana called me. *(hugs him)* She told me that we could make our wish come true.
Branko: Which one?
Dušan: To dance together at prom.
Branko: No, not here, this is too public.
Dušan: Look onto the dance floor.

Branko looks to the dance floor to see two gay couples and a lesbian couple dancing.

Dušan: "At this school, everyone is welcome." That's what Dejana told me. And it seems to be true. So please, may I have this dance?
Branko: *(in tears)* Yes, yes you may.

As the couple is dancing to the final slow song of the evening, Dušan pulls Branko closer to him.

Dušan: There's one more thing I've been meaning to tell you.
Branko: What is it?
Dušan: Branko Jovanović, I love you.
Branko: *(stunned, after a pause)* I love you too.

They seal their dance with a kiss.

Scene 90

The day before his family trip to Albania, Branko is at his third session with Mr Radulović.

Mr Radulović: So you love him?
Branko: I have never felt like this before. It's just indescribable. I have had girls in the past, but this type of love is a first-timer for me.
Mr Radulović: You are feeling the relief of being understood, and be

cared for, and in this case, it comes from a man.

Branko: Exactly, because I could never give to a woman, what I can give to a man. There are all these social expectations for me to take care of a woman, and that's what I felt: pressure. I don't want to be the sole caretaker and the provider for everything. I don't have any of that with Dušan, and that makes me so happy.

Mr Radulović: Would you consider yourself politically liberal?

Branko: I think so, I'm not that much into politics.

Mr Radulović: Well, I guess you picked up some typically female values and with that mix of male and female in your behaviour you need the needs of both to be met.

Branko: Is that an abnormal thing?

Mr Radulović: No, it's actually pretty common. It's not a rare observation I've made in my years as a psychiatrist.

Branko: So what do you suggest I do?

Mr Radulović: Oh, I'm not here to make suggestions, I'm just here to guide you. As you said it yourself during our first session, you're here to get guidance.

Branko: Well, then, guide me onto something else.

Mr Radulović: What do you need guidance on?

Branko: Where I'm going to Albania tomorrow and would I like guidance on how to deal with the wedding and my family?

Mr Radulović: Okay, we can do that.

After the session, Dejana is waiting for Branko in front of the building.

Dejana: *(hugging him)* Did you survive?

Branko: I'm glad you could make it. Did you get what my parents asked for?

Dejana: *(hands him a list of things)* Yeah, here are a few suggestions and addresses you might want to check out during your visit. Albania can be really beautiful if you know where to go.

Branko: Okay, thank you.

Dejana: What did the guy bother you about?

Branko: Well, I stirred the conversation to my family issues and Albania, so I guess the moral of the story was, don't fuck shit up and don't tell anyone you're gay.

Dejana: You really don't need a psychiatrist to tell you that.

Branko: Seven more sessions to go, then I'll be done with it for good.

Dejana: But your dad's pressure won't stop.

Branko: It won't, but if I play my cards right I could ease it.

Dejana: To be honest, I'm so proud of you for being strong in this case. Keep it going like this and you will get out of it. *(hugs him again)*

Branko: Thanks, Dejana, I really appreciate it.

Scene 91

June 30th at around 11 pm, the Jovanović family is at Belgrade Nikola Tesla International Airport waiting for their flight to Tirana. After passing passport control.

Mrs Jovanović: Okay kids, dad and I will go look at the duty-free stores, if you want to, you can walk around yourself and we'll see each other at the gate. They should announce it.

Branko: I think we'll just walk around.

Bojana: I want to get some ice cream.

Mr Jovanović: Okay, you can go there. Your mother and I will be here if you need us.

Bojana and Branko walk away.

Branko: So do you want to get Moritz Eis or something else?

Bojana: My God, I don't want ice cream, I needed an excuse to go to Victoria's Secret.

Branko: Wait, you're taking me to Victoria's Secret now?

Bojana: You're gay, you can handle it.

50 minutes later.

Branko: You know by now I'm getting really uncomfortable watching you pick out sexy underwear, why do you need it anyway?

Bojana: *(checking herself out in a mirror)* A woman likes to feel good when she looks at herself in the mirror.

Branko: Okay. I still don't get this concept.

Announcement: Final call for passengers on flight JU 656 to Moscow

Sheremetyevo at 23:40. Gate A4 will be closing. Final call for passengers on flight JU 826 to Beirut at 23:45. Gate C2 will be...

Bojana: Why don't you just listen to the announcements and tell me when we need to leave.

Branko: Uhm, okay.

Announcement: ... to Abu Dhabi at 23:40, the flight has been delayed by 90 minutes. Please await gate information. Flight JU 168 to Ohrid at 00:20 is ready for boarding. We kindly ask all passengers to go to gate A1. Flight JU 216 to Tirana at 00:25 is ready for boarding. We kindly ask all passengers to got to gate C7. Flight JU 526 to Thessaloniki...

Branko: Boki, we need to go. Gate C7.

Bojana: *(running to the cash register)* Let me at least just buy this swimsuit!

Branko: Okay, but hurry up!

With C7 being the last gate at the airport, Branko and Bojana find themselves running across the entire airport.

Branko: Damn, why did we get the gate furthest off from the main terminal?

Bojana: *(out of breath)* No clue, but at least I have a cute swimsuit now!

After clearing security and meeting up with their parents, the family finds themselves on an airfield in front of a small propeller plan.

Mr Jovanović: Ah, what a great moment this is. Our kids' first flight.

Mrs Jovanović: It's so nice to witness this.

Bojana: I just find it exciting that we'll be in Tirana in an hour.

Branko: And I just can't wait to get out of here.

Scene 92

On the plane, Branko keeps on looking down from the window while his sister is taking a nap next to him.

Branko: *(to himself)* Flying is exactly what I expected. Being in the air like a bird, cruising at high speeds and looking down at the city lights from above. Each of these lights represents a street or a house, with people living there. I wonder what they're doing down there. How many of them are sleeping, how many are partying on a Friday night? How many of them are families, friends or lovers? You know, it makes you realise just how small you are as an individual. Part of a greater good that is above you. And not in a degrading way.

Flight attendant: *(interrupting his thought process)* Would you like a sandwich?

Branko: Uhm, yes sure.

Bojana: *(waking up)* Uhm, could I get one too? How much is it?

Flight attendant: Oh, the service is for free madam.

Bojana: Awesome.

Flight attendant: Would you like cookies with that?

Bojana: Yes, please. *(to Branko)* This is awesome!

After ordering their drinks the two are enjoying their snack.

Bojana: I think my favourite part of flying is the food. Yours is probably looking down at the ground and shit, but hey, there's free food! *(bites into her sandwich)*

Branko: No comment.

Bojana: Oh please, your next five paintings will have the frame of an airplane window.

Branko: How did you...?

Bojana: I've been watching you paint since I was five, I think I can figure out your thought process by now.

Branko: You know me well. Maybe too well.

Bojana: I grew up with you. *(laughs)* It's part of my job as a sister.

Branko: *(annoyed)* Eh...

Shortly before landing into Tirana Bojana looks to Branko again.

Bojana: Remember when I first told you about finding out where uncle Nenad lives?

Branko: Yes, of course, how I could I forget, that was a revolutionary moment.

Bojana: Could you have ever imagined that within a matter of months we would be on a plane to that place?

Branko: No, not at all. But I did feel like it meant that we would see Nenad again.

Bojana: True.

Branko: Are you excited about seeing Milenko? This is the first time we'll see him since he moved to Malta.

Bojana: I know. And I don't know to feel about it.

Branko: Why?

Bojana: I feel like he and dad are going to fight again, you know, because he didn't manage to do anything and that he's a failure etc.

Branko: He did manage to move to Malta.

Bojana: Only to work at a construction company. Let's face it, dad is ashamed of him.

Branko: He's ashamed of me too.

Bojana: Not on an educational basis though. You at least show potential for a future. I overheard him speak to mom about letting you go to Zagreb or Ljubljana.

Branko: Why those two?

Bojana: Do you think he'd let you go to Sofia?

Branko: Yeah…

Bojana: All I'm saying is that your cultural capital could be the key from saving you from this fucked up situation.

Branko: Oh I don't think that it could be the key. I think it is the key.

The plane touches down on the ground.

Announcement: Ladies and Gentleman, welcome to Tirana Mother Theresa International Airport. The local time is 1:30 in the morning and the temperature is around 26°C. Thank you for choosing to fly Air Serbia, enjoy your stay in Tirana and a have a good night!

Branko: This announcement, Boki, this announcement is the start of a new chapter in our lives.

Scene 93

After passing passport control and grabbing their baggage the family is reunited with their uncle Nenad waiting for them at the airport with his future wife, Diellza. (For the sake of equality Mr Jovanović will be referred to as Dragan and Mrs Jovanović as Jadranka)

Nenad: *(happy)* Brother, is that really you?

Dragan: Yes, yes it is.

Nenad: *(opens his arms)* Come here.

After being introduced to Diellza, the family is in Nenad's jeep on their way to their house.

Diellza: So, welcome to Tirana. I know that you can't see much at night, but I promise you that it will be beautiful during the day.

Nenad: It's really nicer than I initially thought it would be.

Branko: I find it intriguing to be in Albania.

Diellza: To be honest with you, I felt very scared when I went to Belgrade for the first time, but seeing the city and meeting the people made me realise that we are slowly getting past this entire war bullshit that plagued us in the past decades. So, trust me, I can understand why you feel a little uneasy, but trust me, Tirana has its nice sides.

Bojana: I like her already. Good choice, Nenad.

Nenad: Thanks, sunshine.

Branko: *(to Bojana)* Heh, haven't heard that one in a while. Makes you nostalgic.

Bojana: Oh shut up, you're only 18.

Jadranka: Thanks for taking us in Diellza. It does mean a lot to us.

Diellza: Oh please, you're Nenad's family, you're welcome here at any time. Besides, I would love to show you my home country.

Dragan: Pardon me for asking, but I thought you were from Kosovo?

Diellza: Oh, I'm actually not. I was born in Shkodër in the north of Albania, but my family moved to Prishtinë when I was 5.

Jadranka: *(slightly uncomfortable)* Oh, that's nice.

The family arrives in front of a villa on the outskirts of town. As they enter the villa Diellza walks them through.

Diellza: Here we are. Welcome to our home.

Bojana: Wow, this is huge.

Diellza: *(to Jadranka)* So you and your husband will have a room on the ground floor, while Bojana and Branko will be on the first floor.

Your eldest, Milenko will have his own room next to yours. My parents, Nenad and I are on the second floor and my sister is next to Bojana and Branko's room.

Jadranka: Wow, this is a huge house you have here.

Diellza: Come, I'll show you around.

The two women leave the scene.

Dragan: So, this is what became of you?

Nenad: I'm afraid so.

Dragan: I'm proud of you my brother, you made it, you made yourself a life. I'm sure our parents would've been proud.

Nenad: I hope so too, but don't see me as the more successful man. I think you've made more out of your life than I have.

Dragan: What do you mean.

Nenad: *(pointing to Branko and Bojana)* Look at your angels. They're all grown up now. I'm 44 and I still don't have kids and with Diellza already being 42, I don't think I ever will.

Dragan: *(quieting down)* That's a shame, my brother.

Bojana: You can always adopt. There are so many unwanted children waiting to find a home. They'd love it here.

Nenad: I've talked to Diellza about it. Maybe after the honeymoon, we'll bring up the topic again.

Bojana: I would be happy for you, and I'd love to have some cousins.

Nenad: *(smiling)* Let's hope for the best then. *(pauses)* You must be very tired, come on, let's go to bed and we'll explore the city tomorrow.

Dragan: Deal.

Scene 94

The scene opens the next day on Skënderbej Square in Tirana. The family is standing at the side of the square as they are observing the horseman in the middle and a huge Albanian flag waving through the wind.

Branko: *(taking pictures with his phone)* It's quite cool here.

Diellza: This square is basically the lifeline of the city. Here you can see the Tirana International Hotel, the Palace of Culture, the National Opera, the National Library, the National Bank, the Ethem Bey Mosque, the Clock Tower, the City Hall, the National Historical Museum and the Ministries of Infrastructure, Agriculture and Economy.

Nenad: Imagine it as your one and only go to place. The square was designed during the Roman occupation of Albania and has been re-vamped during the socialist regime of Albania in the late 70s.

Dragan: *(looking around)* This is highly impressive.

Branko: To some extent, I can see some parallels to Belgrade, but at the same time it's very different.

Diellza: I would say that the architecture is similar in many buildings due to this classic socialist building regime, but the layouts of the cities are completely different.

Branko: I think that's an obvious difference to spot. It's also much warmer here than in Belgrade.

After a while, they're all walking through the street with Branko and Bojana walking in the back.

Bojana: *(whispering)* Do you think dad and Nenad are getting along?

Branko: I guess. I mean they have a lot of catching up to do.

Bojana: I'm just afraid that the national tendencies will escalate again.

Branko: *(in a indifferent tone)* I think he's too busy thinking about what will become of me, rather than national tendencies.

Bojana: I wouldn't be quite sure. I see that he's being uncomfortable most of the time.

Branko: He's a Serb walking through the streets of Tirana, I don't think that you can really blame him for being a little uncomfortable.

Bojana: Are you uncomfortable?

Branko: Well not really, but I'm also not a bigot.

Bojana: You have a valid point there.

Diellza looks to the kids.

Diellza: Come on! Hurry up, I want to show you some cool places!

Scene 95

The next day the family is vacationing in Durrës, a seaside Albanian town, about 40km west of Tirana. After less than an hour in the car, the family arrives at the beach.

Bojana: Now, I do not know about you, but I didn't go swimming in forever. I so can't wait to get in there. Branko?

Branko: I'll come with you.

Jadranka: I'd like to take walk across the beach, Diellza would you like to come with me? You could show me around.

Diellza: Sure, I'd love to.

After leaving the group Branko and Bojana stand by the water.

Bojana: Thanks for playing along.

Branko: Huh?

Bojana: Mom and I talked in the morning. We agreed that dad needs to spend some alone time with his brother. That's why we split up.

Branko: I see. *(looks back to his dad)* I wonder what they're talking about.

On the other side of the beach:

Nenad: The kids have really grown since I last saw them.

Dragan: I worry about them every single day.

Nenad: Isn't that normal if you have kids?

Dragan: Uh. I guess. They're everything I have, along with my wife.

Nenad: And that's a beautiful life you're living.

Dragan: It was beautiful.

Nenad: Why, what happened?

Dragan: Branko got very sick.

Nenad: *(worried)* Why? What happened to him? Is it bad?

Dragan: It's bad, but it's treatable.

Nenad: What happened?

Dragan: Recently Jadranka found out from one of his friends that he came out as gay in school.

Nenad: *(after a pause)* And you don't know how to deal with that yet?

Dragan: I'm sending him to therapy, it's only a matter of time until he'll be fixed.

Nenad: You're doing what?

Dragan: I'm fixing my son.

Nenad: *(angry)* Are you out of your narrow mind?

Dragan: What? What have I done wrong?

Nenad: The same thing you've done wrong when you convinced everyone to cut me out of the family because your view of the world didn't accept what I was doing. I was dating someone you and our parents didn't approve of! And now you are doing the same thing to your son. What will you do if he doesn't get "fixed"? Will you kick him out too?

Dragan: He will get fixed.

Nenad: But what if he doesn't?

Dragan: I guess I'll just let him live his life without the family.

Nenad: You are repeating the same mistake. Come on! You can't be this stupid.

Dragan: Okay, listen up, the only reason why I was able to come to terms with your situation is the fact that there was a national difference that can be overcome if you have the patience to do so. Diellza didn't choose to be Albanian.

Nenad: Neither did Branko chose to be gay.

Dragan: Being gay is a choice! I've spoken to professionals.

Nenad: Oh God. "Professionals" you say?

Dragan: Branko was manipulated into thinking that he's something he's not. I'm just trying to protect my son. Am I that wrong?

Nenad: Quite frankly, yes, yes you are that wrong.

Dragan: Then I guess there's no reason for us to speak about this topic then. How can I help you prepare for the wedding?

Nenad: Well, I will need some help over the course of the coming week, and I was thinking that you and Milenko, once he arrives, could come with me.

Dragan: What about Branko?

Nenad: Diellza will probably need his help with carrying some stuff to the venue.

Dragan: Okay, sounds fair.

Nenad: I really need this to be perfect. Diellza is everything I have and I want to give her the wedding that she deserves.

Dragan: Don't worry, you can count on me.

Nenad: Thanks, brother.

Scene 96

A few days later, Bojana and Branko are with Diellza in a café after going shopping for the house.

Bojana: Wow, it's really cool to spend time with you Diellza. I can't wait to call you aunt Diellza.

Diellza: I bet that we'll make a good family. I really enjoy spending time with you.

Branko: We recently overheard uncle Nenad regretting that he doesn't have kids, how do you stand on that?

Diellza: Well, I am too old to have kids at my age. Unfortunately. But we would like to adopt, I feel like it's important to have a child and bring it up.

Branko: *(smiles)* That's such a nice thought.

Diellza: Nenad shared with me what your father recently shared with him.

Bojana: What is it?

Diellza: Well, your father isn't quite alright with Branko being gay.

Branko: *(scared)* Oh fuck.

Bojana: Yeah, we know that.

Branko: Diellza, please I don't want to cause any problems at the wedding, and I re-

Diellza: Please, stop that. You are our invited guest, and you will soon be my nephew. And I will accept you, no matter what.

Branko: *(stunned)* Huh?

Diellza: If I learned something through your uncle it's that love has no boundaries. If two consenting adults love each other, no one has the right to decide or judge but the people themselves.

Branko: But God judges against that?

Diellza: Nobody should care what other people say about what Allah would say. I was raised in a Muslim household, yet chose to become an atheist, because I don't see a point in this entire religious bullshit.

Branko: Well, I always found comfort in religion.

Diellza: You found comfort in your beliefs, and that's good. But no one in your religious group should have the right to tell you what you can and can't believe. If you're truly gay and you can feel it, and the feeling is pure, then that's how God made you.

Branko: I do doubt it at times.

Diellza: Because you want to change or because others want you to change?

Branko: Because others want me to change.

Bojana: That's our main problem. Our father believes that he can "cure" Branko of whatever satanic spiral he got himself into, without understanding that it's utter bullshit.

Diellza: Nenad was very mad at your father. He felt like he wants to turn the entire family against you.

Branko: I just hope that it's not going to be too much of a drama.

Diellza: Well, the wedding is in two days. Let's just hope things don't heat up too much.

Bojana: Does our dad talk about it a lot?

Diellza: As far as I know they talk about it a lot.

Bojana: He's worried, but I feel like he'll come around.

Diellza: That's what I hope too, but I wouldn't bet on it. If I were you I'd take the scholarship.

Branko: You know about the scholarship?

Diellza: Yup, I heard you can get your first year abroad financed. Try it. After one year, you might want to stay and work for your money, or you can return and study for free in Serbia.

Branko: It's too much change at once though.

Diellza: Yes, but it will guarantee you that you'll make it mentally, should your dad not come around.

Branko: But I don't want to move.

Diellza: Maybe you'll have to.

Branko: But I'll be alone.

Diellza: And maybe that's the price you have to pay. Though Nenad and I have also talked about it, and should it get too bad, you can always come to us. Tirana will always welcome you.

Branko: That might be a sentence I never thought I'd hear, but, thank you. It means a lot to me.

Diellza: You are very welcome.

Branko: Ah, I feel so at ease now.

Bojana: Why that?

Branko: I have a support system.

Diellza: And you can count on us. Come here. *(she hugs him)* In two days, we'll be a family.

Scene 97

As the group returns home they find Milenko, Branko and Bojana's older brother in the house, who has just arrived from Malta.

Milenko: *(smiles)* Aah, my little peoples, come here. *(hugs them)* I haven't seen you in ages. You alright?

Branko: Yeah, we've been good. You?

Milenko: Ah, I'm loving my life in Malta.

Bojana: We've heard you have someone.

Milenko: Ah yes, Marija, my lovely lady.

Bojana: How long has been? Half a year.

Milenko: I guess so. Marija and I really managed to work through a lot.

Marija: *(approaching)* Has anyone called me?

Bojana: *(very surprised)* Oh my God! Is that her? Oh my God! It's so great to meet you. I never thought Milenko would find someone and yet here you are. And damn, you look damn fine.

Marija: *(smiles)* Thanks, I'll take that as a compliment. You must be Bojana, Milenko's sister.

Bojana: Yes I am.

Marija: So, I take it that you must be Branko?

Branko: Yup.

Marija: Well, it's so nice to finally meet you. I met your parents and they're pure angels.

Bojana: *(smiling the pain away)* Uh huh, they're great.

Marija: Well, Milenko and I wanted to go out to the city, would you like to join us?

Bojana: Yeah, that sounds like a great idea.

Branko: Sure, I'm in.

After commencing the evening, the group sits down in a café in the old town. Since they are speaking Serbian, no one can understand them.

Milenko: *(interrupting the previous conversation)* Say, would you mind going through a little family crisis that we are having right now?

Marija: Are you sure that you want me to be here?

Milenko: Yeah, back me up on this one.

Bojana: What is it?

Milenko: *(looking at Branko)* Well, I talked to our father and he told me, that you've been having some devious thoughts. And I wanted to-

Bojana: *(interrupting him)* Stop it right there! Don't you even dare take his side!

Milenko: He told me you went insane as well, listen Branko is sick.

Branko: I didn't even do anything.

Marija: *(confused)* What is going on?

Branko: I'm gay and your boyfriend is bashing me for it.

Bojana: Oh wow, you came out to someone again.

Branko: Yeah, on my own.

Bojana: Wow, I'm very proud of you.

Branko: Thanks. *(looks to Marija)* Anyways, your boyfriend is bashing me.

Marija: Milenko, are you serious?

Milenko: Come on, you cannot possibly be on their side?

Marija: Has the move to Malta not taught you a single thing about human rights? Listen, just because you're uneducated doesn't mean that you can be a bigoted twat like that.

Milenko: Marija, I…

Marija: Don't even try. You'll shut up about this or we're going to have a serious discussion about your morals.

Milenko: Okay…

As Milenko goes over to pay the bill

Branko: You have no idea how thankful I am.
Marija: No worries, just remember that you will always have people on your side.
Branko: Thank you!

Scene 98

After the wedding ceremony, everyone's in the garden celebrating young and diverse love.

Branko: Say, do you think that our father actually came to terms with Nenad?
Bojana: Yeah, I do think so.
Branko: Because I feel like it's a bit weird.
Bojana: I feel like there's a divide in the family. Not because of Nenad, but because of you.
Branko: Because of me?
Bojana: Of course. I mean, our father fought with our uncle, our brother is fighting with his girlfriend. You really raised an extremely important question in our family.
Branko: Oh come on, I wouldn't give it that much importance.
Bojana: I think that it's more important than you think. It's not primarily about accepting you as an individual. It's about the principles the family has. It's mostly about morals. That's what makes this so complicated.
Branko: Do you think that will make our family a massive chaos?
Bojana: I think we already are.

As they speak, Nenad gets up on stage to speak to his guest.

Nenad: Uhm, hello. Hello. *(in Albanian)* Thank you for coming! *(in English)* So, I wanted to thank you all for being here. I want to thank Diellza's family for accepting me as one their own, even though I come from Serbia. I would like to thank everyone for their love and support, and I wanted to say a special thank you to my family, who came here from Serbia and Malta, just for me. So this next bid will be in Serbian for you. *(in Serbian)* Dragan, I remember the day you married Jadranka. It was a beautiful day and we were on this splav floating on the Sava river. Back then you were pregnant with Milenko. And the cycle goes on, it's my turn now, and then you're next. Marija, I've known you a few days, but you are a very kind person, and I hope that you can stay part of our family.

Everyone is looking at Nenad with awe.

Boki, you have always been my pretty little princess, and I truly hope that you will get to have a fairytale wedding, just like you always dreamt of it. And Branko, whatever happens, and whatever you'll have to do, just remember, that he will be worth it. *(in English)* Thank you.

Bojana: He DID NOT just say that.
Branko: Oh, but I believe he did.
Bojana: Look, dad is walking over to him. This can't be good.

Dragan: What the f*ck were you thinking over there?
Nenad: Brother, it's my wedding, I can hold my speech.
Dragan: You are not allowed to play with my son's life like that.
Nenad: So, it's okay to wish Milenko and Bojana all the best in life and leave Branko out? He deserves to get married one day just as much as you and I deserved it.
Dragan: To a woman, the right way.
Nenad: Oh, please, grow up.
Dragan: You're the younger one, you should listen to me.
Nenad: No! I'm the younger one, that means I should be able to look up to you. But instead, I got nothing but judgement from you!
Dragan: I'm not judging you. You're simply wrong!
Nenad: Nope, you're wrong. But you'll never be able to see that. And that, brother, is extremely sad.
Diellza: *(running to them)* What's going on, why are you fighting?
Dragan: It's nothing. My brother still likes to pick on me from time to time.
Diellza: What's so wrong about that?
Dragan: He's putting shit in my boy's mind.

Diellza: I'm sorry to put it this way, but the only person putting shit into his head, is you.

As the fighting escalates on one side, Milenko runs over to his siblings.

Milenko: Do you see what you have done to this family?
Bojana: Would you leave our brother alone you primitive uneducated construction worker? Don't make this more pathetic than it is.
Milenko: Oh, so now we have a big mouth.
Bojana: *(shouting)* I'll shut my big mouth if you shut your big mouth you useless fuck.
Marija: *(approaching)* What's going on here?
Bojana: Your boyfriend is misbehaving.
Marija: *(yelling)* Milenko, come with me, right now!
Milenko: I have something to settle.
Marija: *(getting louder)* You come with me right now, or I'll cut your fucking dick off.

From the other side of the room, the threat could be hurt.

Dragan: *(to Nenad)* Look at what you've done. Now even Milenko has to pay for your sin.
Nenad: The only people to blame here are Milenko and you!

They watch as Marija takes Milenko further into the back.

Dragan: I'm going to check up on them. Make sure that the only healthy relationship in this family survives.

He runs off after them.

Scene 99

In front of the garden, Branko's mother is sitting on a bench, crying. Branko runs out from the venue to get some fresh air to breathe until he notices his mother.

Branko: Mother?
Jadranka: *(turns away)* Don't look at me.
Branko: *(approaching her)* Mother, what's wrong?
Jadranka: It's about your father, I can't see him acting up like that.

Branko: *(sitting down next to her)* Oh, I see.

Jadranka: *(angry)* I can't stand watching him hurt you.

Branko: I don't think anyone except Milenko can stand that.

Jadranka: I do agree with him. I don't think that what's happening with you is normal. It's not. It's a serious illness. But you're my son, and I love you. *(cries)*

Branko: So, you're accepting me?

Jadranka: Don't get me wrong, I don't think I'll be able to ever accept it, but I guess I'll have to learn to live with it.

Branko: I guess that would be the best option for all of us.

There is a short moment of silence.

Jadranka: I believe that you will see the right way one day. But you will see it yourself. I can't force you to see it. I think that's the main point.

Branko: I understand.

Jadranka: This situation is a burden for all of us. I think your father is not able to see that, and now he's ruining his brother's wedding.

Branko: Oh come on, I don't think he's ruining the wedding.

Jadranka: I saw the situation unfold. That wasn't a discussion that was a heated argument.

Another short moment of silence.

Jadranka: I just want this to be over and to fly home.

Branko: We're flying home tomorrow. Let's just enjoy this while it lasts.

Jadranka: I don't think that there is anything to enjoy anymore.

After a few moments, Bojana appears.

Bojana: You won't believe the shit storm that is going on in there.

Jadranka: What happened?

Bojana: Marija just broke up with Milenko and confessed to our father that he was abusive with her.

Branko: That he was what?

Jadranka: *(putting her head into her palms, crying)* This cannot be true. Did I raise a single normal child?

Bojana: Mom, Branko and I are normal children, and as far as we know, it's only a claim.

Branko: What did she claim exactly.

Bojana: That he would push her away too hard or hit her from time to time. I guess she just snapped.

Branko: Oh fuck. This night seems to be going down the road to hell anyways.

Bojana: I do not wish to know what it will look like tomorrow.

And yet there is another short moment of silence.

Jadranka: Kids, could you listen to me for a second.

Bojana: What is it?

Jadranka: Could you just try to live your lives and make the best out of them? Bojana, go out with your friends whenever you want and Branko, go see your boy without paying attention to what your father says. We can't go on like this. We must start living like a technical family until we all can come to the same middle ground. Promise me you won't let yourself be controlled by him?

Branko and Bojana look at each other silently.

Branko: Yes, we promise.

Bojana: Technical family it is.

Scene 100

Sunday, July 10th at around 1 pm: Tirana International Airport. The family reached security control as they are flying back to their respective homes. Nenad and Diellza are standing in front of security saying their goodbyes.

Nenad: Now, I know we never really got along in this family, but there's still room for us to grow.

Diellza: It really meant a lot to us that you came here for the wedding and we will make sure to start seeing you more frequently.

Jadranka: Thank you for your invite and for being so kind and welcoming.

Diellza: Please, no need to thank us. We just wanted you to be part of our special day.

Jadranka: Thank you.

Nenad: Brother, I hope to see you soon and to stay in touch.

Dragan: I hope so too.

Nenad: Take care, everyone!

Dragan: We will, bye.

After passing security the family gathers around the gate for Belgrade as that plane is leaving first. (Dragan and Jadranka will return to being Mr and Mr Jovanović)

Mr Jovanović: Well, I guess this it. Another family fallout.

Mrs Jovanović: Don't even start it.

Mr Jovanović: I'm not. I just don't know if I want to speak to Nenad ever again.

Mrs Jovanović: You did that once, and see where that got you. Nowhere! All you need to do is calm down.

Marija: You people are really sick. You shouldn't behave like that towards each other and yet you do. No wonder Milenko turned out the way he did, and I really hope that Branko and Bojana will manage to make something out of their lives.

Milenko: Oh now, you're talking again. Stop it.

Marija: *(yelling)* Or what? Are you going to hit me again? Do it! There's security everywhere, you won't stand a God damn chance!

Bojana: I think we should all just keep our peace.

Marija: *(walking over to Bojana)* You are such a kind angel, don't let them ruin you. *(to Branko)* You too, Branko. Stay safe. Now if you don't mind, I'm going to sit at another gate and read a book up until our flight to Rome. Alone.

Marija walks out of the group.

Milenko: Brother.

Branko: Yes?

Milenko: I fucking hate you. Faggot!

Act 5

Scene 101

Following his arrival from Albania, on July 11th, Branko met up with Dušan in a quiet cafe in Belgrade's downtown area of Vračar to discuss the events of the wedding.

Dušan: This sounds all so terrible. *(hugs him)* How did you even manage to convince your parents to see me?

Branko: On the last night, my mother encouraged us to take a chance and just live our lives, so I'm trying to come up with some sort of action plan.

Dušan: Any ideas of what you want to do?

Branko: I'm thinking of taking the scholarship. It's not a permanent thing and I would be gone for a year. Who knows, maybe I'll like it there.

Dušan: I support your decision. It's really the best for you.

Branko: I'm still a bit sceptical.

Dušan: Just push through with it. I believe in you.

Branko: And what will become of us?

Dušan: Oh come on, many gays have long distance relationships. If they can do it, we can do it too. Besides, all the cities they offered you are not that far away. If you pick Zagreb, I can be with you in under six hours by bus. Trust me, you have nothing to worry about.

Branko: Should I go for Zagreb then?

Dušan: Well, it is the closest city and you don't have a language barrier. I think it might be best for you not to be too far away, but to still be away.

Branko: I guess you're right.

Dušan: Well, it's your choice in the end. I don't know anything about the quality of the universities.

Branko: Well, I don't think that Zagreb has a bad university.

Dušan: See! Besides, Croatia is beautiful, you will be so close to the seaside, the Plitvice lakes and, oh my God, just move to Croatia.

Branko: I'll think about it, you make it sound bearable there.

Dušan: Oh, come on. If you really need a second opinion, talk to

Dejana. I'm sure her international outreach will be able to tell you which city fits you best.

Branko: Well. I think you have a point there.

Dušan: Branko. I love you, and I only want the best for you, so don't let anyone get you down. Okay?

Branko: Okay. Thanks. I love you too. *(kisses him)*

Scene 102

The next day during his session with his therapist, Branko is dealing with his emotions of regret, sadness and frustration.

Mr Radulović: You see, Branko, personally, I am worried that we might be looking at something much more serious.

Branko: What do you mean by that?

Mr Radulović: Well, I would like to look into the possibilities of a classification. Many gay men end up with clinical depression, Borderline or some light form of PTSD usually caused by their environment. The way you're re-telling me your story in Albania seems like you are having some difficulties in handling your stress.

Branko: Some difficulties? I don't think it's anything out of the ordinary. Every family has their fallouts, and everyone feels sad from time to time. Every gay guy has a coming out. That doesn't mean that I'm clinically depressed.

Mr Radulović: How do you feel about your family? Describe it in as much detail as you can.

Branko: How I feel about my family?

Mr Radulović: Yes, how do you feel about the people who know you the best. Your parents who raised you and your siblings whom you grew up with. How do you feel about them, being on the other side from you?

Branko: Well, I feel, betrayed. I feel like the people who know me best have turned against me, at least to some extent. At the same time, I know that they know me better than anyone else, and I want to believe that they know whats best for me. However, so far that has only caused pain and a lack of understanding. They don't understand me and the way I feel, just as I can't understand why they turned against me that much. It's just way too confusing. I don't think that I can deal with all of this pressure anymore. My instincts are telling me to trust them, but my mind is telling me to do my own thing.

Mr Radulović: So you feel like you're in a conflict with your instincts and your own mind?

Branko: I feel like I'm in a conflict with everything. It's not like my entire family is against me. There are people who support me. My sister is always by my side, even against our parents. And I just feel this immense quilt that I unleashed chaos in the family.

Mr Radulović: Support is always a concept we need to be careful with, Branko. Think about who supports you and how much you mean to those people and ask yourself if that's real support.

Branko: It is real support.

Mr Radulović: Is it? Even from your uncle's wife whom you've known for a few days? Is that support?

Branko: You sound just like my father.

Mr Radulović: Well, maybe your father and I simply have a common viewpoint there.

Branko: I don't even want to think about that.

Mr Radulović: Branko, I'm not saying that no one supports you, but try to set your priorities. Look at who supports you in a way that's good for you.

Branko: I'm trying to do that since the day I was outed.

Mr Radulović: And that's why you're here. So we can work on that.

Branko: But, I do not want to work on that with you. I feel like you're an instrument my parents use to control my thinking and me.

Mr Radulović: You know that you are not obliged to be here. You can leave at any time. Your parents might not like it though.

Branko: I feel like that's not important anymore. I want out.

Mr Radulović: Very well, this would conclude our last session then.

Branko: *(standing up)* Very well.

Mr Radulović: I will send my bill to your parents in the next 5 to 7 days. Until then you have time to tell them yourself that you cancelled the sessions.

Branko: Fair enough. Thank you for your time.

Mr Radulović: *(standing up)* You are most welcome. *(shaking his hand)* Have a nice life.

Branko: You too Mr Radulović. You too.

Scene 103

After therapy, Branko met up with Dejana in a café in central Belgrade.

Dejana: *(impressed)* And you just walked out of there?

Branko: I wasn't really in the mood to take any more of that bullshit.

Dejana: And how do you think your parents will react?

Branko: *(indifferent)* I don't know, all I know is that I will have to push through. I don't think I'm really left with another option.

Dejana: I am so proud of you for not giving up on who you are, and should you need any help, you know I'm there for you.

Branko: Thanks, Dejana. You're what my therapist would call, "true support".

Dejana: Okay, enough with the "true support" bullshit. How do you see your life continuing?

Branko: I see a bright future.

Dejana: Do you?

Branko: Definitely. I've decided to take the scholarship and get out of Belgrade for a year.

Dejana: Well, that's fantastic! I'm happy for you!

Branko: Yeah, I feel a bit sad about leaving Belgrade, but Dušan told me that if I go to Zagreb, it's not all too far away.

Dejana: Zagreb is beautiful. It's really European and much cleaner and more organised than Belgrade. I feel like you'll like it there.

Branko: What about the other cities at hand?

Dejana: You mean Sofia or Ljubljana?

Branko: Yes.

Dejana: Well, Ljubljana is definitely more beautiful than Zagreb if you ask me, but it's much smaller. I don't think you'll like it there.

Branko: Small cities can have their charm.

Dejana: That's true, I just wouldn't say that you're a small town person.

Branko: But Ljubljana is a capital.

Dejana: With 250.000 inhabitants. It's not a large crowd.

Branko: Hm. I guess you're right.

Dejana: Sofia, on the other hand, is much bigger. It's a large city. Very similar to Belgrade. I think you'd like it there. If I were you I would either choose Zagreb or Sofia.

Branko: I guess I'm shifting more towards Zagreb.

Dejana: Because you don't want to be too far away from Belgrade?

Branko: Exactly.

Dejana: Does it have to anything with Dušan?

Branko: Not quite. I was actually about to talk to you about that.

Dejana: About Dušan?

Branko: Yeah.

Dejana: What's wrong?

Branko: Nothing is wrong, he is a great guy and all, but I, I just can't handle so many things at once, and I was thinking…

Dejana: of breaking up?

Branko: Is that a terrible thing of me to do?

Dejana: No, it's not. If you don't want a long distance relationship but can't stay in Belgrade for obvious reasons. I would go for the scholarship.

Branko: I might even go for Sofia then. If you recommend it.

Dejana: You shouldn't make a choice based on a recommendation. You should make a choice on how you feel.

Branko: But I don't know what I feel.

Dejana: When you get home, make yourself a tea, switch off all of your electronic devices and use the time to think about it. You'll find the solution in you.

Branko: That sounds like a good idea.

Dejana: Trust me, it helps. Now, regarding Dušan. I don't think that you want him out of your life, but if you don't want him as your boyfriend because you're moving, just tell him that.

Branko: But he wants a long distance relationship.

Dejana: So? You don't want one, and that is your choice, and that's completely okay. Don't worry about it too much.

Branko: I'm thinking about breaking up with my first boyfriend. Don't tell me not to worry too much.

Dejana: This might sound harsh, but there will be so many more men in your life. Dušan is just the first stepping stone. Maybe he's the right one, maybe he's not. If he is, he'll still be here for you once you come back and if he's not, then the right one will come along.

Branko: Urgh. This is so frustrating.

Dejana: Yes, but you have no other choice than to make a choice.

Scene 104

After abandoning his therapist and talking to Dejana, Branko is eating with his family at the dinner table.

Branko: I have decided to take the scholarship.

Mrs Jovanović: Really, which city will you apply for?

Branko: Sofia or Zagreb. I'm not quite sure yet.

Mr Jovanović: Uh, don't go for the Bulgarians.

Branko: So you don't mind me going?

Mr Jovanović: I see this as an opportunity for you. Maybe it will help you see the right way. Education should help.

Bojana: Branko is already on the right way.

Mr Jovanović: I don't want to talk about that right now. But, what will become of your therapy?

Branko: Well, I told Mr Radulović that I'm no longer going to go to sessions. I don't intend on taking therapy anymore.

Mr Jovanović: *(getting angry)* Okay, are you out of your mind?

Branko: No. I just don't feel like I need therapy.

Mr Jovanović: You are out of your mind? Say, do you have a single brain cell left in your mind?

Branko: Dad, would you please stop?

Mr Jovanović: Stop what? Caring about you? I'm sorry that put such an emphasis towards raising my son.

Branko: Dad, you know I don't mean it like that, it's just…

Mr Jovanović: What? What is it now?

Branko: *(yellig)* You never listen to me! Every single thing I suggest or want seems to be irrelevant until someone else suggests it or convinces you of it. My words don't really matter in the situation.

Mr Jovanović: That is not true, you are telling a lie!

Branko: Am I? Because you didn't want to let me do anything with my art studies up until Dejana convinced you. And you support your girlfriend beating son in Malta without any hesitation at all! I'm not having this.

Mr Jovanović: Are you serious right now?

Branko: I'm dead serious.

Bojana: And he's right.

Mr Jovanović: You shut your mouth!

Branko: *(extremely mad)* You know what. I'm not dealing with this right now.

Branko stands up and grabs his keys from the counter.

Mr Jovanović: Where do you think you're going?

Branko: I'm going to see my boyfriend.

Mr Jovanović: Come back here this instant!

Branko: Forget it. I'm out.

Mr Jovanović: Branko?! BRANKO!

Branko slams the door.

Scene 105

After running out of his flat, Branko picks up the phone.

Dušan: Hey. What's up?

Branko: *(fast paced)* Can you meet me in front of Delta City in like 20 minutes?

Dušan: What's happening?

Branko: Can you, or can you not.

Dušan: I'll be there. Just tell me what's going on.

Branko: I'll explain later. *(hangs up)*

After hanging up Dušan stands perplexed in front of his phone.

Dušan's Mother: Was that your boyfriend?

Dušan: Yes. I'm going to meet him in 20 minutes. And something tells me he might need a place to stay tonight.

Dušan's Mother: Oh please, you know he's welcome here anytime.

Dušan: Thanks, mom. *(hugs her)*

20 minutes later. Delta City.

Branko: *(running towards Dušan)* Thank God, you're here.

Dušan: What happened?

Branko: I had yet another fight with my parents and I just couldn't handle it. And... And... I don't know. *(starts crying)*

Dušan: *(takes him into his arms)* Calm down, everything's okay.

Branko: Can we take a walk?

Dušan: Of course we can take a walk.

The two start walking towards the river, as Branko explained the situation to him in detail.

Dušan: To be honest. I don't really know how to solve your problem. I think you might just need distraction up until something changes. Your father obviously doesn't want to move away from his viewpoint.

Branko: And your suggestion is to just do nothing?

Dušan: Do you seem to have any other options?

Branko: Not really.

Dušan: Tell you what. We're going to calm you down. You can stay with me for the time being until your dad cools off. I'll text Dejana and we'll go out drinking tonight. I think you need a good group of friends around you.

Branko: Thanks, my love. I really do value having you around.

Dušan: Don't worry, I'm going to take care of you. *(kisses him)*

Branko: I love you.

Dušan: I love you too.

Scene 106

That evening, Dejana, Dušan, and Branko are sitting in the ok.no pub in central Belgrade.

Dejana: So what is it going to be? Zagreb or Sofia?

Branko: I feel like I'm more leaning towards Zagreb.

Dejana: *(to Dušan)* That's your influence right there. *(laughs)*

Dušan: Is it such a sin to want your partner close to you?

Dejana: No, it's not, it means that I'm going to keep my friend close to me too. *(smiles)*

Branko: Guys, would you stop making such a big deal of this? It's only a year.

Dejana: Yeah, I know. We're still going to miss you.

Dušan: But we are happy for you. You're going to live a better life.

Branko: I hope so.

Dejana: What's your plan for the coming period? How are you going to bridge the time between Belgrade and Zagreb?

Branko: Well, I'll go sign up tomorrow and then I'll make my way home. I hope my parents are not too pissed about me being gone.

Dejana: They'll come around.

Dušan: They probably know you stayed with me. You might have an issue there.

Dejana: Tell them you stayed with me. That way you have an alibi.

Branko: That's a good idea. Thanks!

Dušan: Did you put any thought on how you're going to find a place to stay in Zagreb?

Dejana: You could call Luka.

Dušan: Who's that?

Dejana: Ah, just some guy. He was representing Croatia at the competition in Budapest. He lives in Zagreb.

Branko: I guess I could try to ask him.

Dušan: You never told me you know someone in Zagreb.

Branko: Well, I met him once.

Dušan: But you have his contact.

Branko: Isn't that kind of normal?

Dejana: *(interrupting Dušan before he can say something)* Let's see if he can help you find a place.

Branko: I'll text him in the coming days. Once I have my confirmation. Otherwise, I guess I can also apply for student accommodation.

Scene 107

The following day, Branko makes his way to the ministry. Upon arrival, he's greeted by Bojan and finishes the signup.

Bojan: Okay, so Zagreb it is. *(Hands him a form)* Sign here and then we're done here. We'll transfer you the initial money in the coming days.

Branko: *(signs the form)* Sounds good.

Bojan: Do you have any more questions?

Branko: Actually, yes. Do you have any tips on how I could find accommodation?

Bojan: Ah, yes. I wanted to talk to you about that. *(looks onto his computer screen)* Since we're sending two of you to Zagreb, the other girl asked me to tell her who the second spot is, for a potential flatshare.

Branko: Well, I would be interested in that.

Bojan: That's great, and here. Milica Jahović. She was with us in Budapest, you should know her. Could I give her your number?

Branko: Oh, she already has my number. And I also have hers, I can call her.

Bojan: That's even better. Then my work here is done. *(stands up to shake his hand)* Branko, it was so nice to see you again, and I wish you all the best in Zagreb.

Branko: *(shaking hands)* Thank you. It was nice to see you as well and I thank you for the opportunity.

Bojan: It is our pleasure, we look forward to working with you in the coming months.

Branko leaves the ministry and gives Milica a call.

Milica: Hello?

Branko: Hey there.

Milica: Hey! *(excited)* My God, Branko. I haven't heard from you in ages, what's up?

Branko: *(dramatic)* Urgh, so much stuff has been going on, I'll tell you all about it when I have time. But I wanted to ask you something.

Milica: Yes?

Branko: Since you're the other one going to Zagreb.

Milica: OMG, you're coming to Zagreb with me?

Branko: Yes.

Milica: *(screams)* YAS! Oh my God, this is great. Did Bojan tell you about the flatshare?

Branko: He did. What's up with that?

Milica: Well, my mothers best friend lives in Zagreb and she has a friend who is a real estate agent and she found us a small little flat with two rooms close to the downtown area for around 2000 Kuna per month.

Branko: And that's how much?

Milica: Well it's less than 300€ a month for the both of us.

Branko: Oh wow, that's extremely affordable.

Milica: Yeah, I would be renting it from the 1st of September. Would you be in for it?

Branko: Definitely.

Milica: Do you already have an appointment at the embassy for your visa?

Branko: Not yet.

Milica: Let's do that together then. I'll need to come to Belgrade to get my documents, so we can agree on a day to do that together?

Branko: Sounds like a plan.

Milica: Great, I'll text you later then. I have to go now.

Branko: Same here, bye.

Milica: Bye!

Milica hangs up and Branko joyfully walks towards his bus.

Scene 108

After the ministry, Branko returns home. He looks around as no one is to be found. After a while, Bojana steps out of the room.

Bojana: *(in a very scared tone)* What are you doing here?

Branko: I came back.

Bojana: You came back?

Branko: The situation got heated, so I spent the night with Dušan.

Bojana: Dad didn't call you?

Branko: No, he didn't call or text me.

Branko goes over to his room, yet Bojana interrupts him before he can open the door.

Bojana: *(scared)* Don't go in there.

Branko: What? Why?

Bojana: If dad hasn't called you it means you don't know.

Branko: Know what?

Bojana: *(shaking)* What happened here after you left yesterday.

There is silence for a moment. Branko is shocked.

Bojana: Dad got angry. Very angry. He yelled, he screamed, he was mad. He proclaimed you were no longer his son and... and my God, did he snap. I never saw him like that.

Branko: And what's all that about the call?

Bojana: He said he'd call you to tell you that you are no longer welcome here and that you can take your scholarship and go.

Another moment of silence fills the room.

Branko: What happened to my room?

Bojana: I don't know. Neither mom nor I had the guts to enter the room after dad went in.

Branko: Do you think he destroyed something?

Bojana: I didn't hear any smashing or anything similar, to be honest.

Branko: So, should I look?

Bojana: I'm afraid you don't want to see what's in there.

Branko: Well, I guess I don't really have another option.

Branko stands up and walks over to his room. He opens the door only to find his room in the condition he left it, with the exception that there are two suitcases which are located in the middle of the room. Branko walks over to the suitcases to find a note attached to it. "PACK YOUR THINGS"

Branko: *(shaking)* This isn't happening. This isn't happening. THIS ISN'T HAPPENING.

He takes his phone and takes a picture of the scene.

Scene 109

After packing everything that was important to him, he picks up the phone.

Dušan: What's up?

Branko: *(shaking)* I will need to stay with your for the next few days.

Dušan: What happened?

Branko: My dad... *(stutters)* kicked me out of the house.

Dušan: Fuck. *(in a fast-paced tone)* Get out of there and come here!

Branko: I'll be on my way.

After finishing the call he looks up to Bojana who's looking at him.

Branko: *(trying to calm her down)* I'm pretty sure this is not permanent.

Bojana: *(starting to cry)* I know, but I don't want to lose you like this.

Branko: You are not losing me.

Bojana: *(crying)* I don't want you to go. Why does this have to keep on happening to our family?

Branko: *(hugging her)* Boki, it's fine.

Bojana: I don't want to lose you. *(hugs him tightly)*

Branko: You are not losing me. I'm going to have a better life. A life outside of this mess. And that's all you need to think about right now. It's the best option for me.

Bojana: *(drying her tears)* I love you. I don't want you to go. *(hugs him again)* But, at the same time. I don't want you to get hurt. You have to go. And that's all the more painful.

Branko: I can stay a little longer if you want to.

Bojana: *(crying)* No, leave. Leave, before dad gets here.

Branko: Are you going to be okay?

Bojana: *(calming down, heavily breathing)* I'll try my best.

Branko: Then this is goodbye for now then. *(hugs her)*

Bojana: Text me while you're still in the city. We can still see each other.

Branko: I will, I promise.

Branko leaves the house. As he shuts the door he hears Bojana crying in the background.

He leaves the house and starts heading towards the bus stop as he runs into Ivan.

Ivan: Ey, what's going on?
Branko: Don't even ask.
Ivan: Leaving the neighbourhood?
Branko: It's all your fault, you moron.
Ivan: Oh wow, easy there.
Branko: You shut your big fat fucking mouth. It's the goddamn reason why I'm in this situation and I will sure as hell not take any more bullshit from you. Do me a favour and tell Petar, my so-called "friend", to get fucked in his goddamn fucking ass for the prick he is.
Ivan: Wow, easy there.
Branko: I have nothing to say to you, bitch.

Branko turns around and continues running to the bus stop.

Scene 110

After arriving at Dušan's place Branko is in total distress. After making him some tea, Dušan sits his boyfriend down.

Dušan: I've talked to my mother. You can stay as long as you want to, it won't be a problem. We'll take care of you.
Branko: I love you and your family. You have been so kind to me.
Dušan: You only deserve the best.
Branko: It's just such a confus-

Branko is interrupted by the bell.

Dušan: *(stands up)* I'll get that. That must be Dejana.
Branko: You called her?
Dušan: I have to show you that you have support.

Dušan opens the door as Dejana storms in.

Dejana: I came as soon as I could. *(walks over to Branko)* What happened? *(hugs him)* Are you okay?
Branko: *(still shaking)* I'm fine. I'll be okay.
Dejana: Look at you! You're not fine. Oh God, you're so cracked.

Branko: Don't say that.

Dejana: It's the truth. Face it, you're going to a tough time right now.

Branko: Aren't you supposed to help me?

Dejana: I'm here to listen to you.

Branko: *(sighs)* Oh well. I guess it's pretty clear what happened. I'm no longer wanted in my family.

Dušan: That is not true! I'm sure your father just overreacted. He'll come around.

Branko: No, he won't. That's the whole point of this discussion. This permanent state that my dad doesn't want to accept.

Dejana: Since when is being gay considered being a state? My God, I don't want to live in this country anymore.

Branko: Well…

Dušan: Personally, I think this is all just the beginning of a huge process.

Branko: I just don't know what to do.

Dejana: Well, you took the offer from Zagreb. You'll have to survive the remaining time here and then pack your things and go.

Branko: That's much easier said than done!

Dejana: I know, but you have no other option. I'm sorry to say it like this.

Branko: Well then, it'll come one way or another.

Scene 111

During the night Branko and Dušan are lying in bed talking about various things.

Dušan: Say, where do you see us going after your move to Zagreb?

Branko: *(snuggling up to him)* Well, we still have way over a month to see where this is going.

Dušan: Yeah, but have you thought about how the relationship would look like after you move to Zagreb?

Branko: Well, I'm going to be in Serbia quite a lot if I cooperate with the ministry, so I guess I'll try to visit you as much as I can and I think that you'll do the same.

Dušan: That's true. I always think about the countless calls we're going to have and constant texting. I feel like that will be very difficult to manage.

Branko: Yeah, but it's the only way we can keep this relationship alive.

Dušan: Yeah, and that's the point. I- *(interrupted by a knock on the door)* Yes?

Dušan's mother opens the door.

Dušan's Mother: Branko, sweetie, your father just rang at the door.

Branko: *(shocked)* What? *(starts shaking)* How did he find this place?

Dušan's Mother: I'm not sure. I didn't let him in yet.

Branko: Please don't let him in. *(gets up)* I'm going to get dressed and go outside and see what he wants.

Dušan: Are you sure you want to do that?

Branko: Yes. If he's here, he must have a reason for that.

Dušan: Do you want me to come with you?

Branko: *(scared)* No, that would be a terrible idea.

Dušan: Mom, could you please go with Branko. I don't want his dad to take him away.

Dušan's Mother: If that's okay with Branko.

Branko: I think it might be a good idea.

Dušan's Mother: Then I'll accompany you. Let's see what your dad wants.

Dušan: It's probably something terrible.

Dušan's Mother: Now, let's stay positive here for a moment. Maybe he wants to apologise to Branko and set things straight.

Dušan: Oh, he wants to set something straight.

Branko: I really hope that he's here to apologise.

Dušan's Mother: Well, there's only one way to find out. We need to get out there.

Branko: I'll go put on my shoes. *(walks over to the hallway)*

Scene 112

After walking down to the entrance of the building, Dušan's mother and Branko meet his father.

Mr Jovanović: There you are. You're coming home with me right now!

Branko: *(angry)* Why? You were the one who kicked me out.

Mr Jovanović: I gave you a warning.

Branko: *(yelling)* "Pack your things" is not a warning!

Mr Jovanović: DON'T YELL AT ME! You ran away and I'm taking you home with me right now!

Branko: I did not run away, you kicked me out! And I am not coming home with you.

Mr Jovanović: You are my son, you have to.

Dušan's Mother: I'm really sorry to meddle with this, but your son is 18, he can choose to stay here if he wants to.

Branko: And I want to stay here.

Mr Jovanović: And who are you to interfere. Are you his boyfriend's mother?

Dušan's Mother: Yes I am.

Mr Jovanović: You are a terrible parent, miss.

Dušan's Mother: *(getting angry)* I at least care about your son's well-being. Something you failed at massively. If I were you, I would be careful about whom I'd call a terrible parent.

Mr Jovanović: Would you like me to interfere in your children's lives?

Dušan's Mother: Of course not.

Mr Jovanović: Then stop interfering in my son's life!

Dušan's Mother: You abandoned your son! I took him when you didn't want to and you should be ashamed of that.

Mr Jovanović: Listen, madam, I really don't want to make a scene here, but

Dušan's Mother: *(interrupting him)* Then don't! Leave.

Mr Jovanović: Not without my son.

Branko: I'm not going with you! Stop disturbing me.

Mr Jovanović: I can stand here all night if I want to.

Dušan's Mother: I will call the police if you do.

Mr Jovanović: It is my right to take my son with me!

Dušan's Mother: *(screams)* NO, IT IS NOT! LEAVE THESE PREMISES RIGHT NOW!

Mr Jovanović: No.

Dušan's mother takes out her phone to call the police.

Dušan's Mother: *(on the phone)* Hello, is this the police? I have a man stalking my houseguest who appeared in front of my house and refuses to leave, could I have a unit sent to

Mr Jovanović: You see what you have done, you piece of garbage?
Branko: Oh, trust me, this is all you. It's all your mess. Don't blame me for it.

Dušan's Mother: *(on the phone)* Okay, thank you. Have a good night. *(hangs up the phone)* A unit will be here soon. Branko, go up to the flat. *(hands him the keys)* I'll settle this with your dad. Let me in when I ring.
Branko: Okay. *(he goes over to the entrance)*
Mr Jovanović: *(screaming)* Come back here! BRANKO! YOU DON'T HAVE ANY RIGHTS. DO YOU HEAR ME? YOU HAVE NO RIGHT TO DO THIS! BRANKO!

Scene 113

Branko re-enters the flat.

Dušan: *(kisses him)* Oh my God, are you okay, I heard screaming!
Branko: *(shaking)* Your mom just called the police and they'll bring my dad away.
Dušan: Oh shit. I'm sorry it has to be like this.
Branko: Don't be. In some bitter far away place in my heart, I really do believe that he deserves this.
Dušan: Oh, please, don't start talking like that.
Branko: I find it to be appropriate given the situation.

Dušan's Mother re-enters the flat.

Dušan's Mother: I'm sorry we got to this kind of extreme situation. Your father left before the cops came. I really hope he learned his lesson.
Branko: I'm so sorry you have to go through all of this stress because of me.

Dušan's Mother: Don't be. *(hugs him)* I find it heartbreaking that something like this can happen to a child. I cannot understand these people who abandon their kids like, just for their own pride. I might be a liberal and your father might be conservative, but we both agree on one thing. We should base our lives on love. Your father just has a broken understanding of that.

Branko: *(touched)* Thank you so much for your kind words.

Dušan: Do you have any idea of what we should do?

Dušan's Mother: That's extremely difficult to say. I would say, try to find out how your father found you?

Branko: I think I know the right person to call.

Branko makes a call, Bojana picks up.

Bojana: Branko? Is that really you?

Branko: Yes it is. Did Dad come home yet?

Bojana: Uhm, he came home hours ago from work.

Branko: Oh. Well, he was here a few minutes ago, trying to take me back. I still need to figure out how he found me.

Bojana: *(anxious)* He found you? Shit.

Branko: Yes, and I'm not quite sure what I should do about it.

Bojana: Do you have the Find my iPhone app on your phone?

Branko: I think so.

Bojana: Delete it! I think he spied on me through that as well.

Branko: What? Is he really tracking me?

Bojana: Yes, I'm pretty sure. Otherwise, he couldn't- *(pauses)* Shit, I heard the door. I'll text you the rest.

Bojana hangs up and Branko lowers his phone.

Dušan: And?

Branko: I think we need to have a group discussion about this.

Branko deletes the Find my iPhone app from his phone.

Scene 114

Three days later. Bojana, Dejana, Dušan and Branko are in a hidden LGBT café in downtown Belgrade.

Dejana: You should move to my place, you know that you can have the guest room. Bojana and Dušan can visit you, but your dad can't.

Bojana: *(very worried)* I feel like that's a good idea, concerning the fact that dad knows where Dušan lives.

Dejana: Branko, what do you think?

Branko: I'm really uneasy about the whole thing.

Bojana: Why?

Branko: Listen, I would feel comfortable staying with Dejana, but I don't want to spend time apart from Dušan since we're about to be separated for a year.

Dejana: Then just move in with Dušan.

Dušan: *(shy)* Deki, I can't accept this. You're doing too much.

Dejana: Don't think about it, it's the only plausible solution for now. You shared your first night in that bed, you can share a few more. It'll only be for a month and a half anyway. Plus, you'll have your own bathroom.

Bojana: Oh, she has a good point.

Dušan: I guess that it couldn't hurt for the time being.

Dejana: There we go. Trust me. You'll be in a better place.

Bojana: I really support Dejana's opinion on this one. Dad is currently extremely unpredictable, and it might be smarter to move you to another location for the time being.

Branko: Alright, we'll move in with you.

Dejana: Yay! My dad's not at home anyways. He's with my brother on an adventure trip in Thailand, so it'll all be laid back.

Dušan: Sounds good.

Dejana: You'll provide your own condoms, right?

Branko: *(gasp)* DEKI!

Dejana: Oh come on.

Bojana: *(laughs)* She's funny, I like that.

Scene 115

A few days later Dejana, Dušan and Branko are having breakfast in her beautiful kitchen.

Dejana: Can I tell you guys a story?

Branko: Uhm, sure.

Dejana: When I was in Madrid, on a holiday with my girls, I met this girl at a bar. Julie was her name. She was from Poland. We drank a few too many drinks that night, and I lost my friends in the crowds. After not being able to find them, she offered me to come back to her place and text them tomorrow. And then it hit me. Julie was hitting on me. And you know what I did?

Dušan: You felt flattered and rejected her offer?

Branko: You went with her and passed out on her bed?

Dejana: I started making out with her. My friends found me and gave me their blessing, I went to the hotel room with her and had what I would call one of the best sexual encounters of my life, with what I would call, the best orgasm someone else ever gave me.

Branko: *(confused)* When we talked in the club you said that you never tried anything with a girl?

Dejana: Yeah, I lied. I didn't feel comfortable telling you yet.

Branko: Are you trying to tell us that you're bisexual?

Dušan: Or a lesbian?

Dejana: Actually, none of the above. Because the next morning, as I woke up, I realised that Julie was nothing for me. The sex was better, but I couldn't see myself loving her, or showing any kind of romantic emotions towards her. And that told me a lot about homosexuality.

Dušan: In what way?

Dejana: Well, I imagine sex being extremely painful for the two of you and that it would be maybe easier, even better to have sex with a woman. But your love for each other is so strong that even in contrast to nature, you still hold on strong to each other.

Dušan: What the fuck did you suggest?

Branko: Yeah, our sex is amazing!

Dušan: That's not what I meant. I was rather pointing to the fact that your theory doesn't add up at all.

Dejana: In what way?

Dušan: We don't see our sex as a by-product of our sexual identity, we see it as a part of it.

Dejana: Hm. Interesting. Maybe I am bisexual.

Branko: Do you still crave the touch of a woman?

Dejana: In a sexual way? Definitely. I'm just not emotionally attached to them.

Dušan: Your case might be special then.

Branko: I find it interesting. You tried it and decided that it was nothing for you. That's very noble.

Dušan: Doesn't every gay person go through that process?

Branko: Yes, they do, but straight people hardly ever do. That's why I find it noble.

Dejana: *(smiles)* Well, in that case, I take it as a compliment.

Branko's phone rings.

Branko: Oh, that must be Bojana. She's waiting.

Dejana: Where are you guys going again?

Branko: To church. I haven't been to mass in ages.

Dušan: Less religous manipulation for you.

Branko: Oh come on.

Dušan: *(bitter)* You know what I think of the church.

Branko: I know, and I'm not going to have this discussion with you again. I'll see you tonight.

Dušan: I'll see you tonight. Come on, give me a kiss.

They kiss, then Branko leaves to meet with his sister.

Scene 116

Branko and Bojana leave the church after lighting candles and decide to go for a walk.

Branko: This was extremely refreshing, I haven't been to church in so long.

Bojana: *(looking at the pavement)* It felt a little bit weird going without our parents.

Branko: In what way?

Bojana: I don't think I'm that religious as I believe myself to be.

Branko: I really? I find comfort in the fact that there is a God.

Bojana: If there really is a God, would your situation be just?

Branko: No, it wouldn't. But if there was no God, would there be any hope?

Bojana: If there is no God, you're responsible for your own happiness, which means that you need to build your life in Zagreb according to your own standards.

Branko: That's true. But can I do that in a completely lifeless state?

Bojana: That you can't. Well, you can, but you'd end up like a zombie.

Branko: Dušan doesn't really approve of me being religious.

Bojana: And you two have functioned properly?

Branko: Well, yeah, I guess so.

Bojana: I think I'd leave a man who'd criticise the things that make up my identity.

Branko: Even though you're questioning your orthodox identity?

Bojana: Yes. Because it's my orthodox identity. That's none of his business, I can question it all I want, he can't. And you should do the same with Dušan.

Branko: But I don't want to start a fight.

Bojana: And if you think like that, he might not be the right one for you.

Branko: What?

Bojana: Has that thought ever crossed your mind?

Branko: Not really. He was always there for me and he loves me. So he's the right one for me.

Bojana: Which is a good foundation, but can you build on it?

Branko: What do you mean?

Bojana: I mean: What are the things that connect you? Once this entire bullshit is over, where will you stand?

Branko: Well, we both have different ideas about our future. So I guess we'll be on two different roads.

Bojana: And that's where we have the poison in the relationship. Now you're good, but the minute you move to Zagreb it's going to be two different worlds.

Branko: What are you saying?

Bojana: I'm telling you to enjoy the time you have left with him, because once you move, your life might go uphill, but for your relationship… It's all downhill from there.

Scene 117

During Branko's visit to the church, Dejana and Dušan are sitting in the living room watching Netflix.

Dejana: Say, what was that deal about religion?
Dušan: Let's just say that I'm not very fond of Branko's religious views.
Dejana: Are you kidding me? Have you fought about that yet?
Dušan: Not really, we agreed to disagree.
Dejana: You know that's quite wrong?
Dušan: I just don't see why he would believe in such fairytales. The Orthodox Church is turning against us gays, and he knows that.
Dejana: To Branko faith is not what the institution says it is. It's his spiritual belief and the light that keeps him burning.
Dušan: Deki, do you believe in God?
Dejana: Well, I keep religious traditions alive and I like to go to church, but I wouldn't consider myself a believer.
Dušan: And why do you defend Branko in his fanatic sides?
Dejana: He grew up like that. It's part of his identity just as much as his homosexuality is. You can't just deny and ignore it.
Dušan: Well, I hope that he will come to his senses.
Dejana: You know, I'm discovering different sides of you.
Dušan: What do you mean?
Dejana: Your mainstream gay side. Your "I'm a special snowflake and I feel attacked by everything" side.
Dušan: Branko is being attacked.
Dejana: By his family not by his beliefs. If anything, they keep him alive during this madness.
Dušan: You're not going to turn against me now, are you?
Dejana: I'm not.

There's silence for a moment.

Dejana: All I will do is speak my mind.

Scene 118

After being at church, Branko returns to Dejana.

Branko: Hello.

Dejana: Hey, how was your day?

Branko: It was nice. Boki and I went to church and then we sat at Coffee Dream for hours. Yours?

Dejana: Nothing and special, Dušan and I were watching Netflix.

Branko: And, where is he now?

Dejana: He went to his parents' place to get some stuff.

Branko: Oh, I see.

Dejana: You know, I talked about your religion with Dušan today...

Branko: Funny you mentioned that. Bojana and I had the same conversation.

Dejana: Yeah?

Branko: Yes, she suggested a breakup.

Dejana: What? Oh God, no. That won't fix anything.

Branko: Is there anything to fix?

Dejana: Sure there is.

Branko: Get him to appreciate my religion?

Dejana: Get him to appreciate you more!

Branko: And how do I do that?

Dejana: That's easy. If you love someone, set them free. If they love you back, they will come back.

Branko: And how do I "set him free"?

Dejana: Suggest an open relationship.

Branko: Are you out of your mind?

Dejana: Think about it. Your relationship will be sex deprived after a while. Let him have fun with other people and see how he appreciates you during that. If you notice him taking less care of your relationship then it's simply not meant to be.

Branko: And you think that'll work?

Dejana: Definitely. Plus, through your hookups, you'll meet like-minded people in Zagreb way faster. The situation there isn't any better than in Belgrade. Maybe it's a little bit more laid back than here.

Branko: This doesn't make any sense to me.

Dejana: Give it a few days, think about it. Maybe it could be a good solution for you.

Branko: Urgh. I don't know. I'll think about it.

After texting Bojana about it.

YES! Definitely do that

What if it's not good for me?

The current situation isn't good for you either

just think about it for a few days

and talk to him afterwards

Okay…

He looks up from his phone.

Dejana: And, what did she say?

Branko: She approves of the idea.

Dejana: Then I'd say, that it's definitely worth a shot.

Scene 119

A few days later, on August 9th, Branko wakes up on his 19th birthday to find the bed empty.

Branko: *(to himself)* Dušan? Where are you?

He stands up and walks into the living room and finds Dušan, Dejana, Bojana, Milica, Jelena, Sara and surprisingly, Vesna, are waiting for him there.

Everyone: Surprise!

Dušan: *(approaching him)* Happy Birthday my love. *(kisses him)*

Branko: Oh wow. This is. This is. Thank you, guys.

After he goes through all the people he reaches Vesna.

Vesna: *(hugs him)* Happy Birthday!

Branko: Why did you come?

Vesna: I heard what happened. And I wanted to let you know that I accept you for who you are. Yes, I was mad at you, but you being gay had nothing to do with that. The truth is, I still love you, as a friend this time.

Branko: Thank you. *(he hugs her tightly)* You don't know how much that means to me.

Vesna: Trust me, I do. Remember my aunt.

Branko: The one with a German girlfriend?

Vesna: Exactly. I consider you normal, and extremely lucky.

Branko: Extremely lucky?

Vesna: Dušan is an angel. He's the best possible catch you could've gotten.

Branko: Thank you.

Vesna: How have you been in spite of your situation?

Branko: I've been alright. I found a support network, and I'm moving to Zagreb by the end of the month.

Vesna: Ah, yes. With this girl *(she points to Milica)* I forgot her name. She's from Novi Sad, that I remember. She told me you were moving in together.

Branko: Yeah.

Vesna: And, are you excited?

Branko: I guess I'm having mixed feelings about it.

Vesna: Oh, come on. Don't be so sceptic about it. I'm sure it'll all be just fine.

Branko: Thank you. I really hope so. *(pauses)* How are the others?

Vesna: Katarina found herself a new boyfriend from another school. I haven't seen Ivan in ages. Apparently, he's going to start studying law here in Belgrade. And Petar is going to study economics. I broke up with him a few days after prom night. Dating him was a huge mistake.

Branko: Don't say that.

Vesna: Huh? I thought you hated him?

Branko: Yes, I kind of do. But I was also his friend since our early childhood. He's a good guy. He simply reacts completely mad to things he doesn't understand. It's been like this ever since he was a little boy. He would get mad at maths for being too hard. Looking back at it, it was kind of silly, but that just stayed part of his character.

Vesna: Do you think that played a role in him not accepting you as a gay?

Branko: Oh most certainly. I see the root of it there.

Vesna: Well. If you say so.

Branko: I do. *(he pauses)* I still think it's good that you two are no longer together. You were a terrible couple.

Vesna: Oh come on.

Branko: Facts are facts, sweetie.

Scene 120

As the party progresses, Milica and Branko talk about their move.

Milica: So the flat is not furnished. But we got a high scholarship payment, so I suggest we take buses to Zagreb on the 29th, go to IKEA on the 30th and move in on the 31st or 1st.

Branko: Where would we stay in the meantime.

Milica: Oh there's an air mattress in the flat. The old tenant will leave by August 15th.

Branko: Oh, well, that's great. Does that mean we could move in even earlier?

Milica: We could. Why? Do you want to?

Branko: I'm not quite sure yet.

Milica: Let's just do it at the end of the month. We'll have the entirety of September to explore the city.

Branko: Okay, you're right.

Milica: Do you feel okay

Branko: I feel good. I just want to get this move over with.

Milica: Trust me, me too. But we should use the time we have left here.

Bojana approaches the two.

Bojana: *(to Milica)* You'll take care of my brother?

Milica: Easy there, we'll share the chores.

Bojana: Eh, I don't care. Branko may clean the entire place on its own.

Milica: Don't worry, your brother is in good hands *(hugs him)*

Branko: I'll send you lots and lots of pictures.

Milica: Oh come on. Don't let her see Zagreb just through her phone. Bojana, is it?

Bojana: Yes.

Milica: You can come visit us anytime.

Bojana: Trust me, I was already planning on doing that. I don't care about what my parents have to say to that.

Milica: I'll be looking forward to it.

Branko: Me too. I can't wait for us to spend some quality time away from all the pressure.

Bojana: Trust me, even the pressure will become less with time. I'm quite sure of that.

Branko: Well, we're only left to hope.

Scene 121

A few days later, during the afternoon, Branko and Dušan are enjoying a snack in Dejana's living room on their own.

Branko: You've been awfully quiet today.

Dušan: I don't like the state I'm in right now.

Branko: What do you mean by that?

Dušan: This eternal waiting state. I feel like we're just waiting for you to move and for our relationship to die out.

Branko: Trust me, I'm scared as well.

Dušan: I'm scared for us, Branko. And I don't know what to do. I feel like we're steering towards a breakup and I don't want it to be over!

Branko: I think I might have an idea.

Dušan: You do?

Branko: Yes.

Dušan: Will you talk to me about it?

Branko: I don't know how to say this.

Dušan: Simply say it?

Branko: Well, I was thinking that we could try an open relationship.

Dušan: *(confused)* A what?

Branko: An open relationship.

Dušan: I heard you the first time. I just can't believe you'd suggest something like that. Why do you want to sleep with other men?

Branko: It's not about sleeping with other men.

Dušan: Oh please, that is the definition of an open relationship.

Branko: It's about the distance! Think about it for a second.

Dušan: Huh?

Branko: If we stay monogamous, we'll both spend our days counting down when we'll see each other again. This will become tiring and it could mean the end of the relationship. If we decide to open it, just for the year while I'm abroad, we can both go our separate ways physically, but still be together emotionally.

Dušan: This is a bit too much to swallow right now.

Branko: Take your time to think about it.

Dušan: I will.

Dejana walks into the house with grocery bags.

Dejana: Hey guys, could you please help me unpack? I'll make dinner and then we can watch Netflix.

Branko: Sounds like a plan.

Scene 122

The next day, while Dušan is away, Bojana visits Branko at Dejana's. He tells the two about his suggestion.

Dejana: So you actually suggested it?

Branko: Yes, right before you came home.

Dejana: Aaaaah, no wonder he was so awkward during Netflix time.

Bojana: How did he take it?

Branko: I'd say he took it well.

Bojana: Did he give you a reply?

Branko: He's extremely unsure.

Bojana: What about you?

Branko: What about me?

Bojana: Do you like the idea?

Branko: I came to like it. I feel like it's the only way to save our relationship.

Dejana: At first you were sceptic though?

Branko: I still am. But then again, it's a lockdown situation.

Bojana: I feel like you need to have the freedom to explore yourself in Zagreb. Dušan is just going to hold you back and pull you back to Belgrade. That's really not good for you in your current state.

Dejana: I agree with Bojana.

Branko: So if he says no, I should break up?

Dejana: I wouldn't think of it as a bad thing. You're just going your separate ways.

Bojana: Besides, there are plenty of fish in the sea.

Branko: I'll have to think about this. *(pauses)* Boki, how's the family?

Bojana: They're good. Mom and dad don't talk much about you. You can feel that mom is sad. Dad is pretty indifferent about the entire situation. It doesn't really make me happy to see him indifferent like this, but oh well, what can we do about it?

Branko: Nothing, really.

Bojana: I feel like it's going to be a wild ride with the two of them.

Branko: Oh well. Maybe things will change once I'm in Zagreb.

Bojana: I think they're slowly preparing for that because as long as you're here there's this thought that they might still come and see you. I know that mom really wants to see you. I think she knows that I started visiting you.

Branko: Well, if she's ready to see me, I wouldn't mind talking to her.

Bojana: I'm not quite sure if she's ready. But maybe she'll come around before you leave.

Branko: I really hope so. I would be happy to see her.

Bojana: I'll see what we can do.

Later, after Bojana left, Dejana consults Branko again.

Dejana: Are you sure you want to see her?

Branko: I think so, why?

Dejana: I mean, your family turned against you, and they're not showing any signs of improving.

Branko: Well, the process has to set in.

Dejana: Personally, I think you should focus on yourself and your move to Zagreb first. Belgrade is no longer where you belong.

Branko: But this is my home!

Dejana: And it will always stay your home, that won't change. Now, you're faced with a choice, your family or your life. And I think you should choose your life.

Branko: I am choosing my life, but I want to see my mother before I leave.

Dejana: I'm afraid she's going to try to talk you out of this.

Branko: Trust me, I know that deep down, she knows what's best for me.

Dejana: I sure hope so, I really do.

Scene 123

Three days before Branko is scheduled to leave for Zagreb, Dušan comes back to his suggestion, while the two are alone in bed.

Dušan: I thought about what you proposed.

Branko: Is this conversation going, where I think it's going?

Dušan: I want to talk about an open relationship.

Branko: Do you want to consider it?

Dušan: Actually, at first I didn't want to. After that, I realised that if we keep our relationship closed it is much more likely to break, and primarily, I don't want to lose you.

Branko: So you would be in favour of it?

Dušan: The thought kind of pains me. That someone else would be allowed to touch you, to kiss you, to sleep with you. I know, it's just sex and there's no emotional attachment, but I'm afraid that it will bug me after a while.

Branko: That is a rational fear, but if we set the rules correctly, we might save the relationship.

Dušan: Okay, so what would be the rules?

Branko: You can only sleep with a guy once?

Dušan: That'll make me a whore.

Branko: But having a fuckbuddy aside would put you at risk of falling for them.

Dušan: But maybe a fuckbuddy can be a stable hook?

Branko: I disagree.

Dušan: Okay, let's say we have to change guys. How often would we be allowed to have sex with others?

Branko: As much as we want? Why would we put a limit at that?

Dušan: Why? Because if you can have unlimited sex with others, what would be the benefit of having sex with me?

Branko: I love you, that would be the benefit.

Dušan: *(upset)* Oh, no, no, no! I'm not buying it.

Branko: Well, what do we want to do then?

Dušan: If you ask me, I think we should end it for good.

Branko: I'm sorry, are you serious?

Dušan: Yes, you're leaving in three days. Give yourself a fresh start.

Branko: *(starting to shake)* Dušan, please don't do this to me.

Dušan: It's for your own good.

He stands up and gets dressed.

Dušan: I'll get my things and let your process this.

Branko: Dušan! Don't do this to me.

Dušan: I'll stop by the bus station to say goodbye. But for now. *(he sits on the bed)* This is goodbye.

He kisses Branko one last time and gets his things. Branko lies there, mesmerised.

Dušan: This is for your own good. I love you.

He shuts the door, Branko breaks out in tears.

Scene 124

In the hall Dušan sees Dejana.

Dušan: Deki, I'm leaving.

Dejana: You're leaving? What's going on?

Dušan: That's a long story. I want to thank you with all my heart for letting me stay here and for helping Branko and me survive this. Unfortunately, our relationship didn't.

Dejana: Did you just break up with him?

Dušan: Please, understand that I had no other choice left.

Dejana: Out!

Dušan: What?

Dejana: Get out of here!

Dušan: Hey, I'm sorry.

Dejana: *(shouts)* GET OUT!

She kicks him out of the house and runs over to the guest room.

Dejana: Branko, oh my God, are you okay?

Branko: *(in tears)* I can't believe this.

Dejana: *(hugs him)* There, there, cry it all out.

Branko cries in Dejana's arms for about 10 minutes.

Branko: *(slowly gaining consciousness)* I can't believe that he broke up with me. I can't believe that I've lost him.

Dejana: That's okay, these things happen. He had a bad side anyway, and you don't need this kind of negativity in your life.

Branko: And what am I supposed to do now?

Dejana: You have to move on. I know this sounds extremely hard at the moment, but you have no other choice.

Branko: This all doesn't feel real. I thought he was the love of my life.

Dejana: Our first love never turns out good. You're young. There will be so many other guys in your life. Don't obsess over this one.

Branko: This new beginning scares me now. I have no one.

Dejana: That is not true! You will be moving in with Milica, I'm sure that she'll take great care of you.

Branko: And what about you?

Dejana: You can always call me, text me or send me a pigeon with a note. I will be there. You have your sister as well. You are not alone!

Branko: I feel lonely.

Dejana: It's going to take some time, but trust me, you'll be good in no time. Why don't you get some sleep now?

Branko: I don't want to sleep.

Dejana: What can I do for you?

Branko: I don't know.

Dejana: Uhm, okay. How about I go into the kitchen, get us some ice cream and two ciders and put on Netflix. Will that help?

Branko: I guess it's a start.

Dejana: Come to the living room. Let's start operation "Healing"!

She walks him to the living room, gets the ice cream and the ciders and puts on Netflix.

Scene 125

The day before his big move, Branko's mother and Bojana ring at Dejana's door.

Dejana: *(opening the door)* Hello.

Bojana: *(hugging her)* Hey!

Mrs Jovanović: Good day to you Dejana. How are you?

Dejana: I've been good, how are you?

Mrs Jovanović: Ah, it's been alright.

Dejana: He's waiting for you in the guest room, I'll show you the way.

Mrs Jovanović: Thank you! *(to Bojana)* Could you please stay with Dejana, I would like to talk to him alone.

Bojana: Of course.

Dejana brings Mrs Jovanović to the room where Branko is packing his things and leaves them alone.

Mrs Jovanović: Hello, my son. *(hugs him)*

Branko: Hey mom.

Mrs Jovanović: How have you been?

Branko: I've been alright. You?

Mrs Jovanović: I'm okay. Please, don't lie to me. I know you're having difficulties.

Branko: Why?

Mrs Jovanović: I overheard Bojana on the phone yesterday, it sounded like you were upset.

Branko: That's none of your business.

Mrs Jovanović: Listen Branko, your father might not have accepted you with open arms, but I want to. Nothing will change a mother's love for her son, and definitely not something like your sexual orientation.

Branko: Are you serious?

Mrs Jovanović: Yes. I want to understand you and I want you to be happy. I would also like to meet your boyfriend when you're back in town.

Branko: He's no longer my boyfriend.

Mrs Jovanović: Oh, so that's why you were upset.

Branko: I'm over it.

Mrs Jovanović: I'm not an expert in gay stuff, but I know something about breakups and when Marko, my high school boyfriend, broke up with me, it took me three months to get over him. Don't tell me you can lay him off that easily.

Branko: I'm not quite sure. He left me because I was leaving. And now I don't know if it was worth it.

Mrs Jovanović: Oh, my sweet sweet boy, trust me, I will make sure you take your chance and go to Zagreb. It's not good for you to stay with us. Your father will be very angry with you.

Branko: But can I visit you?

Mrs Jovanović: Soon you will have a home here in Belgrade, after a few months maybe.

Branko: Why then?

Mrs Jovanović: I wanted to tell you in person. Your father and I are getting a divorce. I couldn't handle his family drama anymore and the way he was treating you. Once it's finalised Bojana and I will be moving into a new flat. And I will be waiting with open arms for you once you come back from Zagreb. That is unless you find a way to stay there, then you can always keep on visiting us.

There is a moment of silence.

Mrs Jovanović: Are you okay?

Branko: I feel like everything is breaking apart.

Mrs Jovanović: You haven't been home in almost two months, things changed. And things are changing for the better, I promise you.

Branko: Are you sure?

Mrs Jovanović: I guarantee you. I love you Branko.

Branko: I love you too.

They hug it out and join the others in the living room.

Scene 126

The scene opens the following day, August 29th, 2016, at Belgrade's main bus station (BAS). Branko arrives with Dejana to the terminal.

Branko: Oh wow, so I guess, this is it.

Dejana: We knew it would come down to this. I'm happy for you.

Branko: I'm excited.

Dejana: Promise me we'll skype regularly.

Branko: Oh definitely.

Dejana: Oh look, there's Bojana!

Bojana approaches them, she goes in for a hug immediately.

Bojana: I will miss you more than anything.

Branko: Stay strong, we'll make it through this

Bojana: I don't need to stay strong. I know you're in better hands now.

Branko: Will you come visit me?

Bojana: I was thinking I could come during autumn.

Branko: We'll keep in touch. How's mom?

Bojana: She's very happy. She was happy to see you and is excited for what the future holds.

Branko: Well, I guess this is a moment to celebra- *(sees Dušan in the distance)* He actually came?

Dušan approaches the group.

Dušan: Hey guys.

Dejana: What do you want?

Dušan: I just wanted to say goodbye.

Bojana: You did that three days ago.

Branko: Guys, it's okay. He told me he would come.

Dušan: I just hope that we can see each other again as friends.

Branko: Listen Dušan, what happened between us was special, and I

S. RADAKOVIĆ   PAGE 203 OF 210   ZAŠTO?

will never forget the times we shared together. I love the memory of you, but I no longer feel like I'll be able to love you, and I just need my time to move on, and then yes, we can meet again, as friends.

Dušan: Please, take care of yourself.

Branko: I will.

The two hug each other one last time and Dušan leaves.

Bojana: Are you okay?

Branko: Yeah, I feel ready for this.

Dejana: Let's get you to your bus, shall we.

They assemble in front of the bus and Branko leaves his luggage in the hold and comes back to say his final goodbye.

Branko: Dejana, you became my friend in a very short period of time, and I can now say that you are my best friend. And I love you for all the things you've done for me, and I will cherish them forever. I promise you, this is not the end of our friendship.

Dejana: This will last a lifetime. Come here Branko. *(she hugs him tightly)* I love you too.

Branko: Boki, my sweet Boki. I love you more than anything in the world, and I will make sure that you stay happy and healthy, even from afar. I will stay your big brother and will protect you, just like you protected me. You've been by my side in the family from the very beginning, and I love you for that.

Bojana: I love you too big brother. Stay safe.

Branko: I will.

They hug one last time. Branko enters the bus and is off to Zagreb.

Scene 127

Five hours later, the bus reaches Zagreb's main bus station (autobusni kolodvor). Milica awaits Branko at the terminal.

Milica: *(hugging him as he leaves the bus)* Welcome to your new home.

Branko: Thank you. When did you get here?

Milica: A few hours ago with a bus from Novi Sad, come I'll take you to the flat.

Branko: Thanks.

Milica: How was your journey?

Branko: It's been alright. No major problems.

Milica: That's great to hear.

As they're in the tram driving to their flat in the centre of Zagreb (Kvaternikov Trg), Branko observes his surroundings.

Branko: Zagreb is so clean and nice. Why do we still think of Croats as primitive people from the Balkans?

Milica: Senseless nationalism, that's why. I don't understand it either. It's great here. A bit expensive at times, but we have a scholarship.

Branko: True, we will be living like kings.

Milica: Wait until you see the flat.

At Kvaternikov Trg, Milica shows Branko a beautiful flat with a gorgeous interior and a beautiful terrace, two rooms, one for each and a big kitchen with a living room.

Milica: Welcome home, Branko.

Branko: This is where we'll live?

Milica: Uh huh.

Branko: For the price you mentioned?

Milica: Yup.

Branko: I'm in heaven.

Milica: Let's plan heaven then.

Branko: What do you mean?

Milica: *(takes out IKEA catalogue)* I mean every little detail of this house.

Branko: *(excited)* OMG, yaaaas!

Scene 128

A few days later after they have finished building the furniture in the house, they made their first meal together as roommates in Zagreb. They sit at the dinner table and enjoy the meal.

Milica: You know, I'm really looking forward to university. I can't wait for all the fun to begin.

Branko: Me too. This is a wonderful city.

Milica: I know right. Especially since everything is so close from here. I can walk everywhere.

Branko: I really like it here.

Milica: Do you have a favourite place so far?

Branko: I really liked the upper part of the old town. Otherwise, I love the entire city.

Milica: It's great. It's really European. Can you believe that we're now living in the European Union?

Branko: No, I'm still trying to grasp it.

Milica: It's so bizarre. I really hope that this is a never-ending dream.

Branko: Trust me, I believe it is.

Milica: Do you feel okay?

Branko: I do, why?

Milica: Well, I mean, your life in Belgrade kind of fell apart and now you're in another city trying to make a life for yourself.

Branko: Yes, and? I'm sure that I will find friends once university starts and I have you and you have me.

Milica: That's true. I want this flatshare to be like a second family.

Branko: A big happy second gay family?

Milica: Oh yes!

Branko: Ah, I already feel welcome.

Milica: So what are your plans tomorrow?

Branko: I have a meeting really.

Milica: Really? With whom.

Branko: Oh, don't you remember?

He tells her the details of the meeting.

Scene 129

That evening Branko texts with Bojana.

Are you sure everything is fine?

I'm still worried

Yes, I'm 100% sure

Don't worry about it

Milica and I are getting along really well

and the city is beautiful

I love it here

Have you explored all of the city yet?

Not really

Tomorrow I'm going for a walk

I want to explore some of the green areas of the city

Like a park?

Yes

Park Maksimir, next to the stadium

of Dinamo Zagreb?

Yup

And you're not scared of hooligans?

I don't think that there's a game tomorrow

I think dad said something about a game

Hmmm

No, idea, not my field of interest

How have you been?

How are the others?

I've been good

I was in the city with Dejana today

She's also fine

Mom's fine

Dad's alright

I haven't heard anything from Milenko in ages

Nenad called recently, they're also fine

I miss you…

Aw

Don't worry, I plan to maybe come once during
the end of September before my studies start

I still need to talk to Dejana if I can stay at her place

I don't think she'll say no

Same

I just need to figure out my university schedule

Is it complicated?

You have to do some stuff online
I'm not yet quite familiar with

It'll be fine

If you say so

Yeah

Milica and I wanted to go to a bar now

Do you mind if I text you later?

Of course not

Enjoyy! 💕

Thanks

I love you 🖤

Love you too 🖤

Take care

Scene 130

*Park Maksimir, at sunset. Branko approaches the park to find Luka, from
the competition in Budapest waiting for him.*

Luka: *(looking at him in disbelief)* So it's true. You actually moved
here.

Branko: Yes, it's true.

Luka: Oh my God. That's amazing. Come here. *(hugs him tightly)*
Welcome to Zagreb, my friend!

Branko: Thank you. Can we take a stroll through the park? I wanted to take a look at it.

Luka: Sure thing.

The walk through the park as Branko talks Luka through all of the events of his life and vice versa. After both are finished Luka approaches Branko again.

Luka: My God, I'm still in disbelief of the events in your life. When you stopped texting I thought you were busy with your bf, but now I see the whole picture.

Branko: It was all a chaos.

Luka: Why didn't you decide to tell me sooner that you were coming? Why did you call me two days ago? Just like that, out of the blue!

Branko: I wanted to see how it will all play out. Besides, to that extent, I was busy with my boyfriend.

Luka: You don't have to justify yourself, I was simply confused.

Branko: And I can understand that, but now you know, and we can move on. Deal?

Luka: Deal.

There's a moment of silence.

Luka: So how do you like Zagreb?

Branko: It's nice. It's really nice. It's clean, it's organised, it has structure. It's the opposite of Belgrade. I find it very refreshing.

Luka: And the people?

Branko: I haven't met anyone yet, I only know you.

Luka: Oh, I see.

They reach a bench.

Luka: Wanna sit down?

Branko: Sure thing.

Luka: *(sitting down)* So, why do you want to get the contact between us running again?

Branko: Isn't that obvious? *(sitting down)* I know only Milica and you here, I'd like to have a base of people.

Luka: Is that the only reason?

Branko: Kind of. Why?

Luka: When you called, I felt, weird. We really had a great time in Budapest, and I am very fond of that memory and when you told me that you moved to Zagreb, you moved something in me.

Branko: Luka?

Luka: I don't know how to explain this.

Branko: Say no more. *(he approaches him)*

Luka: *(laughs)* Oh God, this is so cliché.

Branko: Shut up and kiss me.

The two kiss.

Branko: A part of me missed you too. But it never felt so close as it feels now.

Luka: Let me take you to a special place.

Branko: A special place?

Luka: Trust me, you'll like it.

Luka takes Branko to the upper part of the downtown area onto a bench from the whole city can be seen. The couple sits on the bench arm in arm.

Branko: *(smiles)* Luka, can I ask you a simple question?

Luka: Sure thing.

Branko: When you look around, what do you see?

Scene falls.

Annex

The journey to writing Zašto? was long and hard. It all started back in 2014. On February 25th that year I was on a bus from Leipzig to Prague with my physics class from school. We went to Leipzig on a field trip to explore job opportunities at a company known for innovation. It was all part of a project which intended to give us an insight into studying and working in Leipzig. I was 16 at the time and in 11th grade (second to last year) at the German School of Prague.

On the trip back to Prague I decided to write a monologue which I called "Scene 1" as an experiment to sort my thoughts as a gay teenager trying to find a purpose in life. "Scene 1" was finished after around 45 minutes typing on my iPad. I invented a character, which I named Branko in order to reflect a Serbian version of me. A path my life would have taken if I grew up there.

"Scene 1" quickly became "Scene 1 + 2" and "Scene 1 to 3" and I started developing other characters known as Petar, Ivan, Dejana and Vesna. After a while the project became known as "Vukojebina" which is a vulgar term in Serbian for "No Man's Land" and after that, the provisional name of the project became "Zašto?", the name it still holds today. In the original version of 2014, which I will not publish due to personal reasons, "Scene 1" became the actual first scene of the book, and some of the original elements of "Scene 1" are preserved in scenes 1, 5 and 130 of this version. It was important to me to keep elements of "Scene 1" in the book, yet I deem it too personal to publish.

When I finished the first Version of Zašto? back in July 2014, I tried getting it to a point where I could publish it, yet it took me too much time to correct it and as a 16-year-old, I was not ready to master the challenge of writing a book. Looking back at it now, that was a good decision. I was able to write a lot at 16, but it wasn't really good or thought through in a manner that would be worth publishing.

In 2015 and 2016 I have had multiple failed attempts at rewriting Zašto?, never being fully satisfied with the results I recieved, so I chose to give up until New Year's Eve 2016-17. I made a resolution to publish my first book in 2017 and quickly went back to the concept of Zašto?. Instead of rewriting the original story, I put a new more thought through story on top of the old one, holding on to key elements from the original. And that made me write faster, and with more motivation. 19 at the time I started this, I quit my side job and focused solely on my university studies, travels and Zašto?. The Zašto? you are holding in your hands (or on your digital device) today.

I am 20 now, not much older than when I started all of this. Fairly young to be an author, yet I aspire to bring out more content to the masses on topics that touch me on a personal level. I want to put my country out there on the map and show that there is hope for the people in Serbia if we manage to do things right. And I want to be the type of author that people can look up to. I don't want to be famous, I want to make an impact. No matter how small the impact may be.

I really hope that you enjoyed this book and liked reading it. If not, I'm sorry I couldn't meet your expectations. In all cases, I would like to personally thank you for reading my book and supporting me by getting a copy. It really means a lot to me, when I know that someone somewhere is holding this book (or viewing it on a digital device), reading this text and is thereby supporting an unknown young author achieve his dream. And for that, I would like to wholeheartedly thank you!

С. Радаковић

The team behind the book

By no means was I alone in my journey. Even though 99% of the text is written by me (more on the other 1% later), I was accompanied by multiple teams of people over the years who helped me write the book. These so-called "lector groups" were my backbone and they would read with me as I was writing. I have had two steady lector groups over the years, one in 2014 and one in 2017. The 2017 lector group will get its special dedication on the next page, but first I would like to talk about the people who contributed to the book before it got this far.

The 2014 lector group

Comprised of Isabel Carstensen, Marlene Gröblacher, Philip Helf and Darko Milivojević. These four have helped me write the first and original version of the book. We had a shared Facebook group and they were there for most of the process. Unfortunately, after the 2014 version dissolved into dust not much work has been done and to this day, contact has been sparse between us.

My former teachers in school

Ms Probst, my former sociology teacher was my number one fan in regards to my project. She helped me alongside the lectors and was always happy to give me feedback on the project. I want to thank her for all of her support over the years. She has been so kind on so many levels and I really could not have imagined a better support system from a teacher.

Mrs Hönig is my former English teacher and was partially the language backbone for this piece. I would like her for making English class fun and interesting enough for me to actually enjoy working with the language that brought me to finish this piece.

The fantastic four

I mentioned on the previous that I had two lector groups, one in 2014 and one in 2017. These four people helped me write this piece and were there for me every step of the way for as long as they have known me. I would like to take the time to dedicate a small passage to each and every one of them and give you an insight of what the people I was working with were like.

The job of the lectors was to read the book and give me feedback. I would usually upload a few scenes and let them read through it and gather feedback. I would also discuss issues with them and asked for their help whenever something was too challenging for myself. I would like to thank them for what they have done for me and not just only for being amazing lectors, but also for being the best friends I could ask for.

Isabel Carstensen

Isabel and I met on her first day of school in Prague. She moved to the city in the summer of 2010 and ended up being in my class. We were sitting next to each other on the first day of school and after that, we started talking to each other on a regular basis and eventually became good friends and later on best friends in school. Coincidence took it upon itself that we both started studying at the University of Potsdam in 2015 after our graduation. She hasn't left my side in seven years and I am fairly confident that she won't up until the day I die.

On February 25th, 2014 she was sitting next to me as we were returning from our school's field trip to Leipzig while I was writing "Scene 1" (read pages 211 to 212). She was the first to ever read something that would become part of Zašto? and is the only person who was part of both lector groups. Her style of correcting is probably the most honest I've seen and she has always been very precise and voiced on the things that she didn't like about the book.

As a person, she is probably the purest human being I've ever met and the most one. She always listened to my problems and helped me develop as a person (like all of the other people in this group too, but she has been doing it for seven years by now and that is an achievement worthy of the Nobel Peace Prize). No matter how annoying, boring or dramatic I got she was there. And for a gay teenager going through the stress of school is though and if it wasn't for Isabel, I would've probably hated my time at school. Yet I always knew that there was this one girl I could always count on as a kid and that I can still count on to this day. Thank you for everything!

Anđela Čagalj

Instagram icon, future Croatian president, my personal stylist and former roommate, Anđela has been in my life since the 17th of June 2014, shortly before the 2014 version of Zašto? was finished. Back then she lived in Belgrade and we used to see each other from time to time when I would be in town and it would always be cool to hang out. She also read Zašto? in the summer of 2014 and claimed it as a "good read". In the fall of 2015, we both moved to Berlin and moved in together. We lived together until the beginning of 2017 and two weeks after moving out, I started writing this book. I wanted to keep Anđela in my life as she has been and still is a very valuable person in my life and one of the few people in Germany who still know me from before.

She is responsible for the "coolness" factor of the book and has been actively engaged in correcting my writing style to make the characters sound like actual teenagers and not like entitled self-absorbed politicians. She is also responsible for scene 30 of this version which was co-authored by her and my biography (read page 218).

Anđela is probably the person who knows more about me than most of my family. We lived together for one and a half years and in that time had a marriage like style of life. Well, except for the romance part, because, you know, I'm, you know. You get it. We spend so much time together and we take the longest walks (we're too cheap to sit in a café all day) and have the deepest talks. I don't think that there is a single topic on the planet about which Anđela and haven't talked about in the past three years. Habibti, thank you!

Amina Balajo

Amina and I met by chance on the 9th of November 2016 at our university. A month later we were already best friends at university and hung out on a weekly basis even outside of uni. She visited me in Prague over New Year's Eve 2016-17 and was my witness when I made the commitment to bring Zašto? back to life. She joined the lector group from the start and was by far my harshest critic. Since she studies English as a language she is also the backbone of my grammar and sentence structure (especially commas).

Even though we haven't even known each other for more than one year we have been extremely close and for some reason whenever I can't make a definite decision and ask her for her opinion, I end up taking that choice. So far, not a single one of them with regret. And that's what I love about Amina's advice, it's tailored to minimise regret and always helped me live with my decision. I highly value that and I really want to thank Amina for putting up with my decisions.

She is also responsible for the great summary you can find at the back of the book. I knew that I could hand this task to her as she never ceased to amaze me with her writing skills! Thanks for being yet another role model for me!

Nick Ludwig

The person on this list I've known the shortest. The story of how we met is long and detailed but let's say that we met during the writing process of the book and have known each other for half a year. The past four of these six months he has been known as my boyfriend, so far my longest relationship to date. He is the only person on this list who didn't follow the story as I was writing it and the only one whom I didn't tell anything about the ending before I published this book. That's because the ending of the plot was planned to go differently up until the very last second when one of our relationship situations inspired me to change it.

Nick has contributed a lot in terms of his opinion on the manner I should do things, he edited and prepared the most amazing cover and is responsible for my emotional support and emotional distress during the creation of this book. Both of which had helped me write it and push through with it. He might've not done anything for the text itself but without his help, the publishing of this book would've not been possible to execute this easily. I do not know where this relationship will take us in the coming period but as for the period of the creation of this book, I can openly say that I love this guy with all my heart. And that shall stay in this book. Eternally.

About the Author

Stefan Radaković was born on the 7th of August 1997 in Prague, Czechia in a Serbian household. He spent a brief amount of time in Spain during his early childhood before settling with his family in Prague, Czechia. After one year in a Czech primary, he switched to a German School in Prague, the same school he graduated from. After his graduation, Stefan moved to Berlin,  Germany, to start his studies in 2015 (Economics and Sociology at the University of Potsdam). Stefan started to work on „Zašto?" in 2014 while in school and finished it in 2017. His favourite activities include walks around the city he mildly detests and writing on his personal blog, usually lamenting about societal phenomena. The decision to write a play in 2017 is a bold one, but Stefan is no stranger to a challenge: Through dedication and hard work, he became a self-published author in autumn of 2017. He will continue to pursue a career in writing.

(Text by: Anđela Čagalj)